# EXODUS

## AN OLD FARTS CLUB STORY

### MICK WILLIAMS

ENIGMA
HOUSE
PRESS

**Enigma House Press**
**Goshen, KY**

www.enigmahousepress.com

This is a work of fiction. All of the characters, names, incidents, organizations, and dialogue in this novel are either the products of the author's imagination or are used fictitiously.

*Acknowledgements*

*As always, this novel wouldn't exist without the help and inspiration of many people. Since the last book, my memory didn't improve much so, if I miss you, please accept my apologies and know that you are appreciated.*

*So, massive thanks, in no particular order, to...*

*Barry Ashley, Madison Culler, Kenneth Morris (Eagle-Eye), and anyone else that took a look at this and said "Er, hang on. That's not right!"*

*Tony Acree, Lynn Tincher, Sarah Gardiner, and all of my fellow authors at Hydra Publications, for their encouragement, friendship, support, and their skills at putting this story into your hands.*

*The Kentuckiana Authors Group, especially my favorite romance author, Mysti Parker, who could format a maze to look like a straight line.*

*Steve Zimmer and Holly Marie Phillippe from Imaginarium, for everything they do and for being who they are.*

*Ron Fertig and Kenny Vessels, who are in here but don't know it (at least not yet!) and Dario, who doesn't have dreadlocks or gold teeth, and will probably never see this. His banter and laughter (not to mention gorgeous cocktails) breathed life into my bad guy like nothing else could.*

My supportive friends and family on both sides of the pond, for everything (especially my brother Steve and his lovely wife, Max, for letting me take over their kitchen table at a time of need to get this done!)

The people that put the Sparkle in my life, you know who you are. You're always there, even when you're not.

Cathy, who gives me the love, space and support...and keeps the cats off me.

And, finally, to the veterans who went to strange and dangerous places and laid down their lives to protect our freedom. Novels like this are, obviously, fiction. Our veterans are fact, and the Old Farts Club is based on a group of men from Louisville, Kentucky, that frequents a well-known fast food place near my old home.

These men are real sons and fathers, who left their families and went off to foreign countries to preserve the freedom that we are able to take for granted. Some of them, on their return, struggle to enjoy the same freedom. Amazing groups like the Wounded Warrior Project exist to help them. Go online, check them out and, if you can do something to help, do it.

Our veterans are the reason you're able to.

Thank you and much love to you all.

Mick Williams.

Stoke-on-Trent, England. April 2018.

The Jamaican guide threw back his dreadlocks and laughed through a row of gleaming teeth.

"Look at it, mon. It look like the ocean's on fire."

Dan Wilkerson gazed out across the ravine. Beyond the miles of varied greens, and the curl of the bay in the distance, the rising sun bounced off the ripples of the Caribbean and lapped toward them on the tide like liquid flame.

He gestured to his wife and plucked a cell phone from his pocket. "Evelyn. Come on, babe. Stand beside me and let's get a picture of this." He waved the phone in the air. "It's no good for anything else anyway, all the way up here. No signal."

His wife of five years nestled beside him and snuggled into his shoulder as the morning breeze swept her long blonde hair across his face. She shook her head and looped the strands behind her ears as he focused and tapped the screen to capture the moment.

"Come on, lovebirds," said the guide. His thick accent

sounded relaxed. "We still have some climbing to do if you want to get to Nine Mile before the crowds."

They climbed back into the open top Jeep and continued their ascent. The road was narrow and rutted, barely wide enough in places for the rugged tires to grip, but the guide drove with confident and daring speed.

"I never had you pegged as a Bob Marley fan, Dud," said Evelyn as they strained against their lap belts.

He smiled. The boys back home had nicknamed him Dud. It still sounded strange coming from his wife. "I'm not a huge fan, babe, but you know what they say about when in Rome. We're in Jamaica. We can't come here and not see the resting place of a legend, regardless of the occasion."

The night before was an impromptu fortieth birthday party for Evie. Over all-inclusive cocktails, the couple befriended the bartender and picked up the name of Marley's hometown, Nine Mile. High up a mountain in the St. Anne parish, the reggae singer's home was isolated within a compound which sight-seers would flood before lunch. Mario, the bartender, pointed them toward the Tourism Office at the side of the hotel. "See the manager in there, mon. She'll get you out early, no problem."

After drinks, they'd made their way around the expansive hotel until they reached the office. $180 later, they left with an invoice, and set their alarm. The guide still picked them up half an hour early the next morning.

The first hour of the drive, from the hotel in Montego Bay, had been luxury compared to the ride now. Houses, daubed in bright paint, balanced on hills that lined the smooth roads as they drove out of town. The road grew rougher the further out they traveled, just like the buildings. As they wound up the mountain road, an occasional shack broke through the dense green; small, thrown together buildings of corrugated metal tacked onto flimsy looking wooden frames.

"Homelessness is an issue in Jamaica, mon," said the guide. Tattoos danced across his forearms as he fought the steering wheel. "Squatting is illegal, so people build temporary homes. When the police or government appears, they dismantle and move to a new place."

"When you consider the size of the homes closer to town, that's ridiculous," said Dud. "Still, it's the same everywhere."

Below them, an expanse of green swept across the landscape, broken by veins of red. "And what caused the red lines?"

"That used to be our main economy," shouted the guide over his shoulder. "The red comes from the mines. Jamaica used to export aluminum. Aluminum comes from bauxite ore. The ore is red and gets into everything, mon. It's no good for you; it contains lead. Still, it kept the country going for years. Now, other countries do the same thing and Jamaica is struggling. That's one reason for the other houses we passed." He cast back his head and laughed again. "We are fortunate though, we have a thriving drug trade." Gold teeth sparkled in the morning light as he lurched and corrected the wheel before the Jeep ran off the road.

Dud pulled his lap belt tighter and swung a protective arm around his wife's shoulders. She gave him a nervous smile.

"You can't see the areas from here," continued the guide, "but it's still mined. The government closed most of the railway network, but there's still a quarter of it left for transporting the bauxite. And then there's the trucks and an overhead system called RopeCon. But listen, mon, I should be telling you about Marley."

At that point, he burst into a full-throated rendition of No Woman No Cry, then slammed on the brakes. Evelyn gasped as the belt pulled against her stomach. Over the guide's shoulder, Dud saw a wide van coming down the mountain toward them.

"I was going to mention we haven't seen much traffic coming the other way."

"No, mon. Later, it will be a test. That's why I prefer to get out earlier."

He maneuvered the Jeep to the road's edge as the large van approached. Gravel and stones slid and bounced over the precipice as the tires held on with an inch of rubber off the road.

Dud gripped the edge of the Jeep. The trees below looked like tiny plastic models. "Good thing we're not afraid of heights, babe."

Evelyn gripped his arm, her knuckles white. "Speak for yourself. I didn't think I was, but I'm not so sure now."

The van edged alongside them and inched forward. The guide craned his neck to see over the front of the Jeep and then the side, his tongue sticking out between his gold teeth. Bit by bit, the Jeep crept along as the van did the same. Metal clattered as the Jeep's wing mirror flexed on its hinge against the van's wide body, and still the two vehicles hugged. Larger chunks of road crumbled, skittered away, and vanished from sight as Dud gripped the roll bars overhead and offered up a silent prayer. He turned to Evelyn. "I don't like Bob Marley this much."

After a lifetime of scraping metal, the van sped away in a shower of gravel and drove off into the distance, leaving the Jeep and its occupants shaking.

The guide turned in his seat and smiled. "Holy shit,

mon. That's the closest I've been to sliding off the edge. Okay, let's finish this ride."

He stamped on the accelerator as if to show the vehicle who was in charge, and they shot off up the mountain road again.

Within a mile nerves had settled, and the three enjoyed the breathtaking views. The Jeep continued its steady climb, and the guide pointed out distant landmarks as the road leveled and slight grass banks bordered the road.

"You can open your eyes now, babe," said Dud with a smile. "No more big drops."

Off to the side, another hill rose parallel to the one the Jeep climbed. A huge concrete slab lay flat against the side of it. Dud pointed it out to the guide.

"Water catchment."

Dud unbuckled his lap belt to get his phone.

"Water is a precious resource, and I'm sure you've noticed that when it rains here, it rains," grinned the guide. "The water runs down the concrete and into a huge catchment at the base. All the towns up here have them to get as much use as possible from what Mother Nature gives us."

Dud took pictures just before they rounded a curve. The guttural throb of a large motorcycle engine chugged toward them from further up the road. As the guide completed the curve, not one but three bikes came toward them. The trio took up the entire lane before them and straddled the center line. He had no choice but to swerve across the road as he slipped by them.

This time, the Jeep left the road.

The guide wailed and Evelyn screamed as the tires left the gravel and bounced across the rough grass. Dud reached for the roll bars again as the guide slammed on the brakes and the Jeep skidded sideways. Gravity took over and the wheels nearer the road lifted until the vehicle tipped and rolled down the incline.

---

He woke to the sound of happy birds and pouring rain. Dud opened his eyes and closed them again as raindrops hammered against his pupils. His bruised ribs protested as he rolled to one side and then, panicked, he snapped awake.

Evelyn. The Jeep.

He struggled to his feet and looked around. The brow of the hill peaked a hundred feet above him. Divots of grass tracked the path the Jeep had taken as its roll bars had dug into the ground. He pivoted and followed them as they continued another fifty feet further down the incline. His eyes settled on the Jeep. It lay on its side, wedged up against a huge tree, as if it had sought shelter and fallen asleep.

Smaller boughs had broken off under the impact and lay draped across the top of the vehicle. Nothing moved as he half ran, half slid toward it, the grips of his boots sliding across the wet grass. He muttered his wife's name until he slammed into the underside of the Jeep. Stomach churning, he edged around to the rear, fearful of what he might find.

"Evelyn? Evie?" His eyes glistened as the rear seats came into view.

They were empty. So was the driver's seat.

He stepped back. How long had he been unconscious? The sun had gone from being a threat in the east to being dominant overhead. And the birds were singing. The crash would have made a tremendous noise and scattered nature in every direction.

His wife and the guide had both been wearing their lap

belts. If they'd survived, one of them would have woken him before going to get help.

Dud spun on the spot like a slow-motion ballerina and studied the area.

They were nowhere to be seen.

2

The older man leaned back into the plastic seat and spoke with a slow drawl through barely parted teeth. "So, you'll be 'English'."

"Yes, I am," replied the younger man.

"No. I mean your name. They call me Sarge, cos I've served the most tours. At this table, you're 'English'. On account of the fact you sound like one of those hard-nosed actors that always plays a bad guy."

"Oh. I can cope with that," replied English. "So, come on then. Can I join?"

Sarge considered him. "Well, there's a ritual to go through before you can join the club."

'English' Keith Watson thought he'd heard it all before, but he massaged the stubble on his chin and met the old man's gaze. "Really? And what would that be, Sarge? Nothing too elaborate, I hope. I doubt McDonald's likes its customers dancing on the table."

Over a month, English had been meeting the regulars in the diner a few mornings a week. The ragtag group of veterans called themselves The Old Farts Club and met daily for support and a glimmer of old comradeship. And coffee with endless refills.

The diner sat inside the entrance of a large Walmart. Shoppers streamed by the entrance as the steady group of five men sat at their usual table. One seat sat empty today.

"No, nothing like that." Sarge twisted the brim of his baseball cap as if it helped him to concentrate and seated it back on his head in exactly the same position. The logo of the 101st Airborne Division sat proudly, dead center in the faded fabric. "Just tell us a story. But one we've never heard before. And it's got to be a good one."

English leaned back against his seat and thought for a second. He peeled the pickle off his Big Mac and tossed it onto the wrapper, took a bite and swallowed. Then he leaned forward again. "Okay," he said. He looked around the table and paused for effect. "The first night I met my wife?" he whispered. "I stabbed her."

The group leaned forward, like a scrum, as if the extra foot of distance would make everything clearer. One guy, toying with a small canvas bag, coughed 'bullshit' into his hands and smiled.

English continued. "We both went to the same college. Before I got into computers I used to run for the school. The wife ran too. Still does, she's a fitness freak. Wears me out. With the running, too," he smiled. "Sorry, English humor. Anyway, they ran this lecture on the campus where some highly rated coach from America came over to do a talk about scholarships. Everyone sat at these massive round tables and she sat opposite me. She was gorgeous, and I kept hoping she'd move so I could check her legs out."

"How long ago's this then?" asked the guy with the pouch.

"About twelve years ago, mate." English glared at the

man's face. Something seemed different about him, but he couldn't quite place it. "I did two tours and loads of training, but she wanted me out of the service. Can't say as I blame her. So anyway, she's sat right across from me and they're bringing these dishes in with all kinds of seafood on them. I'm allergic to it, and I'm bloody starving, and she orders a salad and steak, so I tell the bloke I want the same. She starts sifting through this salad. Next thing I know, she's turning red. Like I said, she's gorgeous, but her face is swelling up like a puffer fish and she's gasping for air. The whole table's sitting there watching her gag, but I knew what was happening. There were nuts in her salad. She had an allergic reaction. I always carry an Epi-Pen with me cos seafood messes me right up. So, I run around the table and I can see her legs now. She's got this mini skirt on and they're sticking out cos she's shaking but they're still amazing."

"Is this about to get romantic?" asked Sarge. "Only it's been a while since I got that way. I'd go to war for the right cause, but don't start throwing women at me."

"No, definitely not romantic. I lifted the hem of her skirt up, checked her legs out once more and slammed the pen into the meat of her thigh. She might have been choking, but she still landed a bloody good slap across my face that sent me flying. Anyway, she recovered and, as a thank you, she took me out for a meal. Something similar to White Castle. Nothing dangerous." He sat back and picked up his burger. "So, that's it. The first night I met the wife, I stabbed her."

"I don't know about White Castle not being dangerous," said the oldest man at the table. "They don't call them sliders for nothing."

Sarge looked around at the men. "So, do we let the young 'un join the club?"

The guy shuffled his pouch, still smiling. "I'd say so. That was entertaining. Of course, it helps when the narrator sounds like Harry Potter."

"Agreed," said the old guy. "Do the intro's, Sarge."

English wiped his hands on a paper napkin as Sarge stood and pointed. "Okay, English. The old fella here? That's Numbers."

"White Castle's don't agree with me," said Numbers. English shook his hand. "Ron Cole. I served in Vietnam, though not with Sarge. Logistics and planning. That's my forte, hence the nickname. Been retired a while now, like Sarge. I could have arranged you the wedding of a lifetime."

"Pleased to meet you, Numbers," said English.

"And this here," continued Sarge, "is Marbles."

English reached across the table and was met with a firm grip. "And is that because you're a bit mental, you know, like you've lost your marbles?"

"What language is that?" said the guy with a frown. "I'm Lucas. Lucas Durrant. And no, they call me Marbles cos of these."

He pulled open the drawstring that tied closed the small pouch he held and emptied its contents onto the table. An assorted collection of eyeballs rolled around until he cupped them in his hands.

English recoiled. "Shit! I've read about them collecting ears in 'Nam, but eyeballs? I was right the first time. You're bloody mental."

Marbles laughed. His blue eyes glistened under the fluorescent light until he leaned forward and plucked one of them out. He sat upright again with a gaping hole in the left side of his face.

"Well bugger me," said English. "I'm sorry mate, I had

no idea. That's a bloody good eye. Hope I didn't offend you."

"No offense taken. They're all glass. A sliver of shrapnel ruined the original, but the ex-wife's father is a top eye doctor. Not only did he hook me up with a perfect match," he said as he popped the glass eye back into its socket, "but he gave me a little collection to have fun with."

English noticed a couple of different designs, a blazing sun and a smiley emoticon, before Marbles scooped up his collection and dropped it into its pouch.

"Used to be if it had wheels or wings I could operate it but, once the eye thing happened, they won't let me near anything now." His real eye sparkled. "I still have a few toys though. So, what about you? What's your area of expertise?"

"Tech," said English. "Computers. Programs. I worked the front line, but if you need something hacked or programmed, I'm your man. I run a computer repair service now. Self-employed. It's nice, and I get to make my own hours."

"And, you might have noticed, we're missing one man," said Sarge. "Dud's on vacation with his lovely wife, sunning himself in Jamaica. He'll be back next week so we'll introduce you then."

Numbers reached into his pocket. "All right, English. I assume you have a cell phone." He placed an iPhone on the table. The others followed suit.

"Of course. Doesn't everyone?" English placed his face up and waited.

"You're in the club. Trade your number with everyone else. We're all here to support one another. Anything you need, just call. Keep your phone handy though, cos it's a two-way street."

Area codes and cell phone numbers bounced back and

forth across the table until they were all hooked up. Then the theme song to the A-Team played from Sarge's phone. He glanced at its screen and held up the device so the others could see it. "Speak of the devil, and he shall appear. It's Dud!"

3

Using the Jeep as a ledge, Dud attempted to climb the huge tree to gain extra height but its trunk wasn't rough enough for his grip to find purchase. Splinters jabbed a million pins into his hands every time he flexed his fingers.

Next, he tried to right the Jeep. The vehicle rocked back and forth against its roll-bars but remained stubbornly upright. Defeated and exhausted, he left it rested against the tree.

Even with no signal, he alternated calls to Evie with calls for help over and over until the battery light flashed red. Resigned, he trudged downhill with his thumb extended toward the passing traffic. His shirt hung like a wet towel, stuck to him with a combination of blood and sweat, and his whole body ached and throbbed as he swiped away insects. The trees chattered with the sound of them and red welts had already appeared beneath the blood where some had feasted on him. He walked for two hours and waved at numerous drivers that trekked uphill, but none of them slowed. If anything, the sight of him, bruised and bloody, encouraged them to speed even faster up the treacherous incline. Vehicles traveling in the opposite direction did the same.

Just as he considered standing in the road, a fluorescent yellow tour bus slowed, screeched to a stop a few yards ahead of him and allowed him to board.

The smell of ganja stung his nostrils. It permeated everything and hung in the air, even in town and back at the hotel, like an illegal after shave.

He explained his story to the driver who spoke back in broken English until a woman in the seat behind him leaned forward.

"Jameson speaks the Jamaican Patwa, mon. He might understand you, but you won't have as much luck understanding him unless you've been here a while. Having said that, looking at the state of you, you've been somewhere for a while. I overheard part of your story. Let me see if I can help."

The guide was a young woman, probably late twenties, early thirties. Jet-black hair lay flat against her head and curved around her cheeks to frame a curious smile that beamed as she studied him. Much friendlier looking than the tattooed beast of a man who'd run them off the road earlier. Dud struggled to remember his name and then realized he'd never mentioned it.

The girl shook her head as he told his story. "Gangs roam these hills, mon. You know how, on fairground rides, they say keep limbs inside the vehicle at all times? Here, keep all of you in the vehicle at all times, unless you know who you're with or where you are. In these hills, there is land that hasn't even seen a footprint. Not a good place to be."

At the back of the bus, he traded one accent for another, sandwiched between groups of German and French tourists. He played with his wedding ring, spinning the endless gold circle around his finger for over an hour until the gates of the hotel appeared. As he waited for the doors to open, he pressed money into the guide's hand.

"Thank you. God knows how long I might have been out there. Take Jameson somewhere for a nice meal."

She smiled again. Despite her warnings, the people he'd met so far had been nothing but friendly. "No problem, mon. Thank you. And good luck, I'm sure it will all work out. The police might not be much use, they're always busy, but reception can call them for you."

He held out his hand to shake hers as she pushed a card into his palm. "I know people," she said. "Trustworthy people. And if you need to get around the island, call me."

He nodded his thanks and slipped the card into his pocket as the bus pulled away.

A multicolored pathway of small stones lined with slim palm trees led to two huge entrance doors. 'Follow the yellow brick road' sang in his head as Dud walked past a carved wooden effigy of Bob Marley and into the cool shade of reception.

Two young girls buzzed about behind the desk, checking in new arrivals and directing bikini-clad tourists to pool events. Everyone was having fun as he barged through and leaned against the wooden counter.

"Could you call the police, please? My wife's missing."

The girls' eyes widened at the sight of him, then she recovered and picked up the phone. She spat out a few rapid-fire sentences in the same language as the bus driver, then replaced the phone and addressed him in perfect English. "Please take a seat in reception, sir. Help yourself to a drink and they'll send an officer as soon as possible."

He took her advice, grabbed a coffee off the bar and sat

in a chair shaped like a big hand, its fingers climbing up his back for support. A free Wi-Fi sign hung on the wall in front of him, so he pulled out the phone again. The Wi-Fi icon glowed next to the flashing battery light. He dialed Evelyn's number and clamped the phone to his ear.

For a moment, nothing happened, then the line clicked as if an old-fashioned operator had connected the call and the ringtone burred. Bitter coffee moistened his tongue as his stomach tumbled.

And then she answered.

Tears formed as he opened his mouth to speak. "Evie? Where..."

"Hi. You've reached Evie's phone. Sorry I can't..."

The tears tumbled as he listened to his beautiful wife's voice.

"...so leave me a message after the tone and I'll call you back. Byeeeee."

"Babe? It's Dud. Dan! Call me as soon as you hear this, I'm so worried. I looked everywhere for you but I had to come back to the hotel. The police are on their way, and I'll be back out to get you as soon as I can. If your phone won't work, or you're stuck, make some kind of signal. Love you, babe. I'll be there soon."

He disconnected the call, then stared at the blank screen. The battery had died. How much of his message had got through?

The police arrived thirty minutes later. Two of them, each over six feet tall, marched like gunslingers through the doors. Their waist belts resembled the American version Dud recognized, equipped like Batman's utility belt with snub nosed 9mm pistols secured in holsters. Shiny handcuffs glinted at the rear, stark against jet-black fabric.

He stood and beckoned to them as they walked to the desk. "Over here. Please. Please help."

The gleaming brass badge on the chest of the cop closest said 'Thomas'. Officer Thomas stood eye to eye with him and nodded. "Sir, you reported the missing woman?"

Dud babbled out the morning's events until Thomas put a hand on his shoulder. "Slow down, mon. Come on, take a seat over here and start again."

Dud grew frustrated. "My wife is missing. It'll be dark soon and she's out in the hills somewhere on the way to Nine Mile. We don't have time to slow down. We have to find her."

"And we will," said the voice of reason, "but not if we can't understand a word you're saying."

He took a deep breath and retold his story, from the pick up at the hotel's gate to the trek back down the roadside. The cops took notes and nodded at all the right times. When he finished, they closed their notebooks and stood.

"Please understand, Mr. Wilkerson, we can't consider someone missing until twenty-four hours have passed."

Dud protested as the other cop stepped forward. Thomas continued. "We know Jamaica's reputation and, yes, hundreds go missing here each year, but the majority are runaway teenage girls. Missing adults normally turn up unharmed."

As with other Jamaicans he'd spoken to, Dud noticed that the cop pronounced no 'h'. Missing adults normally turned up unarmed.

"Here is my card. I understand your impatience, but shower, eat and rest. Keep your phone close, get treatment for your cuts and, if you hear nothing tomorrow, call and we'll go from there. We'll talk to the tour operator, too."

Before he could say a word, the cops turned and left the hotel.

---

Evelyn's suitcase greeted him as he entered their room. Since they'd left early, she hadn't had time to repack it after dressing this morning and colorful clothing lay scattered across the mattress.

He repacked it, then took out her makeup case, grabbed her tweezers, and spent twenty minutes perched on the side of the shower plucking splinters, one by one, from his palms. They littered the basin like bee stings until he swept them into the trash.

A hot shower washed away the day. The water took care of the blood and dirt, and he ran it until the mini whirlpool by the drain faded from pink to clear. The heat soothed his aches as he adjusted the shower head until hot water pounded into the base of his skull and across his shoulders.

He knew he should be out there looking for her. After multiple tours in the Middle East, existing alone in isolated places was second nature to him. Evie had been nowhere like this, not alone. And sure, the Middle East was miles of sand instead of jungle, but alone was alone. And danger was danger, no matter how it dressed.

Getting to know her had been a blessing and a curse. An event in his past had led Dud to seek the advice of a counselor; someone to help him make sense of the crazy things men did to one another, and to rationalize the evil in the world. His counselor became a trusted friend and, after a while, invited him to events to socialize and get used to being around people and loud noise.

PTSD should have been something that happened to

other people, but July 4$^{\text{th}}$ celebrations left him cowering in his basement, sweating and tense. The gunfire sound of popping fireworks and each bang and explosion took him back to every skirmish he'd been involved in.

The counselor invited him to a Halloween event, which he attended dressed as Batman. After a nervous entrance, he'd scanned the room of strangers to find someone to talk to. Catwoman stood out in the crowd like a beacon. Three hours of conversation later, he and Evie left the venue together. They'd not been apart since.

Until now.

A million TV channels had nothing of value to watch. He entertained himself by checking out the same program in three different languages before his stomach reminded him he'd not eaten since this morning.

The all-inclusive buffet teemed with people that milled around like ants picking grains from a sugar cube. Dud fixed a plate of meat and fruit and found a corner to eat in. Regardless of how he arranged the food on his plate, his stomach churned each time the fork approached his mouth. Nerves and anxiety gnawed at him, and he retreated to the quiet of the bedroom.

The ceiling fan continued its relentless attempt to circulate the air conditioning as he lay on the bed and stared at its spinning blades. His body cried for sleep, but his mind buzzed, going over the day's events.

The bikes that caused their guide to leave the road were nothing more than a fleeting glimpse. As a mechanic, he knew engines and, although it may have sounded like large bikes, the volume seemed louder because there were three of them and the roar bounced back off the tree line.

The scene replayed in his mind; their guide, confident and assured, whipping the Jeep around the dangerous curves; the engine noise and the sudden and surprising appearance of the bikes, and then the almost controlled skid off the side of the road and down the embankment.

He could make out the silhouette of the three bikers. Tall. Upright. All wearing the same clothing.

And guns. Black shoulder straps had cut a swathe down the front of each man. Each had a gun slung over his shoulder, with the barrels stuck out behind them like antenna.

The phone's screen illuminated, and he scrambled to pick it up. Its battery icon glowed a healthy green, so he checked the volume, laid it back down and closed his eyes.

---

Sunlight, rather than rain, burned his eyes as a sudden, sharp noise woke him. Dud sat bolt upright, used to waking up alert after years of training. The hotel's phone chimed, the age-old sound of jarring, annoying bells. His heart thumped as he lifted the handset. The police had succeeded, and he needed to pick up his wife.

"Hello?"

"Mr. Wilkerson, I'm sorry to bother you. It's Tasha, from the main desk. The tour office asked me to call you. You can call in to pick up your refund at any time."

His head spun as disappointment rushed through him. "Refund? Refund for what?"

"I'm sorry, sir, I have no idea. They just asked me to pass on the message. I do hope you receive good news today."

The call disconnected.

His cell phone still had a blank screen. He dialed Evelyn's number again. This time there was no voicemail. There was no dial tone.

Dud washed and dressed and made his way downstairs. He avoided the elevator out of habit. Always exercise.

A glance at the clock in reception confirmed that, in three hours, Evelyn will have been missing for the required amount of time for the police to get off their asses and look for her. He wandered through reception and opened the door into the Tourism Office. Posters plastered the walls with promises of a great time. None of them mentioned missing persons.

The lady behind the desk looked up as the door closed. It was the same person who took his $180 two nights ago.

"Good morning," she said, her voice breezy and pleasant, "and I'm so sorry about your trip. Perhaps I could arrange another to make up for it? At a discounted rate, of course."

Dud slumped confused into the seat opposite her as his temperature rose from cool to warm. "Say what? To make up for it? Are you being serious?"

She frowned and placed her hands on the desk and shuffled some papers. "Well, accidents happen, but I realize this might be your only time here, so I'd like to make it up to you. Hector will be back soon, I'm sure, but I have other drivers that could show you around."

"Lady, what the hell are you talking about?" His internal thermometer rose again, from warm to hot.

"Hector. Your guide. I've not heard from him and I can't get hold of him. He didn't come to work. That's why he didn't pick you up, and that's why you missed your trip. I didn't know until this morning when I found your details still on my desk because he would have picked them up."

The room spun and Dud clutched the edge of the desk.

"Sir, I'm sorry. I didn't realize it would offend you so much. All I can do is apologize."

He held out a hand to silence her. "So, you're saying that your guide never showed?"

"Yes."

"We went on our trip."

"How?"

"Hector. Your guide. Big guy? Tattoos and gold teeth?"

She laughed, then spoke through a smile. "Are you kidding? Hector is a young man. He drives to get extra money for school. I've seen heavier coconuts."

Dud stood and whirled out of the office. Insects were already singing, and a cloak of humidity hung in the air as he held on to the door frame for support.

The card. The cop's card. He fished it out and dialed the number. The call answered on the third ring and a female voice spoke. "Montego Bay Police Department, how may I direct your call?"

"Thomas, please. Officer Thomas."

Paper rustled and then the voice returned. "That officer is now off duty. If this is about on ongoing investigation, I can pass you through to someone else if you'd like?"

He disconnected and slid down the doorframe until he sat like a beggar in the doorway. Evie was missing, and the police didn't appear to be too concerned. And who had picked them up yesterday? A friend of Hector's? Maybe he'd offered to split the fee rather than lose the job.

Dud felt alone. Isolated.

Those feelings weren't new, but he felt abandoned and lost, too. He needed comfort. The phone had a healthy fan of Wi-Fi lines across the top of the screen. He opened his contacts list and searched for someone reliable. Someone he could depend on.

4

Sarge spun the beck of his cap around until it rested over the back of his neck. Then he answered the phone.

"Dud? You calling to tell us how beautiful the weather is there? Cos if you are, let me tell..."

His stopped as his friend spoke, and the club members leaned in again to listen as his face darkened. Dud's voice chattered like a rabid squirrel through the tiny earpiece, but not loud enough for them to hear any clear words.

"Well, shit son. What can we do?"

Numbers reached forward. "Sarge. What is it? Is he okay?"

He was silenced with a glare.

"Okay. You can get the co-ordinates? Uh-huh. Okay. Send em on over and we'll get to it. Keep your phone close. Uh-huh. Roger that. Don't worry, son, help's coming. Uh-huh. Okay, bye."

He placed his phone back on the table and shuddered. "Evelyn's gone missing over there in Jamaica."

Sarge held up a hand to silence a chorus of chatter. "Questions later. English. You're in at the deep end, son.

Time to find out how good you are. I assume you've got a bunch of those program things that can do just about anything a man can?"

English snapped to attention. "What are you looking for, Sarge?"

"That Google Mapearth thing? With the satellites? I want that, but in real time."

"Surveillance? That's easy. I can count the leaves on trees in Africa."

"Is Mrs. English home?"

"Jenny left the house and went to her mother's. Why?"

"Pack up then, boys. We're de-camping."

"To where?" said Marbles.

"The English residence. We have a spying mission."

A convoy of pickup trucks followed English's Honda out of the city and into the suburbs.

It took twenty minutes to reach the English residence, which turned out to be a two-story patio home sitting on three acres of lush green land. It took a further five minutes to get through an electric gate and drive along a camera-covered winding path to reach the front door. A series of slamming truck doors startled squawking geese as English climbed the steps and fumbled for his house keys.

"So, do all of you English folks like your privacy, or are you just particularly paranoid?" asked Sarge.

"Didn't you know, Sarge?" grinned English. "We've all got a castle back home. This is my American version."

He unlocked the door to the sound of a beeping alarm, lifted his head and shouted "Ready."

The beeping stopped as the rest of the club followed him inside, across a tidy living room, and through a basement door to a dark staircase. Halfway down, he shouted again. "Lights."

Fluorescents buzzed and glared into life along the length of the downstairs room. The section nearest the staircase was a regular living room, with throw rugs and comfortable sofas that faced a large flat screen TV. A pool table sat to one side, with the balls racked up and ready to go. Behind it, the back wall was one long bench lined with keyboards. Above each keyboard, mounted to the wall, hung a monitor.

The rest of the club filed into the room behind him. Numbers gasped.

"Shit. You could probably land a plane with what's in here. And nice table."

English smiled. "No probably about it, I've landed a few. And the table was my English input." He paused for a second, then shouted, "Camera."

The banks of monitors clicked, and each screen displayed a single question mark.

Marbles stepped forward. "I've seen this sound activated shit before. Remind me to tell you the story about the clapping lamp and the noisy lovers. Nice, but I reckon I can do the next part. Here, watch."

He walked to the center of the room and raised his head. "Action!" He grinned and turned to face the monitors. The question mark glared back.

"I'm almost impressed, Marbles," said English. "but this system only recognizes my voice. Action."

The monitors blinked and ready screens appeared on each one.

Sarge adjusted his cap. "Well I'll be damned if it ain't air traffic control. Okay, tech boy. Get the surveillance program running, we have urgent work to do."

English pointed across the room as he walked to the

bench. "Beers are in the fridge. Help yourselves guys, I'll only be a minute."

———————

While he worked, English shouted across the room.

"So, who's Dud? How'd he get his name?"

Sarge walked back with two beers and handed one over. "Dud? Let me tell you something about Danny Wilkerson. He fought in the Gulf War. Desert Storm. There were insurgents in every town looking to become martyrs by killing one of ours. Regardless, he took it upon himself to go into the middle of town twice a week to teach Kuwaiti kids English. He's one of those people that will see the good in everyone, regardless of color or creed. So, imagine this; here's this twenty-three-year-old kid, teaching these young 'uns our language, and one of those bastards cracks open the door and throws a grenade into the room."

English sat back wide eyed. "Shit. That's cold."

"No kidding. They didn't care about human life or collateral damage. Still don't, it seems. Anyway, he yells at the kids to get on the tables. Buddy, he knows he's got a matter of seconds before that thing detonates and shards of hot metal will be tearing through young bodies. As they're all clambering onto table tops, he does the only thing he can, and dives on top of the grenade. He smothered that son of a bitch with his own body."

"But he's still here," said English. "Well, in Jamaica."

"Yep," smirked Sarge. "Because?"

"The grenade was a dud," finished English.

"By the grace of God. He's a braver man than you, me and these guys put together. He earned his name. And that's why, when he asks for my help, I don't even need to know what he wants. I'm just there."

English nodded. "In that case, so am I."

---

A tidy line of four Budweiser's shared the desk space as the men sat at the center monitor. English's fingers were a flurry of movement as he typed commands into the system and the screen flitted and changed. Horizontal and vertical lines scrolled, until they zoomed in and rested over the small island of Jamaica.

"You said questions later, Sarge," said Marbles. "Now's later. Fill us in. What happened?"

Sarge relayed all the information Dud had told him, and they asked him question after question until all he could do was shrug his shoulders.

"That's it. That's all I know. Gimme a sec now, let me get him on the phone and we'll see what we can do."

He dialed and waited for the call to connect. English beckoned for the phone.

"Don't be crazy, son," said Sarge. "This is important."

English sighed "Okay. Well lay your phone on that black box to your side and we can all listen in."

Sarge frowned, but laid the phone down on a small box just in time for Dud's voice to power through a concealed speaker system.

"Yeah. Sarge? I got you. You hear me okay?"

"Dud, you're on loudspeaker," said English. "We've met, but you don't know me that well, yet. I didn't get introduced properly, but we're all here to help, man."

"Well I appreciate that. This English?"

English frowned. "How do you know my name?"

"Come on, man. What the hell else were we going to call you?"

"I like him already," said English under his breath. "Okay. The place where everything went down. Can you give me a rough idea of the location?"

"Yep. You got a pen?"

"Won't need one. I'm pretty nimble, so I'll just type it in."

"Okay, here goes. Latitude 18.455511°, longitude -77.289505°. Can you work with that?"

The club smiled grimly as English sat there slack jawed. "Are you shitting me?"

"I shit you not, my foreign friend," said Dud. "Welcome to the club."

"Thanks. Let me get a pen."

Five minutes later, English had the exact location centered on screen. Five minutes after that, Dud sat in the hotel lobby gazing at one of the two complimentary computers while English hacked into it and mirrored his screen for Dud to see.

"This is the road, right here." Dud traced a finger up the screen.

"You're doing that thing aren't you," said Marbles, "where you're gesticulating or something, knowing full well we can't see you."

"Shut up, smartass. But yes, I am." Dud smiled at the attempt at comic relief, but he was still all business. "Okay, so this is the coast road that winds all the way up to Nine Mile. Can you move the screen so more of the road shows to the north?"

English did something at the other end and the map scrolled to show a few more miles of road.

"It all seems too convenient," said Dud. "The fact that those bikes appeared as we rounded a curve. You know, element of surprise and all that." He followed the road further north until it branched off to the east. There were no other roads for miles after that.

"You seeing that road about a half mile farther on?" said Sarge. "It splits off the main road and vanishes into woodland. It must lead somewhere, right? Otherwise, what's the point of it being there?"

"I see it," said Dud. "It wouldn't be a stretch to reach that from the crash site. I remember the ground leveled out a little by then, so it would be pretty simple if it's just trees under those, er, trees."

"Dud, do you have access to transport?" asked English. "I could guide you in if you could get within the vicinity."

"I love how you talk, man. The chicks must dig it. And yes, I happen to know a girl, although I'm not sure what she could do at short notice. There is another issue, though. My cell phone turns into a useless piece of crap once I leave the hotel. No Wi-Fi, no phone."

"Minor technicality. I could ping you once you get out there."

"Say what?"

English smiled. "I can isolate your phone and then borrow a satellite to make sure it has a perfect signal. Well, when I say borrow, it's more like commandeer, but you get my meaning."

"I do. What are you, a walking Pentagon? Can you give me a few minutes? Let me make a call and see if I can rustle up some wheels. Push comes to shove, I'll head out of town a mile or so and borrow, or commandeer a set of my own."

"Do you have your phone cable with you? The USB that comes with the charger?"

"It's upstairs, in the room."

"Get it," said English. "We'll need that."

"Okay, let's get to it," said Sarge. "Ten minutes and we'll call you back and get the ball rolling. And Dud?"

"Yes, sir?"

"We're going to find your girl. You can count on us."

"Don't doubt you for a second, Sarge. Ten minutes. Dud out."

5

"Damned insects. I hate them."

Eladio Gomez slapped the side of his tanned calf and inspected his palm for evidence of his kill. Whatever had bitten him had either flown or jumped away. The locals had already warned him about the 'bite an bun', a tiny ant with a bite that produced fire-hot pain. Since that conversation he'd done nothing but itch and scratch.

He growled and slid the iron bolt closed across the hatch. Mr. Ramirez would kill him if anything got into the hatch and damaged the product. If Lindsay didn't beat him to death first.

Five more days. In five days, he would follow the cargo home to Columbia, moving out from here under the canopy by truck, then by boat from the dock. A journey of just over nine hundred miles. Each mile presented a challenge, a danger. Nine hundred chances that the product might be discovered or even spoil.

Cuba's borders were more open than ever before which brought in more travelers. More travelers meant more police patrols. More police patrols made Mr. Ramirez anxious.

The product reached Columbia regularly, since they obtained enough for a shipment every two weeks, but this batch contained something extra. A special order that had to arrive in perfect condition. Or, if Lindsay didn't beat him, Mr. Ramirez would kill him.

He slid the rug back into place and wandered away from the hut and along a dirt path to a metal building. Mr. Ramirez liked to keep things simple; the hut for the product and the metal building for its guards. A wavy wall of green corrugated metal sheets helped it blend into the surroundings in case the overhead trees separated enough for one of the tourist planes to get a glimpse through the canopy.

Deaven, one of the two Jamaicans in the group, sat by the radio as he entered the building. They nodded to one another, an acknowledgment that everything was good. Mr. Ramirez would kill Deaven, too, if anything went wrong and, like Eladio, Deaven wanted to celebrate his twenty first birthday.

It would soon be time. Every hour, on the hour, someone from the mainland called to check in. They couldn't miss check-in. That would mean something was wrong, then Mr. Ramirez would leave Columbia and visit. If Mr. Ramirez came to visit, chances are he would kill them. And Lindsay.

Eladio strode across to the other side of the building to join the others. The leader of the group, a huge man, patted a blood spotted sofa. "Come and sit down, mon. You look exhausted."

Lindsay had no concern for his welfare, he knew, but rather wanted to keep a strong team in case of attack. Cuts and bruises covered the big man's arms and legs. As the head of their small militia, he took the brunt of any dangerous work and enforced rules with violence.

Lindsay recruited him from his local gang back home and made promises of money and travel. It will be hard work, he'd said. And dangerous. You might have to do things few people could. Bad things. Eladio mentioned that he'd beaten plenty of people at school. Lindsay had shaken his head slowly, dreadlocks swaying from side to side, as he peeled back the flap of his jacket to reveal the satin black handle of a pistol. Eladio smiled. But don't get attached to anyone, said Lindsay. You never know what's around the corner.

Eladio shuddered as he remembered events from a night three weeks ago.

There had originally been three Jamaicans. D'Andre was another big guy. Eladio told him that his named meant 'manly'. D'Andre had laughed and said he'd show Eladio manly one day.

D'Andre was weak and used the product. Mr. Ramirez's number one rule was to leave the product alone. Lindsay's fists had pummeled D'Andre's face until his manly eyes had swollen shut. As his body grew limp and collapsed against the sofa, Lindsay had continued to kick and pound it like a slab of meat until the sound of cracking bones popped around the room.

Eladio and another guy, Akoni, dragged D'Andre a mile away from camp to bury him. When they returned, Lindsay stalked the room like a proud warrior, the dead man's blood still spattered across his face and running down his thick arms. Stood beneath a bare light bulb that made the wet blood shine, he reiterated the rules through gleaming teeth, spittle flying from his lips. No one flinched until he left the room.

Eladio sat on the sofa, next to what remained of D'Andre, and waited for the call.

'Kenzie Anderson–See Jamaica Tours.'

Dud flipped the card in his fingers to see the young girls number printed on the back. He dialed it and lifted his phone. Her voice on the voicemail message made her sound even younger than she was.

"Kenzie? It's Dud, the guy you picked up yesterday. You said if I needed anything, I should call you. I need a ride, can you help? Call me back. Thanks."

He took the stairs two at a time, ignoring his aches, and retrieved the phone cable from the bedside cabinet. He got back to the lobby just in time to get reseated by the computer before a family dressed in Hawaiian shirts invaded the entire area. The father took in his bruises and sullen look and ushered his family outside into sunlight.

English had created a chat box which sat minimized in the corner of the screen. Dud opened it.

'Back,' he typed.

English's reply was instant. 'Connect your phone to the computer via the USB cable.'

Dud smiled. Who said 'via' in regular conversation these days? He did as instructed and laid the phone, screen up, next to the keyboard.

'Done.'

'Okay. Give me five...and don't touch!'

Nothing happened for a moment, and then a black box filled with green writing appeared on the screen. Strings of random letters zipped across it, as if English was spitting them out, not typing them. Then the phone screen lit up, flashed and the phone switched itself off. Moments later, the carrier logo appeared, and it rebooted and his familiar icons filled the screen. Then it rang. International call.

Dud jumped at the sudden sound and picked it up.

"That's it," said English. "You're good to go."

"Go where? And what did you just do? I thought I'd fallen into The Matrix."

"You can go anywhere. I modified the phone's settings so you'll get a signal pretty much anywhere in the world. Oh, there is one important thing to consider though, something that would interfere with it."

Dud leaned forward as if it would improve his hearing. "And what's that?"

"Keep the battery charged."

He smiled. "Yeah, you really are a smartass, aren't you? You're going to take some getting used to."

"Half smartarse, on my Mother's side. In all seriousness, though, charge when you can. Remember the military saying; eat when you can because you never know where your next meal's coming from. Same with power. You don't know how long you'll be away from a power source. That phone is your lifeline. Keep it charged. A dead battery is a dead phone."

"Point taken. And I assume this number is your direct line?"

"Yep. Store it for future use, mate."

"Will do. I tried to call that..."

A beep sounded in the earpiece and overrode Dud's voice. He lowered the phone and glanced at the screen.

"Guys, I'll call you back. The wheels lady's calling." He hit connect. "Kenzie?"

"Yes. Sorry, I was conducting a tour, but I heard your message. You need a ride?"

"I do. I want to go back out to where you found me."

She was quiet for a moment. "I'm on the other side of the island right now, but I want to help. I'm tired of the negative reputation my home has. It's full of good people, so let me show you. If you drive from your hotel to the airport, there's a car rental place at about the halfway point. Don't worry, it's the only one. Get there and call me back. I'll take care of you, mon."

"I appreciate that, Kenzie. And I already know about the good people here. Don't worry, I'm not about to let one incident alter my opinion. I've been all over the world, there's good and bad everywhere. And the good normally outnumbers the bad."

"I can agree with that, Mr. Dud. Call me when you're ready, I'll keep my phone close."

He said goodbye and dialed English. The call connected instantly and was crystal clear. "I'm sorted for wheels, guys. The battery's at 96%, so I'll be good for a while. I'm heading out and I'll call again when I get close."

Sarge spoke and sounded like he was in a tunnel. "We hear you, buddy. Be safe and we'll talk soon."

"Roger that," said Dud. "Sarge? Where are you? You're all echoey."

"On a sofa at English's place. He's got one of those hands-free boxes. I can't grasp not holding something while I talk, but I guess I'll get used to it."

Dud shook his head. Hands free box? "Okay. Give me a couple hours and I'll be in touch."

"Gotcha. Sarge out."

Dud disconnected the call, wound the cable into a loop and pocketed it next to the phone, then left the hotel.

It took five minutes to give the guard at the gate his details before the guy would open the barrier for him to leave. After a further fifteen minutes of brisk walking he spotted the rental place set back off an exit from a large circle. They had these things in Europe and the Middle

East, but called them roundabouts. The Jamaicans seemed to have no problem with them. Each driver entered and exited from the correct lane. Dud grimaced. Way more complicated than a good, old-fashioned four-way stop. Much easier. Turn based. Regimented. Military-like.

He walked into the rental lot, leaned against the wire fence and called Kenzie.

"Okay," she said. "I have a couple of cars at the back end of the lot for emergencies. Make your way there."

Dud started the walk. Something about this girl seemed unusual, something different. Who kept a couple of cars for emergencies? He determined to find out more once he found Evelyn.

The number of parked cars dwindled the further back he walked until there were just odd vehicles dotted about as if they'd run out of gas and had been left where they died.

"Okay," he said. "I'm here."

"Do you see the small sedans in the right corner?"

"I do, and I like small," said Dud. "That mountain road is frigging scary in places."

Kenzie laughed, which in turn made him smile. It felt good to smile, at least for a moment. He imagined her pearl white teeth as she chuckled and chided himself. Easy fella, he thought, she's young enough to be your daughter. He walked up to the car closest to the fence, a boxy VW with a body made from equal parts paint and rust.

"There's an old Volkswagen here, might have been blue once upon a time."

"Don't be deceived, Mr. Dud," she laughed. "Just because it wear a shabby coat don't mean it's not hiding a firm body."

He let the innuendo slide and pulled at the door handle. "It's locked."

Dud heard the smile in her voice "That's so it won't get stolen. Go around the back and search inside the exhaust. There's a magnetic box with the key in it."

He knelt and threaded his finger into the rusted pipe and, sure enough, brushed against a box. "Kenzie, thank you so much. I guess I'll return this with a full tank of gas when I'm done?"

"That would be much appreciated. Be safe up there, Mr. Dud. I hope you find what you're looking for."

"Me too. Thanks again, Kenzie."

He climbed in, turned the key and drove off toward Nine Mile.

6

As a child, her father had locked her in the closet under the stairs as punishment. No grounding, or cancelation of weekend activities or TV privileges, just total darkness with nothing to stimulate the senses other than the murmur of voices outside the door.

Evelyn Wilkerson sat on the hard dirt floor and massaged her toes. When she first entered the room, those inside had panicked, seemingly terrified of the dark, so she hung back and waited for the milling and trample of feet to die down. As silence settled, she ventured forward with arms outstretched. Objects brushed against her fingertips as she searched for clues to her location. The leg of what felt like a wooden bed was too high for her fingers, but the perfect height for her toes. Bone cracked as she tumbled forward with a curse and apologized to whoever cushioned her fall before struggling upright and moving again.

The silence was broken with whimpering voices as she measured twenty hesitant paces from timber wall to timber wall in one direction, twelve the other. A row of basic beds, covered with canvas sheets, lay pushed against one of the longer walls. Five of them, all taken. The door must have been flush to the wall because her fingers found nothing but rough timber.

She sat on the floor and stared as her nose grew used to the stench of stale sweat. Now she knew what it must be like to be blind too. "I'm Evie," she said in a quiet voice. "Who's in here with me?"

At first there was silence. The room could have held a séance.

"I know I'm not alone, I'm sure I've touched each one of you. Unless I missed someone, there are six of us in here. I know my husband will look for me, so we need to stay together and be strong. So, come on, I'm Evie. Who's out there?"

The first voice to respond spoke through sobs. It sounded like a child, perhaps a teenager. The next was similar in tone, with the same accent. All five of the girls spoke with a thick local accent. Whoever had taken them had a particular type in mind.

So why was she the only white girl in the room?

She drew her knees up to her chest and asked the obvious question.

"Where are we? Does anyone know?"

Silence.

"Were you all taken from the road? Have any of you seen the people involved? Is anyone hurt? And how long have you all been here?"

Silence again. And then, "I was walking home from school. The big man picked me up and threw me in a van. They haven't hurt us. I don't know how long I've been here, maybe two days, but it's always dark. I want to go home."

The young voice again. The first girl to speak. Quiet and timid, afraid of being overheard.

"It's okay. We'll be okay," said Evie. "My husband is a good man, and he has skills and lots of training. He'll find us and then we can go home. What's your name?"

"Lecia. My name is Lecia."

"Hello, Lecia. I'm Evie," she repeated. "How old are you, Lecia?"

"I'll be sixteen next week. We're having a party," she sobbed. "I don't want to miss my party."

Evie reached out into the darkness to offer comfort, but couldn't even see her own arm. "It's okay, Lecia. Don't cry. We'll be out of here soon."

"Do you promise?" asked Lecia. "Do you promise, Evie?"

Evie crossed her fingers behind her back, a habit from younger days. It occurred to her that she could have held her crossed fingers in front of her face, the darkness was absolute.

"I promise, Lecia. Stay strong."

———————

The guide must have left the coast road at some point because different scenery flashed by from time to time. As Dud thrashed the small engine, he drove by tourist locations he'd seen on the small map back at the hotel. None of the signs seemed familiar from when he and Evie had taken the trip yesterday.

The guide informed them that this part of Jamaica had the deepest bay, and was where Christopher Columbus had first laid anchor. And Dunn's River Falls. Their drinking partners, the Canadian couple Dan and Justine, had told them about climbing the Falls before Mario the bartender had mentioned Nine Mile.

A loading dock passed by on his left. A boat rocked on the tide, anchored beneath a huge conveyor that hung across it like a giant's arm. The place looked deserted.

And signs for Ocho Rios appeared at intervals. Back home in Kentucky, he and Evie had flipped a coin to choose between Ocho Rios and Montego Bay. Both looked like paradise. Would the situation have been different if tails had landed, rather than heads?

As before, the large houses faded behind him and the random shacks appeared. The incline steepened and Dud prayed again, this time that he wouldn't come face to face with a large panel van. The tires on the VW weren't bald, but they'd struggle to grip the loose road the way the Jeep's all terrain rubber had. So far, nothing but regular vehicles had passed, and always at a point where the road stretched wide enough to allow them both easy passage.

He shifted concentration back and forth, switching from watching the road and his position on it, to searching out familiar sights. They hadn't timed the trip yesterday, both content to chat and enjoy the sights, so he had no idea how far to drive. Then, the incline leveled out and grass verges met him on either side.

*You can open your eyes now babe. No more big drops.*

He recognized the landscape. Dud eased off the gas and piloted the car forward at a much slower rate as he scoured the trees to his right. There would probably be tire marks in the road, too, where the guide had swung the Jeep across the opposite lane.

About a mile later, the road vanished around a curve. His heart beat faster. This was it. He rolled the car across the road and onto the grass verge, angling the nose down so the VW didn't roll like the Jeep had. There were no rubber marks on the road but the huge tree still stood proud, dead ahead, like a monument.

The Jeep was gone. Maybe the police had moved it, or perhaps someone had stolen it. The tree seemed to have come through the entire event unscathed although the loose branches that had fallen were still scattered on the ground. Some were a distance away as if someone had thrown them. He turned the car to face down the incline and pulled out his phone.

No bars showed on the screen, and no fan of Wi-Fi lines. He grimaced and speed-dialed English's number. English answered on the first ring.

"Dud. Look up and wave, we see you."

He got out of the car and looked up at the blue sky. Off in the distance, angry looking storm clouds were gathering, ready for the daily downpour.

"Funny. Y'all in a drone or something?"

"No drone, pal. Much, much higher than that. You're glowing red on the screen here. Looks like you're nice and warm."

"Ah, thermal imaging. Useful."

"Very," said English, "cos while you were getting in position, we scouted out the area. There's another group of red folks, five or six of them, about three clicks to your east. I can't see through the trees mate, but if I had to guess I'd say the road we talked about leads to a group of shacks. Everything's undercover so you'll have to go for a stroll and check it out."

"I can do that, it's not like I've got plans. I'll follow the road and see where it goes. Should take me about thirty or forty minutes to cover three clicks, so I'll save the battery and call you back when I'm getting close."

"Copy that. And put your phone on vibrate. I don't want to tempt fate, but if it's a bad situation and we need to call you, I'd hate to light you up where they'll see you."

"Good call, English. I'll check in soon."

"We'll be ready. Good hunting, Dud. Club out."

Inside Kenzie's car, the only thing that resembled a weapon was a blunt pen. A few hand-sized rocks had slid down onto the grass, so he filled a pocket and angled his walk so that he intercepted the road after ten minutes. The trees were thicker than expected. Even at a steady, consistent pace, he glanced down from time to time to avoid twisting his ankle on exposed roots or slick leaves. In the distance, the storm broke as thunder rumbled and growled. The overhead canopy hid any lightning flashes, but the humidity rose a couple of notches and sweat soon tricked down his back. It was a relief to reach smoother and lighter ground. He kept away from the road, hidden off to one side, and picked up the pace.

The clock on the phone said he'd been walking for twenty-five minutes when it vibrated.

"Guys. Everything okay?"

"All good, buddy," said Sarge. "Keep your eyes open, you're almost there."

Dud reduced his voice to a whisper. "Shit. I made better time than I thought. So I'm headed in the right direction?"

"Yep. I'm surprised you can't already see something."

"Nah, the trees are dense. Okay, I'll keep this channel open and see what's up ahead." He glanced down at the phone. "Well, when I say channel..."

"We get you, bud. Eyes peeled and be careful."

He dropped into a crouch and slunk forward. As he cleared a thick bush, the road ahead forked. One direction continued into the heart of the forest, the other snaked away to the north.

"Probably a shortcut to Bob's house," he mumbled. He spoke into the phone. "Guys, there's a fork in the road. The heat signatures, are they north or east of my location?"

"As you were," said Marbles. "You're almost standing on them."

"Hey, Marbles. So, the whole club is there, huh?"

"Yep, we're all here buddy."

"Well I appreciate it. Okay, I'm moving on. Talk soon."

He reached the fork and stopped. About a hundred yards ahead, something green broke up the brown wall of tree trunks. Two buildings, one a good-sized cabin and the other a large building covered in green metal. The trees still offered excellent cover, so he edged forward and swung around inside the undergrowth, parallel to the structures.

A light burned in the larger building but the cabin sat in darkness, so he trekked back to the fork, crossed the road, and moved forward again to come up behind it.

"Okay," he whispered, "I've found it. There are two buildings; one window in the smaller one, two in the larger. The small one looks empty, so I'll check that out first."

"The heat sources are a few feet away from you. You're a lonely red dot at the moment," said English.

The cabin's window faced the other building. Nothing moved in the light across the clearing. No noise and no shadows. He inched around the side and ducked as low as possible before skirting the perimeter. His eyes flitted between the two buildings until he huddled beneath the window. After a moment of silence, he rose to one side of the opening and peeped inside.

The interior looked like a log cabin, like something he

could retire to by the lake. A clean fireplace broke up the far wall, facing a couple of comfortable looking sofas. A rug filled the floor between them, heavy coarse fabric that could double as fine grade sandpaper. In one far corner, a wooden table sat empty and a rocking chair filled the other. There were no dishes, ashtrays, items of clothing or any sign that the room was in use. He ducked and edged back to the rear of the building.

"You were right. The smaller building is deserted. It doesn't look as if anyone's been in there for a while. Okay, stay connected while I check out the other. We know there's someone home there."

He skulked back into the tree line and made a wide circle until he came out behind the larger building. As he grew closer, voices bled through the wall panels. He rested his ear against the cold metal and tried to discern conversation, but only mumbles filtered through.

"There's definitely life inside," he whispered into the phone. "I'm going to creep around front and see what's going on in there."

The soft earth masked his footsteps as Dud padded along the side of the building. A small three step staircase led up to a metal framed door. As he skirted around it, a squawk sounded within. He stopped and listened. The tinny sound of a hand-held radio seeped through the door.

"Hourly report. Check."

He pressed his ear to the door.

"All product accounted for and secure," said a thick Jamaican voice.

"And the package? It is safe?"

"The package is safe. Delivery is on schedule."

"Very good."

A loud burst of static signaled the end of the call. Short,

sweet, and businesslike. What was the package? Drugs, probably. Or guns.

Dud continued to edge along the front of the building until he reached the first window. Insects danced in the beam of light that shot through it to cast a bright square onto the dull forest floor. Cautious, he raised his head to look inside.

If anything could be the polar opposite of the smaller cabin, this was it. No wood or cozy fireplace. Sheer white paint covered the inside of the metal walls. Three men, dark as shadows, played cards on a small table against the other window. They wore the same clothing as the guys on the bikes that ran them off the road.

Two sofas looked as if they'd landed where they'd been dropped. One held a young boy and another guy who faced away, deep in conversation. Heavy weaponry littered the other. Dud recognized two SCAR's, 30 rounds per clip, enough to cut him down easily, and some good, faithful AK-47's. Their curved magazines were attached beneath them like deadly smiles.

He dared to move across the window a little, hoping the card game enthralled the three heavies enough to distract them.

A large table took up the center of the room. Empty beer bottles and magazines littered it like a bachelor's coffee table. In the corner, by the door, another young boy was replacing the radio handset.

Dud ducked again and grabbed the phone. "Guys, there's a frigging militia in the other building, but there's no sign of Evie. She's not here."

"Probably a drug gang," said Numbers. "The hills over there are full of them."

"Yeah, but now we're back to square..."

As Dud almost completed his sentence, the metal door swung open. A shaft of light stretched into the clearing and the radio guy stepped out, stood on the top step with his chest puffed out and lit a cigarette. Dud froze and cupped his hand over the phone. The kid exhaled a plume of smoke along with a relieved sigh and dropped onto the first step. Dud reached into his pocket and curled his fingers around a stone, then crept backwards toward the far corner of the building.

The kid whistled a tune Dud didn't recognize as he dropped onto the bottom step and lifted the cigarette to his lips. The corner was six feet away when the kid turned his head.

His eyes widened, and the cigarette tumbled end over end and nosedived into the dirt with a splash of sparks. He lifted an arm and pointed.

"Intruder!"

Dud launched the stone. It left his hand like a final inning pitch at a baseball game. Confident, practiced and accurate. It struck the kid on the forehead and he tumbled backwards off the step and collapsed screaming against the other corner of the building.

As Dud ran, the deeper voices of the bigger and, no doubt, more experienced soldiers followed him into the dense tree line. He fumbled for the phone.

"Guys, they've seen me."

He dropped his head and ran as the gunfire started.

7

"Shit, shit, shit, shit, shit!"

Dud cursed over and over as bullets zipped past his head or thudded to an abrupt halt in nearby trees. Splinters of bark shot across his path as he fought his fears to bring the phone to his ear.

"I was careless, guys, should've gone around the back. And if I get any more frigging splinters, I'll go crazy." He took a breath. "What's ahead of me?"

"Trees," said English. "Then more trees. Hang on mate, let me scout the area."

"Be quick about it, man," said Dud. His words bounced with each jarring footstep, and his body screamed at him to lie down, to curl up into a ball and take cover until the noise stopped.

"All I see is trees when I go non-thermal. The canopy covers everything. Why not swing around and head back to the road? Make a wide circle and skirt past them all. They're fanned out in a line, five of them, and they're moving toward you. Weird though, one of them stayed back, but he's not by the buildings."

As he made a turn, the shooting stopped. Dud heaved a sigh of relief and wiped his sweaty hands, one by one, across his shirt.

"Okay. I need a gun to stand any chance out here. Damn, I'd forgotten how frigging scary gunfire can be."

"You should have taken some weaponry with you," said English.

"Just my luck, there were no guns on the breakfast buffet, just a few mean looking bananas. Make yourself useful English and guide me around these bastards. Get me back to the lone guy."

"Yeah, sorry mate. Okay, run left at ninety degrees from your current path. With the lead you've got, you should be okay for a bit."

Dud cradled the phone and followed instruction. Nothing stood out in the landscape. In every direction, trees stood like a maze around him.

English continued. "Okay, you should be good now. Angle back about forty-five degrees and track back toward the camp. You've just drawn level with the last guy behind you. If you run back at an angle, you'll pass him by a few hundred yards."

"Got it," said Dud. His breath came in shorter bursts as he turned. "It's a good thing we joined the gym, otherwise I'd have been useless by now."

"We don't get wrinkles on the inside, pal." Sarge's voice boomed through the earpiece, a huge reassurance. "We can be as fit as we want to be, God willing."

He pictured Sarge adjusting his cap with every word as something caught his eye. He dived to the ground and scrambled behind a trunk. A twig snapped and leaves rustled to his side as he craned his neck to look past the tree.

The first guy strode forward twenty feet away, his head

turning from side to side, alert and watchful, automatic weapon held out in front of him. They weren't taking any prisoners.

The next guy stood twelve feet beyond him. Same actions. Past him was the big guy. Each time he turned to face Dud, he disappeared behind a tree, or a limb drifted across to obscure his face. The leader waved his arms and pointed silent instructions, nothing verbal. The other two flitted in and out of the trees in the far distance.

"Shit, English," he hissed. "They're right here. God only knows how they didn't see me."

"Sorry, Dud. I must have misinterpreted the distances. I guess that's why you didn't call me Numbers."

"There's only one Numbers," said a small voice in the background.

Dud looked again. The wall of menace continued to move forward. They wore the same clothing, identical to the guys on the bikes that had run them off the road. This could well be them although there were no vehicles at the camp site.

"English, when you were scouting the area earlier, did you notice any other heat signatures, even faint ones?"

"No, just the ones you know about. One of them moved around before you got there, but that's about it. Why do you ask?"

"There's no transport here. No cars, trucks, bikes, nothing. I don't imagine they walk into town, which means one of two things. Either there's more to this camp I haven't seen yet, or someone is missing from the party."

"All the more reason to get out of there and report this to the authorities," said Marbles. "Don't stick around out there, Dud. You know as well as I do, it's not always wise to fight your way out. There's no shame in running."

"Copy that, Marbles."

The search party inched forward about thirty feet away, still moving as one. The leader's arms were visible in tiny snatches before disappearing into the foliage and Dud still hadn't been able to identify him. "Get me back to the lone guy, English. I'll see what my chances are like when I get there."

"Okay. Begin your move and I'll talk you in," said English.

Five minutes later, he spoke again. "Okay, if I've got my distances sorted he should be directly ahead of you soon. Be careful, mate."

"Will do," whispered Dud. "Gonna put the phone in my pocket while I take care of this. I'll leave the line open."

With the phone in his pants back pocket, he crouched and moved forward. Despite the abundance of trees, no decent sized limbs lay around that he could fashion into a club, so he pulled another stone from his pocket. After a few yards, the guy appeared.

The kid from outside the building paced back and forth, muttering and cursing to himself. Each time he turned to walk back, Dud could see his face, smeared in blood. The gash in his forehead looked raw and painful. He stood in a clearing, with nothing around him but more trees and an embankment covered in leaves. The back of the large building beckoned in the distance.

Dud sat for a second and watched him. Fifteen paces away, fifteen back, a pause to either admonish himself or insult his leader, then a turn and another fifteen each way. It was predictable, like watching a video game. But why would he be out here, away from the camp? It made no sense. The leader seemed efficient and in control, so why wouldn't he put the kid back in the camp, hidden behind a window or door?

Each time he walked away, Dud edged closer.

He paced away again, his regular fifteen steps, then turned and walked back. As he walked away again, Dud dropped the rock, rose from his position, and stalked behind him. Before he could turn, he swung an arm around his neck and pushed his head forward with the other hand. A strong bicep curled against the kid's artery as the child kicked and thrashed. Dud squeezed, and ten seconds later young arms dangled loosely; he was out for the count but still alive.

Sarge always said that all life is precious, and he'd instilled this belief into the club. Dud had no trouble following it. The kid had a mother, regardless of his day job. With a heave, Dud threw him over a shoulder and carried him back to the camp.

Inside the large building, he dropped the limp body onto a filthy sofa and searched it. As well as a battered AK-47, he found a knife sheathed in an ankle holster. It was a mean looking weapon with a serrated edge and a loop by the handle to thread a stabilizing finger through. These guys weren't messing around, even the young ones.

He cut the cushion fabric into strips, gagged the kid, and hog-tied him on the sofa.

A quick search of the room turned up nothing other than extra ammo. No means of communication, other than the radio. No wallets, keys, nothing. The kid carried no I.D. either. A faint voice chirped from his back pocket. He grabbed the phone.

"From the scuffle and the faint rise in body temp, we're betting you choked out the lone guy?" said Marbles.

"The wonders of modern technology," said Dud. "He was just a kid. I couldn't kill him."

"Good man," said Sarge. "So, what's the situation? The others are still in a nice line some distance away, but I don't imagine they'll walk forever."

"There's nothing here. I don't get it. Why was the kid outside the camp? I'll take another look. Let me know when I need to leave."

"Will do," said English. "Keep us posted."

Dud checked the kid's ties and jogged back to the clearing. There was no tactical reason for him to have been positioned here. Looking for a height advantage, he turned to run up the incline, slipped on the thick carpet of leaves and tumbled forward. His hands landed on the floor with a solid thump.

"What the hell?" He ignored the biting splinter marks in his palms and wiped away the blanket of leaves to find a block of thick wood. With more effort, he cleared a six by three feet area to reveal a door, latched closed with a heavy iron bolt and a huge padlock.

"Guys," he said into the phone, "I've found something. There's a door cut into the incline. This isn't a hill, it's a bunker."

As he spoke, he heard a murmur. He swung around and lifted the gun. Nothing. Then another noise; a squelch, followed by a faint voice. The radio in the larger building. They were checking in. Unless the kid on the sofa was Houdini, they'd miss it this time.

Dud imagined him, rolling around on his stomach in frustration. He'd probably fallen off the sofa by now. "How far away are my friends?"

"On their way back," said English. "I'd give you five

minutes tops before you'd better think about getting out of there."

Then the murmur started again.

"I can hear something, coming from behind this door. Watch my back."

He pocketed the phone, turned the gun in his hands and hammered against the wood with the grip. After each blow, a scuffle or cry responded from the other side.

"Hello? Is there someone in there?"

There was silence, and then he heard a familiar voice, strong and assertive.

"Dud? Dud, is that you, babe? It's me. It's Evie."

8

The phone chirped, quietly at first, before it rose in volume like a chorus of crickets.

Dud leaned his forehead against the door. "Are you okay, babe? Are you hurt?"

The noise grew even louder as he tried to make out Evie's words. "I'm okay. I told them you'd come for me."

Before the phone drowned out Evie's voice, he reached into his pocket, grabbed it and spoke into the mouthpiece. "Talk to me."

"Whatever you were hammering against," said Marbles, "the whole world heard it. Company's coming and they're not in a tidy line now. They're moving fast, which means they're sprinting. Get out of there."

With nothing to lose, Dud stood, pocketed the phone, and leveled the gun. "Babe! Stand back!"

The hinges were huge steel bars with thick rivets driven through quarter sized holes. The handle sank into the panel and had no fittings visible. That left the lock and bolt. The bolt had to be an inch thick, slid through a loop of steel the size of a child's fist.

He took one step back and pulled the trigger three times. Jagged holes appeared in the panel like splintered Morse code as the rounds thumped into the wood. The steel pinged as the slugs hit it, but it held firm and rattled in place. He tried again, bracing the gun to fight the barrel rise. He went for a third attempt before a different gunfire sounded. Rounds whizzed by as he ducked and rolled to one side.

The bad guys were just visible against the tree line and were running flat out.

Palm flat against the wood, he screamed through the door. "I'll be back babe. Stay safe. I love you!"

He didn't wait for a reply, but used the incline to roll upright and then bolted for the car. The rise of the hill hid him as he raced into the trees and zigzagged with the crack of gunfire sounding behind him. He jumped and cursed, but nothing came close. They were shooting out of anger and desperation.

Faint screaming came from his back pocket. Dud grabbed the phone and spoke as he ran. "They spotted me. Running back to the car."

"No shit, Sherlock," said English. "We were screaming at you to move."

"Sorry pal, didn't hear you over all the gunfire. Evie's here."

"Call the police now. Give them the coordinates and get them out there. Hang on, did you say Evie's there? With you, now?"

"Not with me. She's in that bunker. And she's not alone."

"Bloody hell. Call the police. As soon as you can."

He emerged onto the incline at the roadside. The car

waited a few hundred feet further down the road. "As soon as I get the car going. 911?"

"One step ahead of you," said English. "The internet is conflicted. Some sites say 119 and some say it's been changed to 911 to make the number more universal."

Dud's breath came in ragged bursts. "I can't believe I'm talking phone numbers. I have to get back to Evie."

"You're out-numbered and out-gunned," said Sarge. "Call the police."

"Will do," said Dud as he threw open the car door. With the accelerator mashed to the floor, he shot the car onto the wrong side of the road, corrected it, and raced toward town.

---

Lindsay's deep voice bellowed through the trees. "Find him. Now!"

Sending almost everyone after the intruder had been a gamble, one that hadn't paid off. Deaven was a liability, one of the young ones, but he could map the island with his eyes closed. Lindsay assigned him to radio duty, only to be used in confrontations if necessary. Still, he had spotted the guy when he'd somehow sneaked into the camp under their noses. With the blood running from the head wound into his eyes, he'd be useless in a search, but he could guard the product.

The guy couldn't be allowed to escape. He'd seen little, but he'd already seen too much.

Then the hammering started. Somehow, the intruder had slipped past them and doubled back. The banging sounded like it came from the camp or, even worse, the storage facility. The only person there to stop him was Deaven.

Lindsay Anderson ran as fast as his muscled legs would propel him. The others raced behind, their breathing growing heavy as Lindsay leaped over stumps and roots and opened a sizeable gap between them. He rounded a curve and the green panels of the camp loomed ahead. There was no sign of Deaven, just the back of a large man, balanced on the embankment, slamming the butt of a gun into the door of the storage facility with the weight of his whole body.

He closed the gap further as the man stepped back and fired the weapon. Lindsay couldn't see any damage from this distance, but the ping of metal against metal told its own story. He found another ounce of energy and pushed harder as the firing stopped and the guy ducked out of sight. Then he saw him, lying on the ground. It looked like he was listening through the door. Mr. Ramirez would kill them all if anything happened to this shipment. Especially this particular delivery.

At around a hundred yards, Lindsay stopped and raised his gun. He loved the SCAR. Its French sounding proper name was way too long to remember, but if it was good enough for the U.S. Special Forces, it was good enough for him. It had more control than the popular guns the others used. Let the kids play with their AK-47s.

Even at this distance, the guy flinched as he fired and made himself a smaller target. The heavy breathing of the others sounded behind him as he fired one more volley. The guy looked back before he rolled and dropped over the hill. It would have been a lucky shot from here, but it only took one slug to do some damage.

When they reached the camp, he'd vanished.

Lindsay scanned the trees, his head whipping from side

to side, causing his dreadlocks to slap against his cheeks He pointed toward the road. "Go! After him. He cannot escape."

As his men ran in pursuit, Lindsay checked the door. Pock marks crisscrossed it, but it remained intact. The product was safe. He stormed into the camp, checked the small cabin first and then burst into the main building.

Deaven lay at the side of the sofa, his wrists and ankles tied behind his back. His eyes shined like beacons against his blood-soaked skin, fear ebbing from them in waves. Lindsay knelt and removed the gag.

"What happened? Talk."

Deaven's words were hoarse as he struggled to speak. Lindsay leaned closer. "Cat got your tongue?"

"Choked. He choked me. Forgive me, I'm sorry."

Lindsay felt the heat rise in his face and he breathed deeply to curb his temper. "Pray we find him, to whichever God you serve."

The radio crackled into life with a burst of static and a familiar voice spoke. "Are you there? Lindsay? You missed check-in. You never miss check-in. What's going on? Is my package safe?"

He glared at Deaven and picked up the handset. "Mr. Ramirez. This is Lindsey. All is good. My operator abandoned his post to take a leak at an inopportune time. I will discipline him and it will never happen again. I repeat; everything is good."

"Don't make me come down there."

The radio squelched again. Call over.

Lindsay whirled, stormed over to the prone man and raised his boot. It hovered an inch over Deaven's face. He lifted it, his eyes blazing and nostrils flaring as his thigh muscles tensed. Then he lowered it and walked away.

"I take it back. You'd better pray to every God there is."

———————

The small Volkswagen held the road well, considering the speed it put out. Dud held the accelerator to the floorboard wherever possible, switching his gaze from the road ahead to the rearview mirror and back again.

After ten minutes, the adrenaline subsided and his heavy foot grew lighter. Just once, oncoming traffic had forced him to swerve to the edge of the road. He didn't even contemplate easing up on the speed. Instead, he gritted his teeth as the rubber beneath him rumbled, and he fought for purchase as the car straddled the road and the drop along-side him. Screams and curses rose over the sound of the oncoming vehicles' horn and there were hand gestures in the rearview, but he grappled with the steering wheel and guided the VW back onto solid ground.

To his right, the days' storm raged in the distance and backlit a huge domed structure. Dud remembered the guide talking about bauxite mining. The dome was by the port he'd driven past earlier. A great place to hide.

The dock appeared a few minutes later. He swung the car under a huge conveyor and parked behind a stack of tall steel containers. The phone still showed no signal as he fished out Thomas' card and dialed the number. The call was answered immediately, the reception crystal clear. Bless you, English, he thought.

"Montego Bay Police Department."

"Officer Thomas, please."

"One moment."

Instead of hold music, a voice reiterated what he'd already heard. Despite its apparent lenience toward mild drug use, the Jamaican Police Department will still take action if you're caught in possession of any drugs. Dud chewed the inside of his cheek. What would they do if you were caught in illegal possession of women?

The voice changed. "Officer Thomas speaking."

"Sir, it's Dan Wilkerson. You interviewed me at the Royal Caribbean Hotel in Montego Bay. My wife is missing?"

A slight pause, and then "Ah, yes. Mr. Wilkerson. I assume she has turned up."

"Well, yes and no. I found her, but she's been kidnapped. I need you to send as many men as you can. They're in a camp and they're heavily armed and..."

"Please," interrupted Thomas, "slow down, mon. What is your location?"

Dud tried to describe the crash site and the road that ran off it further north.

"Do you consider yourself to be safe?" asked Thomas.

"What the hell kind of question is that?" shouted Dud. "I don't give a shit about me; my wife is locked in an underground bunker with a gang of gun toting psychopaths. Send someone before I go back in there myself."

"Please calm down, Mr. Wilkerson. I am already rounding up a party. If you're sure you're not in any immediate danger, describe the vehicle you are driving and then park a small distance away. We will find your car and meet you at the roadside."

"Ah. Sorry." Dud climbed out of the car to read back the license plate number, followed by a good description; equal parts blue and rust.

"It will take time to get to you. Please, stay in your vehicle and we will be there as soon as possible."

Dud drove back and pulled over to the side two

hundred yards before the road branched off into the trees. The urge to keep driving right into the camp, gun blazing, overwhelmed him. Common sense prevailed. He also contemplated heading further north and then sneaking back into the camp to take them out with the knife one by one, Rambo style. A silent, stealthy ninja. Searching house to house for combatants in dusty Middle Eastern villages had taught him that it's nothing like it is on TV. Every innocent looking door nudged open with a nervous foot could be the last thing you saw. Never underestimate your enemy.

The Old Farts Club was camped out in English's basement, waiting for updates. He called and told them about the conversation with Thomas.

"Glad you saw sense," said Marbles. "Keep us posted."

A dozen cars passed by and vanished out of sight before a police car grew larger in the rearview. It had no lights flashing or sirens blaring, just sidelights that looked like a pair of eyes in the afternoon sun. Again, not like on TV. Then the car drove past him. Dud frowned, before its taillights flared and it did a dangerous three-point turn in the road and drove back, before angling to a stop a few feet in front of him. The cop from the hotel climbed out. Dud hoped he wouldn't be as reckless in the field.

He frowned again. Didn't Thomas say he was rounding up a party? This guy came alone. Still, he dressed the part; black uniform, pristine pleats, and cuffs. He wore a wedding band on one hand and a flashy gold watch that matched his badge on the other wrist. A baton hung down his left thigh, and a holster tucked snugly up against his right hip. He smiled a bright smile and waved.

Dud tucked the knife into his waistband and pulled his shirt over it, grabbed the keys and pushed the AK under the passenger seat. He climbed out and stood behind the false safety of the door as the cop meandered closer.

"Where's the party?"

The cop paused for a millisecond, smiled again and held up both hands in a universal gesture of peace. "I'm sorry, mon. When you said party, I thought you meant, you know, party. I'm here to help. Officer James."

"That doesn't answer my question," said Dud. "Where's the backup? Where's the party?"

"Right behind me," said James. He didn't miss a beat. "They'll be here any minute now. I was closer and thought we could make a start. You can lead the way if you like?"

Dud unconsciously glanced across at the crash site as the cop grew closer, then caught a glimmer in his peripheral vision. The cop's watch glinted in the sunlight and he turned back in time to see him snatch his pistol from its holster. Before he raised it, Dud dropped and rolled backwards behind the car.

"You're quick, mon," laughed James. "But can you outrun a bullet?"

Gravel crunched as James reached the front of the car. Dud slid the key into the trunk lock and turned it. The lid popped open half an inch with a faint click. If the cop had any sense, he'd come from the road side to prevent any escape. A steep embankment fell away at Dud's back. There was no safe way down there.

More crunching footsteps. So, he had some sense. He'd be hugging the car in case any other vehicles came flying past; left hand out for balance, right hand holding the gun, angled in at the car's body.

Dud ducked lower, edged over to the license plate and waited.

[ 9 ]

Ramirez watched the one hundred and eighty-foot Taiba yacht bob on the current, moored in the harbor that stretched back until it met the azure blue of The Pacific. It would leave soon, to be replaced by a new model almost twice its length. Bigger was always better and nothing screamed status like a gleaming yacht; the equivalent of an English gent having a Rolls Royce parked in the driveway.

He turned away to admire his home. With the ocean at his back, the sun beamed past him and splashed against the curved stone that formed the front face. Shadows of the palm tree fronds beckoned him like curled fingers. Black, cast iron rails held back patio umbrellas that kept the sun off the two armed men that flanked the main door.

The manicured lawns felt lush beneath his bare feet as he made his way toward the house. Abigail gazed down at him from the arched upstairs window above them. Her features weren't clear, she was too far away, but she would smile even though he knew it would be forced. They only took so many beatings and then they retreated. That's when he got bored. She'd be updated soon, too.

A new yacht and a new woman.

Money kept them happy for a while, and they could shop in the village as long a guard went with them. Money didn't matter, and he wanted an attractive woman by his side. As long as they didn't run or call for help, he didn't have to beat them.

Sooner or later, he'd find one that would stay.

The large patio door slid on a well-oiled track as he entered the building. He slid it closed behind him. Damned insects. Abigail had walked across the upstairs landing and now watched him over the railing. She offered a forced smile.

"You should go into town," he said, and gestured to a striking Jamaican woman who stood guard by a downstairs window. The girl stood almost a head taller than everyone else, with a mane of jet black hair tied in a severe pony tail, and he trusted her with his life. "Take Marcia and buy a new dress. We'll have cause for a celebration soon. You'll want to look pretty, won't you?"

She nodded quickly, nervously, and whirled away to her bedroom.

Ramirez shook his head. Time for a new one.

His office lay at the far end of the first floor. A huge window behind the desk opened onto The Pacific, and another window in the side wall allowed the sun to beam in and glow against the rich, hardwood floor. He sat behind the desk, opened the center drawer and pulled out a handful of Polaroids.

Lindsay was becoming quite the photographer. And he'd grown accustomed to his employer's taste. This girl, the new one, was tall and slim and had flawless skin. She curved in all the right places, with long blond hair that trailed down her back to one of those curves. He guessed her age to be late thirties.

In one photo, she stood against a rail, looking out into the ocean. The sun glared off her hair like a halo. In another, she sat at a hotel bar with a man who looked be a good ten years older, sunglasses pushed up onto the top of her head. With her hair swept back, it highlighted a naturally pretty face. And she had a beautiful smile. Not forced.

He felt good about this one. It would be a pleasure to take her from this man and show her how good life should be.

As good a photographer as he might be, Lindsay's choice of soldier grew suspect. He never missed a check-in. Ever. The man himself was a consummate employee, but even they grew comfortable. Like the women.

Ramirez liked to keep the men on their toes. Perhaps they were due a visit. It had been a while since he'd seen Jamaica.

He shuffled the Polaroids once more and slid them back into the drawer. No. There were things to arrange here. He'd give them a little more time.

---

"There's nowhere to run," said James. His voice taunted and smiled at the same time.

*Never underestimate your enemy.*

Dud rested his palm on the underside of the trunk lid as another deliberate footstep crunched toward him.

"We run this island and we hear everything. You might as well go out quickly, here and now. I promise I'll make it quick."

*An innocent looking door, nudged open with a nervous*

*foot, could be the last thing you saw.* James's shiny boot landed just past the rear wheel. Dud scooped up a handful of loose gravel and tossed it to his left. Human instinct would make James lean just a little closer to peer around the car. Dud moved.

In a flurry of motion, he pushed against the trunk lid. It shot up on squeaking hinges and connected with something solid. A yelp of pain and the clatter of metal was all the notice he needed, and he leaped upright and bolted around the open lid. An innocent looking door could be the last thing you saw.

James had staggered back. Blood trickled from his nose and a finger on his right hand bent out at an unnatural angle. His gun was nowhere to be seen. Fury swam in his eyes as he shook his head and glared. "You'll pay for that, mon."

As he reached for the baton with his left hand, Dud took two quick steps forward and crashed a fist into the already bleeding nose. James yelped again as his eyes watered and he barreled forward. Their bodies met with a thud as the cop scratched and clawed at Dud's face. He fumbled to find an eye socket, but Dud responded with a hard knee to the ribs. Bone cracked as the Jamaican doubled over. Another hard knee followed to the face and gristle crunched as James's nose exploded.

He howled and dropped to his knees. Dud's heart pounded and adrenaline once again flooded his system as he pulled out the knife. James looked up in time to see the savage serrated edge gleam in the sunlight.

As he spoke, drops of blood flew from his lips and dripped off his chin. "Stop. Please. I just do as I'm told. I have a family. Let me see them again."

"Who gives the orders," asked Dud.

"I don't know."

Dud twisted the knife. The reflection glinted across the cop's face.

"I swear," begged James, his deep voice rising. "We do as we're told, and we get paid and no one gets hurt."

Genuine fear ebbed from his eyes. The truth.

"Are the police coming?"

His shoulders slumped and his head dropped and shook as the cop admitted defeat. "No, mon. The police are not coming."

The road was silent. Even the insects seemed to have stopped singing in the trees. Dud beckoned with the knife. "Stand up."

James shuffled his feet beneath him and pushed against the road with his good hand. "Please. Please don't kill me."

"And if I let you live, what will you do? Get a group of you together and come for me?"

Tears rolled from his eyes as he licked the blood from around his lips. "No. I swear, I'll leave. I'll take my family and leave Jamaica. And anyway, there's only one penalty for failure. If I stay, I'm a dead man."

"Get in the trunk."

"What?" The cop's face creased in surprise.

"Get in the trunk. In fact, hang on. Put your hands on your head."

"One moment, mon. At least let me take care of my hand."

Dud nodded as James gripped the broken finger. For a second his eyes pleaded for relief, and then he closed them, took a deep breath, and wrenched the bone back into place. The crunching sound merged with the cop's scream and then he sagged and rested his good hand against his knee.

"Don't even think about trying to rush me," said Dud. "Hands up. Now."

James rose with a grim smile as Dud removed the baton and handcuffs from his belt and snatched the radio off its clip and tossed it down the embankment.

"Okay. Now get in the trunk. I don't trust you, but you're fortunate that I hope to be done with killing people. Climb in before I bundle you in there myself."

After a few minutes of bumbling effort, Dud nudged the cop in the chest to send him sprawling into the trunk. He stared down at the prone man. "Don't make me regret not killing you." Then he slammed it shut.

The pistol nestled against the front passenger side tire. Dud picked it up, shot out the cop car's tires, then tucked it into his waistband and walked a few yards up the road. By some miracle, not a single vehicle had passed during the fight and the whole area seemed to be too quiet. The calm before the storm, thought Dud? The storm was definitely coming.

He took out the phone and dialed.

"Dud. What's happening, mate?"

"English, you still got that satellite close? The one you used to watch me?"

"Mate, there's always a satellite close. Give me a sec."

"Dud." Sarge's voice still echoed and sounded distant.

"Hey, Sarge."

"Update, son. What's been happening?"

English spoke again. "Got that satellite, Dud. What do you need?"

"Give me a red dot count. And Sarge, I'm screwed. I can't trust the police, but I know where Evie is. It's up to me to get her."

"I see you," said English, "and another dot close to you,

but it's not moving."

"I know about that one," said Dud.

"Okay, not even going to ask. Back at the range, we still have six healthy dots. They're moving around, but they're grouped together."

"Definitely just six?"

"Yes, sir."

"Okay, so Evie is still locked away. That's good."

Marbles spoke. "Dude, did you say it was good your wife was locked away?"

"She's safe while she's locked up, Marbles. She needs to stay that way until I can come up with a plan to get her back. It's up to me now."

"Dud?" Sarge spoke again.

"Yes, sir?"

"Son, since we formed the club, have you ever had to do anything alone?"

"Well, no but where are you..."

"I've never been to Jamaica, and I hear the sea's beautiful. Reckon you can smuggle a few guys into your hotel room?"

Dud smiled. "I could smuggle the whole 101$^{st}$ Airborne into my room if needed."

"Well, let me speak to the guys and their respective partners, but I'd say if you need a job done right then you might as well do it yourself."

Dud blinked quickly as his eyes welled up. "You're a beautiful man, Sarge."

"Oh, I know. I blame the hair product. Get to the hotel. There are too many people around for anyone to try anything there. Tidy your room and text English the details. We'll combine resources and skills and head your way. Don't you worry, son. The Old Farts Club is coming."

10

Brilliant sunlight warmed his back as Dud walked to the car. He wondered if it was around this time the bikers had ran their guide off the road. What had happened to him? Perhaps he was in the bunker with Evie? She'd said the words 'we are okay'. Then again, most people that kidnapped women had little use for the men that came with them. And with so much open land in these hills, if he'd been killed they might never find the body.

He glanced up the road again. Evie was right there, a simple walk away. What if, this time, he headed south and cut through the forest that way? To come up on the camp from below it and surprise them? The big lock that secured the hatch had to have a key that fit it. Except for the big guy, they didn't seem particularly well trained. He'd come across much worse before and survived. Chances were the big guy had the key. With a little distraction he could isolate him, take him out and get the key. Rather than the Old Farts Club traveling all the way here, they'd arrange a home-coming party instead.

Sarge's words hammered into the front of his mind.

You're outnumbered and out-gunned. As always, he was right. Emotions were taking over, a sure way to get them both killed. Head back to the hotel and regroup. Remove all evidence of his stay, pack everything, and wait for the guys.

Just then, James thumped against the underside of the trunk. As the lid rose on its old hinges, he rolled and blinked his eyes at the bright light. Blood bubbled from his nostrils as he spoke.

"What the hell? What you doing with me, mon? Whatever's happened, I'm still a cop. You can't just make me disappear."

"You can disappear, we're on an island, dipshit," said Dud. "You don't deserve that badge and, anyway, if I wanted you to disappear you'd be shark food by now."

"But you can't leave me here, I need to..."

"What a whiny bitch," said Dud as he slammed the trunk closed again. The thumping continued as he studied the thick trees on the other side of the road. A simple walk away. To love and to cherish, 'til death do us part.

Evie was in there.

He drove the car to the huge tree that had supported the weight of a Jeep, what already seemed like weeks ago, and parked behind it, out of sight and away from the road. When he slammed the driver's door closed, James bleated again from the trunk. The lid opened to the sharp pang of ammonia.

"What the hell, James? This isn't even my car."

"I tried to tell you," said the cop, "but you wouldn't listen. Now you must clean this up."

Dud racked the slide on the 9mm Glock, a cop favorite, and pointed it into the trunk. "I'm taking a walk. Be quiet and I'll keep my promise, I'll let you out in one piece. Make a noise and a stray round might find its way up your ass."

"That's what I'm trying to tell you. I had to go. Soon, I'll need to take a..."

He slammed the trunk closed again and walked south into the fading light, ready to loop around and come up on the camp from behind.

---

Ron 'Numbers' Cole sat upright in a recliner behind the main sofa. He heard every word through the Bluetooth sound system and knew the words that would leave Sarge's mouth before the man had even thought of them. Something like "we'll be there," or "you're never alone when you're in The Old Farts Club". There would be a call to action.

Other than Dud, who was still here if only in voice, The Club gathered in this room; Sarge, all 6'1" of him, with his body tight and trim, even hidden under a baggy t-shirt, jeans and a battered army cap. His mind was still sharp as a scalpel too. Marbles stood three inches shorter but just as lean and, probably, athletically fitter. His visual disability was only considered as such to the pencil pushers that handed out permits and badges to hang on rearview mirrors. English, the youngest of the group at forty-three was, judging by his basement, the sharpest in terms of technology. Standing two inches taller than Sarge, his only disability seemed to be the Honda Accord he drove. As a new member of The Club, they'd talk him into shopping for something fueled with a little more testosterone and a little less unleaded.

Which left Numbers. When it came to logistics, planning and all around 'making things happen', there was no one better. He and Marbles stood eye to eye, the problem being that three years ago he'd been two inches taller. A penchant for the finer things in life had reduced his height by two inches and diverted it to his waistline instead.

And then there was Arlene, his wife of thirty-six years. No military wife ever relied on her husband, but he was her rock and they did everything together. Even if his aging body handled the rigors of whatever Sarge had planned, which he doubted it would, Arlene would never forgive him. She wouldn't stop him, but a different woman would be waiting for him on his return.

As Dud signed off, Sarge stood, walked to the bench next to English and leaned back into it.

"You heard the man," he started. "He's in trouble and he's alone. I'm aware I volunteered us all to help, but I know y'all have responsibilities. There's just me now Deedee's gone, bless her heart. Y'all have wives. It's easy for me to say, but I'd ask nothing of any of you that I wouldn't do myself. Go home, all of you. Talk to your wives and talk to yourselves. If you were in Dud's shoes, what would you do? Call me in an hour or two if you'll take the trip with me. There's no shame in staying, we're not at war anymore and we've all paid our dues, but I must help my man. That's my decision. In the meantime, Numbers, work out a way to get to Jamaica."

"I can't go," said Numbers. He stood, walked around the sofas and joined Sarge by the bench. "This old body won't handle action like that anymore and, even if it did, I'd get back to either an empty house or a cold shoulder. I will get you to Jamaica, though, I've got plenty of favors to call in. And I can coordinate from here. English might be the tech guy, but I've got enough skills to get us by."

English spun his chair around to face everyone. "Dud would do the same for me, even though I've only seen him a few times. Penny will be pissed, but she'll understand. I'm fit, I can keep us ahead of the game in terms of tech and, if I'm to be honest, I can still feel action boiling in my blood. Numbers, you can come down here anytime you like and run things from here. I'll clear it with Penny and record my voice commands into your phone."

"Well, shit," said Marbles, "that leaves me." He pushed himself up off the sofa and joined the others. "Let me go home and talk to Joy. She'll ride my ass, but she knows me well enough. And anyway, there's bound to be all kinds of toys out there. It's been a while since I drove something other than a pickup. And don't those clowns drive on the wrong side of the road? It's been a while since I did that. How could it not be fun?"

"Well, it looks like we're pretty much sorted," said Numbers. "While you all do what you do, I'll plan and make arrangements. Like I said, I have plenty of favors to call in, and I already know how to get you there. English, you'd better introduce me to the wife if I'm using your house. I don't want to walk through the door and be greeted with a shotgun to the face. Marbles, you'd better go and earn some man points with yours so she's still there when you get back." He raised his palm as each man high-fived it.

"And Sarge? You better pack your bikini. It looks like you're going on vacation."

---

Lindsay sat on the step outside the large building while his soldiers milled around, panicked and nervous.

"We have to move them," said Akoni. "Mr. Ramirez will kill us if anything happens, and now that man knows where we are, too. We should move on to the next stage. They'll still be safe there, and it can't hurt to leave them there a day longer and then move out as normal."

Lindsay toyed with the strap on his gun and considered Akoni's words. He was right, the only problem was the hourly check-in. How would they get around that?

Akoni paced again and whirled to face him. "And the man will probably come back with the police."

Lindsay snickered. "The police do not worry me, but that guy does. He found us too easily. There is not enough luck in the world for one man to find us in these hills, but he did. He cannot be working alone."

"He must be, otherwise he would have brought others with him."

Lindsay stood and joined the men. "I don't know, but one thing is for sure; we cannot stay here. Akoni, Deaven, fetch the truck. The rest of you, get your bikes. Load the product and do as Akoni suggested. If we provide food and water, they will be okay for one extra day. Maybe let in ventilation and fresh air now and then. It wouldn't pay for everything to turn up looking like a pot of boiled lobsters."

The men smiled, and then Lindsay watched them walk along the road. They'd reach the fork but, instead of going straight and out on to the coast road, they'd take the other smaller road and follow it. Two hundred yards on, set back beneath a dense clump of undergrowth, was a shed with the van and three bikes.

Ten minutes later the bike engines sputtered and chugged as they rolled into the clearing, followed by the white panel van. Almost as a unit, the three bikers kicked out their stands and propped up their machines. The other two slammed the van doors closed and joined their comrades.

Lindsay strode over and stood among them. "Okay, here

is the plan. We will get the product loaded and moved. Deaven, Mr. Ramirez knows your voice on the radio. We have missed one check-in, so we cannot miss another. You will stay behind..."

Lindsay silenced his protests with a glare, his eyes fierce but focused. "You will stay behind, long enough to finish the check-ins. When it comes time to move the product, the correct time, you will take your bike and join us. Until then, it is vital you complete this mission. Consider it your penance."

Deaven bowed his young head and nodded. This was not a request.

"Once we are all together, we will move forward as normal. Do not worry, this is only a glitch. We've done this many times and always succeeded. And sometimes, it is good to be tested. Perhaps we have become complacent, but this has woken us. We all have a part to play if we are to succeed as a team. Some parts may appear to be more important than others, but don't forget that even the smallest cog keeps the machine working."

He clapped each man on the back. "Load the van and lock it down. We move out now."

Lindsay walked over to the small cabin and laughed as he glanced at the hillside that formed the outside of the bunker. The guy could have shot at the wooden door forever. Or planted charges against it and blown it and the lock to kingdom come. Nothing would have changed. It didn't open and hadn't since the room had been constructed. Behind the three inches of solid wood lay a slab of steel, backed with another row of wooden panels.

Metal jangled as he pulled the key chain from his pocket. The door to the cabin was never locked but the hatch inside was. He slid the rug to one side, opened the lock and lifted the door. The smell of stale sweat drifted up and made him wrinkle his nose while he lifted his gun over the opening and danced its silhouette onto against the floor below.

"Ladies? Put on your nice frocks. We're going for a drive."

11

The C-130 Hercules lumbered down the runway until it reached a ground speed of 85mph, where the pilot eased back the nose and lifted the huge bird into the air. Four propellers spun to power the hunk of metal skyward. Inside the fuselage, the white paneled interior did little to dampen the sound and vibration. The Old Farts Club held on to metal beams and adjusted themselves to accommodate gravity and the tug of G-force. Two hours of flight took them over two states to the panhandle of Florida. The Gulf of Mexico shimmered through the windows.

Sarge smiled as the others gritted teeth and leaned forward as Marbles shouted.

"I fail to see where the fun is in this kind of thing." He'd replaced his glass blue eye with a smiley emoticon. "There's nothing worse than flying and having no control. Don't get me wrong, I've done enough missions, but unless I'm the pilot, there's no better feeling than when your feet finally hit solid ground."

"Oh, come on," said Sarge. "Remember those rides at the fairground? The ones where you wondered if the wooden track would take your weight? And remember when the thing whipped you around and you thought sure, they must have tested it. They wouldn't let anyone on it without it being approved, right? And then you look in the control box. There's a young kid with a face full of acne, and he's on minimum wage and he's got that look in his eyes that says, 'so that's what drugs are' and you wonder, just for a second, is this okay? Didn't that get your adrenaline racing?"

"No, it got my temper rising and that spotty kid had better have left the grounds before I got off or I would have whupped his ass. Frigging ninety degree turns on a ramshackle wooden track. It ain't right."

The men smiled and looked around them. The fuselage of the C-130 was large enough to allow movement, but the constant propeller drone and rush of outside air drowned out everything but shouting. Random objects shifted and bulged behind netting that stretched the length of the fuselage along one side, and basic seating lined the other.

"So how did we end up in first class, Sarge?" said English as he scratched his nails over the canvas seat. He sat with his feet up on the material and reclined as comfortably as possible.

"Numbers knows a guy in the Air National Guard. They do a lot of picking up and dropping off from Louisville. This plane's going by Jamaica so he's arranged to drop us off nearby."

"And when you say drop us off nearby, you mean on a neighboring island right?"

"Almost. We jump out when we get close and make our own way to land."

Marbles spun his head and glared with his good eye. "To land? You mean we're swimming? I didn't pack my shorts, Sarge. I thought we'd land at an airstrip somewhere and then get a cab into town."

Sarge laughed. "Numbers is good, but he's not that good. The flight plan takes this plane past Jamaica so we can't stop. We're bailing out early. It's all right though, we have boats. And I've got plenty of toys wrapped in water-proof bags. It'll be okay."

Marbles glanced around the cabin. "I know you're enjoying this, you sadistic bastard. I don't see any boat, and even more concerning, I don't see any parachutes either."

"The 'chutes are behind the cargo netting," said Sarge. "We'll jump from low altitude, but they can get the plane slow enough that we'll be almost guaranteed not to break anything against the water tension when we hit. They practice all the time. Don't worry, I'm sure we'll be fine."

"That's reassuring, although it's been a while since I practiced anything water-like but singing in the shower. And I still don't see a boat."

"All in good time, my friend," nodded Sarge.

English gripped an interior beam and swayed with the movement of the plane. "Marbles, you were going to tell us about a clapping lamp and noisy lovers."

Sarge sat back and folded his arms over his stomach as Marbles took up his story. "Okay, I heard this from a grunt back in the service. He knew a man who had experience with one of those sound activated lamps, said it was a friend of a friend but, you know. Anyway, the story goes that he and this girl flirted constantly. It got to where, as soon as they made eye contact, buttons and zips didn't count for much. They ripped at each other and the passion took over. Now, bear in mind, this is before CCTV and all that intrusive shit. There was something much more reliable; the old lady across the road, with nothing better to do than knit scarves and watch the street."

The Old Farts Club tuned out the drone of the engines and drew closer.

"So, they do the posturing thing as soon as they get inside her house. She wants him. He puffs out his chest. She sashays to the sofa and claps her hands. The lamp comes on, all dim and romantic. He loses his pants and struts like a prize bull up to her and she lets him get started. Soon there's unbridled passion and the lamps going crazy. Each time they slap together it's receiving a new command. It's on and off, over and over and the rooms lit up like a disco while they're both oblivious in the throes of passion, slamming into each other. Now, across the street is the little old lady. I'm not saying she's a nun, but she's been alone for years. This is more action than she's seen in a month on the Lifetime channel. The lights are going crazy and she thinks 'fire!' So, she calls the fire department. In five minutes, there's a fleet of cop cars and three fire trucks parked outside the house. Just as they open the door, the couple collapse in ecstasy. There was plenty of heat in the room, but no fire. Apparently, once all the explanations had been made, she gave the lamp to the lead firefighter and ushered them out so they could carry on."

"Must be nice to know that passion," said Sarge over the laughter, "but I reckon we can direct that into whatever's waiting for us. I recognize this banter and the joking, and it's no different from any mission I undertook. We do this to avoid thinking about what's next, but let's remember that one of ours is in trouble, and we're going to help him. Sounds like there are genuine bad guys and they have guns and zero worry about taking out any of us. This is not a game. It's as real and mean as cancer so, when we get there, keep your heads down and watch the next guy's back. You've got partners, I've got my daughter. And we all want to see them again."

"Amen to that," said English. "First time we've worked together, too. It could get emotional."

"How much longer until we get there?" asked Marbles.

Sarge glanced at his watch. "A few hours. If it's all the same to you guys, I'm going to get some sleep."

He lay sideways across the seating and closed his eyes. Marbles gazed through the cargo netting across from him and shrugged. "I don't know how you can relax enough to sleep in a tin can like this. And I still don't see a frigging boat."

---

Dense trees and the setting sun made excellent cover as Dud moved deeper into the woods. Based on his current line, he estimated the camp lay at around ten o'clock. This time, the odds were a little more even. With the AK-47 slung over his shoulder, the pistol snug against his back, and the knife tucked into his waistband, he was better equipped than before. Plus, he knew the layout now. He'd sneak around to the far side of the camp, then circle back to reappear to the side of the larger building. That way, the door that had betrayed him before would be at the opposite end. Then, all he had to do was wait.

There had been no bathroom in either of the buildings and, unlike on TV, everyone had to pee. Men rarely took that trip in pairs, and that would be the time to take them out. Dud felt a pang of guilt, plotting to take out a guy literally with his pants down, but this was no time for games.

Evie's life was at stake and, until The Club arrived, he was on his own.

The camp should now be at around seven o'clock to his position. Dud angled in and made a beeline for the center of his imaginary clock. Sweat trickled down his back and, although the canopy only allowed narrow bolts of light through, thunder rumbled above somewhere on the island. The air crackled with electricity, either from the storm or from his own apprehension.

As the thunderclap faded, another sound split the air. It was unmistakable, the guttural drone of bike engines. Foliage still hid the camp, but the sound made a good point to aim for. His clock estimate hadn't been off by much. The engines died and, as he grew closer, the sound of shouting voices took over. Something moved ahead.

Finally, the green metal of the buildings peeped through the trees. As planned, he'd come around to the back of the large building. He crouched, edged closer and listened. The voices were clearer now; the deep, boom of the leader as he issued commands, and the tense replies from his soldiers. The big guy shouted something about moving them from the cabin, but the end of his sentence faded as another engine rumbled closer. A deeper drone, steady and strong. That had to be the van. Where the hell had they stored the vehicles? There was no sign of any machinery at the rear of the building, no flattened grass or telltale tracks.

Dud sloped across until he saw past the side of the building. Sure enough, against the small cabin were three bikes parked in a tidy line on their stands. The white panel van executed a three-point turn so its rear double doors faced the bikes. And then, over the voices of the men came another sound. It was faint at first, but as they stumbled out of the cabin door, half a dozen women appeared, dusty and tired looking, complaining as the soldiers urged them forward. When a curtain of blond hair caught and waved in the breeze, Dud's heart leaped. Evie stood at the back of the line, tall and proud, and looking none the worse for wear. He took out his phone and took pictures of the van, then zoomed in and took close-ups of the people.

One by one, the girls were herded into the van. Dud pocketed the phone, swung the AK-47 off his shoulder, checked the clip, and edged forward. The third girl climbed in as two of the soldiers straddled the bikes, toed back the stands, and kicked the engines into life. He leveled the gun and moved again as the bikes rolled slowly before him.

With the gun raised, he eyed the scene through its sights. At this range, the weapon wasn't accurate enough to fire. The bikers were right there for the taking, but it would only take one round to miss its mark and hit one of the women.

The fourth girl, a young Jamaican no older than sixteen, put up a fight as a soldier manhandled her to the doors of the van. She swung an arm and was met by a hammer blow to the body that doubled her over. Dud's blood boiled as she cried out and dropped to her knees, and he quickened his pace. There'd be more than a bullet for that coward when the time came. As she was dumped through the doors, the next woman held up her hands and climbed in unassisted. That left Evie, out in the open, defenseless and helpless. Her head turned back and forth, no doubt looking for him.

I'm coming baby, he thought, as a loud shout snapped everyone to attention. The door of the large building slammed shut, and the leader lumbered forward. His dread-locks swung as he walked and helped the shadow to keep him in darkness. Dud watched, fifty feet away, as the thug walked over to his wife and took her chin in his hand. He turned her face to the sunlight that streaked through the trees and studied her like a piece of property. She looked over his shoulder, practically into the tree line where Dud hid.

He was forty feet away when the third bike raced into life and distracted him. It spun around and rolled between them. As it did, the guy pushed Evie behind the open door and out of sight.

It was now or never.

He crouched and moved again with purpose. As he reached the final line of trees, the bikes revved their engines and sped away from the camp in a shower of dust. Then the van's engine turned over and the rear door slammed shut. Dud lifted the gun and tensed his trigger finger as Evie's face appeared in the back window. Again, the shot was too risky. The rounds from the AK would punch through the thin skin of the van's panels with ease.

The big guy turned as he swung open the passenger door and finally revealed his face.

Gold teeth flashed and Dud's stomach churned as the guy climbed into the van and raced away after the bikes.

It was the guide.

All Dud could do was take more pictures.

12

Sarge tugged the parachute straps tight across his chest and joined the other men. They performed systematic checks for each other, making sure each clasp was secure and pull cords were loose and ready.

"Sarge, I have a confession to make," said Marbles.

The old man looked up and couldn't help but grin at the smiling eyeball. It contrasted to the rest of his friend's face which seemed deathly serious. "Don't give me that depressing 'if I don't make it back' speech, Marbles. I've never liked them."

"No, it's not that. I've never done a water landing. Made loads of jumps, but always onto dry land."

"I wondered why you made that comment earlier. English, you up to speed?"

English joined the conversation. "Yep, done a few. Can't say I'm a fan, but I picked up a few tips." He walked over to Marbles. "Sounds like we're jumping pretty low, so once you deploy your chute, unclip your chest strap. Once you feel the water, unclip the leg straps too, shuffle them off and swim down and away from the chute. The reserve will fill with water so don't hang around and don't worry about the chute. It's not up to much once the salt water's done with it, anyway."

"And," added Sarge, "count your blessings we're dropping into warm water. I landed in the Channel years ago and came close to getting hypothermia. Still, don't take the time to snorkel or go fishing, get out from under your chute before you get stuck there."

He knelt beside the cargo netting and pulled it back. Three white barrels rolled around behind it. He reached in and pushed one each back to the other men.

"Floatation device?" asked English.

"Nope. Boats," said Sarge.

English rolled the plastic barrel beneath his foot. "That'll be a pain in the arse to balance on, mate."

Sarge shook his head. "Listen up." He rolled his own beside him and stood. "They're surprisingly light. Hold it close while you jump and, after you pull your cord, tug on this rope here." He pointed to a length of rope that ran through a hole into the barrel. "This opens the release. Push the whole thing as far away from you as you can. The barrel splits open into two halves and a raft will self-inflate. As soon as you surface, look for your boat. There's a paddle stowed inside it. Once we're all situated, we'll meet up and find some quiet land to row to."

English gazed at the barrel. "Are you shitting me?"

"I shit you not, son. Tried and tested."

"Well crap," said Marbles. "I gotta get me one of those."

"You can have these when we're done. Numbers got them from an old Navy buddy. I doubt he wants them back."

Marbles rubbed his hands together and smiled as Sarge reached into the netting again. "Hate to add to your burden, but we're all trained for swimming with weight, right? I raided my basement and brought along a few things we might need and divvied them up into three equally weighted bags. They're all waterproofed, but be careful not to disturb them too much. It wouldn't pay for them to go off."

Both men stared wide eyed as he dragged plastic covered pouches out by their straps and slid them behind him.

"Only kidding. Still, take care of them and don't lose them when you land. We need weaponry and I'm not dragging the ocean floor to get them back."

As each man slung a pouch over his shoulder, a buzzer sounded.

"They're playing our song, boys. That's the signal. Get ready to jump."

The door from the cockpit opened and a uniformed man made his way toward them. "Ready to go, guys?"

"I'd say so," said Sarge.

They moved down the plane and stopped by the rear side door as a light lit up beside it.

The guy spun a handle and lifted the door. As it slid up, heat from outside washed over them. "Sure you don't want to go sunbathing instead?" he grinned.

"Another time," said Sarge. "Give me your number so I can trade in my frequent flyer miles." He checked the strap of the pouch over his shoulder, threaded the rope from the barrel across his palm and clutched the plastic to his chest.

English was silhouetted in the doorway for a second. The wind ruffled his clothing before he turned, gave a thumbs up and jumped. Marbles followed.

Sarge stood in the doorway. The ocean flew by below but land broke the horizon in the distance. He turned to the guy and clapped his shoulder. "Thanks for the lift." And then he jumped.

The water rushed up to meet him as he thrust the barrel away but held onto its rope. It grew taught and then snapped. Fabric unfurled, and the raft fell behind him. Then he pulled the chute cord. He knew how it worked. He could jump from planes in his sleep. The pilot chute would appear from the bottom of the container and catch enough air to yank it upwards. The force would cause it to drag the main chute free, which would billow out above him and prevent him from being decimated by the water surface below.

Everything went to plan. Before he entered the water, his peripheral vision picked up other objects floating on the surface. By now, two other rafts would be buoyant, and the other guys would be freeing themselves from their chute harnesses.

He unclipped the chest strap as his toes cut through the water and he slid into the ocean. Next came the leg straps, and he shucked off the harness and unclipped the chute. The weight of the pouch went some way to compensate for the pull of the air in the reserve chute and he swam down and away from the canopy that floated above him. After a few good strokes, he climbed and broke through the surface with a splash. Marbles and English were already powering through the ocean on their way to their rafts, their arms chopping through the current. Every part of his clothing had filled with water, so he swam as quickly as he could until he rolled into his own.

He lay there for a moment to let the burning in his muscles subside. Steam rose from him as the sun beat down and heated his soaked clothing. Over the top of the raft he saw the others paddling toward him. He tugged off his boots and socks and laid them to one side to dry. By the time he'd stowed the pouch and taken off the parachute backpack, they had pulled alongside.

"Well, that was bracing," said English.

"Bracing is one word you could use," said Marbles. "Avoidable will be the one I'll use from now on."

Sarge scanned the horizon. Hotels and resorts dotted the coastline but, to one side, a bay curved into the island and seemed, at least from about a mile away, to be deserted. He pointed to it. "Let's beach over there. I'd say we should pull in the chutes, but it's not like they're conducting a manhunt for us. Hopefully, they'll think one of those parasailing guys lost a load overboard."

As useful as they were, the rafts were not designed for speedy paddling. After twenty minutes, each man dragged his boat onto the deserted beach and stowed it under a large outcrop of rock. Sarge reached into his pouch and pulled out a Ziploc bag holding a cell phone and its charger.

"Let's see if your magic worked on these too, English. It's time to call Dud and let him know reinforcements have arrived."

---

As Dud reached the car, he knew the van would be miles away. There was only one thing to do. He wiped tears of frustration from his eyes, dug out the cell phone and speed dialed English's number. It rang once and was answered.

"Hey Dud, it's Numbers."

"Dude, can you use the thermal imaging thing again?"

"Sure, give me a sec. Where are you? Sounds like you're outside. I thought you'd be back at the hotel waiting for the others. They'll be there soon. They're in the air right now."

"Numbers, I haven't got time to explain. Get the imaging thing up, I need you to track a van."

"Here it is. I see you by that camp, but there are a few images on the road. Which one you want me to track?"

Dud thought for a moment. "Look for the largest. Most vehicles will have one or two people in them. The van has at least seven or eight."

"Is it a tour bus or something? I'm confused."

"A panel van. They've got Evie and some other women. You have to track it if I'm ever going to get her back. Come on Numbers, I'm counting on you. Pardon the pun."

"Got it. There are two signals that could be it, but one is stationary so it must be the other. Wow, it's moving at a fair rate. What shall I do?"

"I'm not equipped to face them alone. Follow it and make sure you don't lose it while I head back to the hotel. As soon as I get together with the guys, we'll head back out again. Promise me you'll track it."

"I promise, Dud. I've got it here, clear as day. Get back to the hotel and recharge your phone. We'll talk soon."

"Got it, buddy. And Numbers? Thanks, man."

"Anything for a brother. Numbers out."

Dud trekked back to the car and threw the guns onto the back seat. A fist thumped against the trunk lid. "Is that you? You bastard. Just shoot me and put me out..."

As the lid rose, Dud stepped back. The stench was overpowering. "Shit, man..."

"Yes. Shit," shouted James. "I told you I had to go. That was ages ago, mon. Why would you humiliate me like this?"

"Are you kidding me? You tried to frigging kill me. You're lucky I don't leave you here. In fact, get out." He motioned with the gun as the cop scrambled out of the trunk.

James held up his hands. "I wasn't being serious about shooting me. Come on, mon..."

"What do you know about me?"

"What do you mean?"

"For God's sake, James. It's not rocket science. What do you know about me? You said the bad guys hear everything. What have you heard?"

"Nothing, I swear. Well, that you were here, driving a piece of shit VW with a blue paint job." He glanced at the car. "It's barely blue, mon. Does rust count as a color?"

Dud wrinkled his nose as the breeze caught the scent of James and wafted it across him. He motioned with the gun again. "Walk."

"What? Walk where? You shot out my car's tires and it's getting late. Come on, mon, you can't leave me out here. No one will pick me up, I smell like a damn goat farm."

"Not my concern. Walk, or I'll put a round through your foot and you can hop all the way instead."

"That's cold," said James as he skulked away. He looked back, his face furrowed like a scolded dog. "Ice cold."

Dud started the car and began the drive back to the hotel.

---

Numbers sat in English's basement and stared at the screen. The voice commands English had programmed into the phone worked flawlessly and it only took him a few minutes to get reacquainted with the computers. Also, the Brit had left detailed notes in case he came across something he was unsure of.

The red dot wound its way along the coast road, stopping and starting a few times, presumably to let other vehicles pass. It was fortunate that it was larger than the other glowing dots as it weaved around and sometimes merged with other traffic.

He tried to imagine how his friend must feel, knowing his wife was racing away, but couldn't quite fathom it. Then he tried to imagine driving a van containing a cargo of kidnapped women.

They couldn't stay on the road for long. It would only take one stop where the women would make noise for their cover to be blown. They'd have to shoot their way clear which would draw attention. If he were planning this, he'd use the coast road to get some distance, and then cut back inside the island and under cover.

Sure enough, the vehicle used the main road for another five minutes, before it turned east and drove inland. Its speed slowed, but it kept moving and meandered around winding roads for another twenty minutes. At one point, it stopped and remained stationary for five minutes. Maybe it was refueling or someone needed a toilet break.

Then it moved again.

And then the dot vanished.

13

"They're taking us somewhere to kill us."

Lecia, the young girl, leaned against the cold metal and hugged her knees. The floral dress she wore barely covered her thighs, and petals stretched as she tugged the fabric down to cover herself as much as possible. Tears streamed down her face, and she rocked back and forth in her seat as the unused seat belt flapped around beside her.

"I'll never see my family again," she mumbled. Her eyes lifted and looked at the people around her. "And I'll never get to celebrate my birthday."

Evie checked the interior of the van for the umpteenth time. The windows and floor were all solid. In the center of the rear doors, a scratched and hollowed out square sat where someone had removed the interior handle. A solid sheet of plywood formed the partition between the passenger compartment and the front of the van. Their captors were so confident of their security, they hadn't even cut in a window.

"Lecia? Be strong, honey," said Evie. "My husband is right behind us. He heard me back at the other place, which means he knows I'm here, which means he knows we're all here. He'll come for us."

Lecia continued to rock as the other girls sat, stone faced and silent, as if they'd already accepted their fate.

Through the rear windows, Evie watched a two by two frame of landscape, and tried hard to remember the route they were taking. As they left the camp, the green buildings grew smaller through the windows. She held on to their security. Locked in an underground room, with no light but regular food and semi-regular toilet breaks, meant that their captors wanted to look after them. Despite their imprisonment, they were still cared for. Now, moving to a new location, that security, as false as it may have been, had been taken away. They were headed into the unknown.

In a sordid way, the appearance of the coast road was a beautiful sight. The sun had been working for half a day, but grew tired and sloped away to the west, setting the ocean alight and shooting spears of orange light through the trees that lined the roadside. It flashed inside the van like a firework display.

Evie blinked back a tear and hoped she'd see the sight again on her own terms. For herself, and for the girls sharing this cab ride from Hell with her, she had to stay strong. And definitely long enough to see Dud again; her loyal husband who would do everything in his power to rescue them.

As she grew accustomed to the bouncing rhythm of the coast road, which rumbled beneath her like a reggae song, the van took a sharp turn. It left the smooth asphalt and traded it for bumpy soil, gravel and grass. Gasps echoed between the girls as they slid across the vinyl seats and fought to stay upright.

The view from the small windows, of the steady road and the constant buffer of the ocean, changed. Now, nothing but trees filled her view. No landmarks. No indicators of where they were going, no information she could give to anyone who followed.

Nothing but trees.

Then she noticed the road. Everywhere she'd been in Jamaica, the roads were asphalt or gravel. Sometimes new and smooth. Sometimes, like the mountain trip to Nine Mile, rough and potholed. But always asphalt or gravel.

This road glowed as if it had rusted. Dud had pointed them out on their trip. She thought back to the guide's... check that... her captor's speech. The mines in this area transported product that turned the roads red. Bauxite.

Were they heading to a processing plant? Is this where the girls, and she, would be processed? She was under no illusion, they were hostages. The girls in this van meant something to someone, and there was always a price involved. Flesh for money. The oldest business on the planet.

The van meandered for ages, always climbing, bumping and throwing them around as it trundled forward. Occasionally, as they turned a corner, Evie caught glimpses of a huge green valley that stretched out behind them. Other than a sliver of ocean on the horizon, there was nothing else. Still no buildings or towns, no other traffic, just acre after acre of nondescript trees.

The essence of time vanished. All that mattered was that they were here for now. Still alive. Still able to breathe. Still able to see things like the sun, the ripple of the ocean, and leaves blowing in the breeze.

Then the van stopped.

The girls sat bolt upright, and the tension ratcheted up a notch as they heard shouting voices. Aggressive sounds from men communicating, issuing orders and demands.

After a few minutes, the truck lurched reassuringly onward again. While they were moving, they were safe.

They drove through a gate, like some kind of checkpoint. Two men stood, one on either side of the road, and toyed with rifles while they stared through the small windows. Evie caught their eyes and shuddered at the coldness in them.

The truck turned another corner, and she tried to pick out anything among the scenery she could use for direction. The ocean still sparkled, impossibly far away, and what looked like a huge covered water chute ran off high over the top of the trees and faded into the distance. Huge legs supported it at intervals, like power lines.

Then the girls gasped and darkness filled the van.

---

Dud steered through the gate of the rental car compound, his knuckles white as they had been for most the drive from the camp back into town. He'd barely noticed the trunk lid flapping up and down like a guillotine as the car bounced and jumped over potholes and rough gravel. The trunk smelled as if it had been party to a sewer explosion and he hoped the fresh air would help to ease the stench.

As he passed the gate, a young man leaned out and looked through the side window. Dud pulled over.

"The cars you have here, do you clean them, too?"

The man looked offended. "Of course we do, mon. Just because the lot doesn't have gleaming signs don't mean we don't take pride in our work. We have excellent cleaning services. Inside and out."

Dud fished out his wallet and handed over an American twenty-dollar bill. The kid's eyes lit up like it was Christmas. "The trunk of this car had an unfortunate afternoon. I'll give you this twenty to take care of it."

After a quick glance at the rear of the car, the kid held out his hand and Dud slapped the twenty into it. "Park it up, mon. Leave it open and I'll take care of it in a while."

With the car parked against the wire fence, Dud dug out the cell phone and dialed Kenzie.

"Mr. Dud. Are you calling with good news?"

He took a deep breath and exhaled slowly. "Not really. I saw my wife, but I've lost her again." He paused and swallowed to choke back a tear. "She's been taken, Kenzie. I have help coming because I can't trust the police, but I have another favor to ask. Could I borrow another car?"

The line went silent for a moment, and then, "I know all about the police. What did you do with the other one? And though it barely counts as a car, it counts to me, mon. I rely on those cars."

"Oh, it's okay," he said as the breeze sent the smell drifting over him and he held his breath until his stomach calmed. "There was a toilet incident. It'll be cleaned, I promise, but I have someone following Evie. I need to collect my friends and get back out there as soon as possible. So, I need your car."

"How long will it be before your friends arrive?" she asked.

"They're on their way, but it's not like they gave me their itinerary. Sometime this afternoon."

"Mr. Dud, will you have dinner with me?"

Dud paused and played the words through his mind again to be sure he'd heard them properly. "Dinner? At a time like this? And Kenzie, I'm a married..."

"I don't mean it like that, mon. I'm at your hotel. We just dropped off a tour group. If you have time before your friends arrive, I would like to talk to you about something. It's important and anyway, if you're taking my other vehicle, you owe me. Give me as long it takes to eat lunch to talk."

"Okay." He glanced at the phone to check the time. "I'm on my way back there now. The buffet starts soon and I need to eat, anyway. Wait in the hotel foyer and I'll meet you there."

"I can do that," she said, and then paused. "Mr. Dud, you should come quickly. A police car just came through the gates."

At the mention of the authorities, Dud half walked half jogged back to the hotel. Sure enough, as he rounded the corner, police lights flashed a disco through the black gates. His already racing heart skipped. Were they here with good news, and Evie was upstairs in their room, cleaned up and waiting for him? Or did they come bearing bad news?

As he walked through the gates, the woman from the tourist office sat on a bench and dabbed at her face with a tissue. She looked up at him with red rimmed eyes.

"They found him," she sobbed. "Hector, your driver? His body was in a drainage pipe outside town. I don't understand, though. They say he died from an overdose, but Hector would never touch drugs. Something's not right."

Dud reached out and squeezed her shoulder. "I am so sorry. Something is definitely not right, but I hope the police can solve this for you."

He walked off feeling a guilty relief. This latest development, and the lack of good news, justified his actions. The woman would get no satisfaction from the police, just as he wouldn't. The only way this would be resolved would be through the Old Farts Club.

A busking wooden effigy of Jamaica's most famous son guarded the entrance to the lobby. Dud breezed past him and recognized Kenzie's bob haircut silhouetted against the dying sun that fought for life behind her. She lounged cross-legged in one of the oversized chairs that littered the place, flicking through a program of tours that the office out back provided. At first glance, with the ocean still licking at the front of the man-made beach, the view looked like paradise. The palm fronds still swayed in the dying light and boats drifted in slow motion in the distance.

Dud knew the reality.

As he drew closer, he raised a hand to wave, and she closed the brochure and stood to greet him.She met his gaze with eyes of coffee brown swimming in brilliant white. In another life, and with a few less years between them, he may have been tempted. Standing, she had the posture of an African warrior; tall, erect and proud, with her toned muscles softened by relaxed clothing. Her eyes flickered with experience, even though he could tell she was easily fifteen years younger than him.

"I'm sorry about your wife," she said, "and I'll do anything I can to help."

The mention of Evie snapped him out of his spell, and a cold wave of guilt swept over him. "Thank you. You said you had something important to say, so let's eat and you can tell me everything."

He followed her to the buffet and copied her choice of food; fish, jerk chicken, fruit and pastries. A balanced diet. He ordered a large beer to complete the meal.

The area looked as if it could seat a couple hundred people. It was teeming with bodies but they found a table, nestled against a handrail, that looked out onto the Caribbean. Other than plane lights flitting about in the distance, nothing other than boats moved, as if the island had wound down for the evening. Dud knew his was just beginning.

As they pulled their chairs beneath them, he caught her eye. "So, tell me what's going on with the police? And what is it you wanted to talk about?"

Tucking hair behind her ear with a finger, she speared a piece of chicken and swirled it in sauce. "Mr. Dud, I haven't been completely honest with my motivation."

"Oh?"

"Four years ago next week Yanika and I, that's my sister, were shopping at the market in Ocho Rios. Mama wanted bread to go with the chicken she'd marinated. I picked up the bread, but Yanika wanted to surprise everyone with dessert. She ran across the road to another stall to haggle for cake."

Dud tore chicken from bone with his teeth and leaned closer as the noise in the restaurant got louder.

"She waved her hands while she talked to the stall owner. And I can still see her smile when he gave in to her and picked up the cake."

She placed her fork on the table and dabbed her eyes with a napkin.

"A crowd of people walked by wearing Jamaican football shirts, talking about the World Cup. Once they passed, I looked again and she was gone. I leaped up and ran across the road and walked every inch of the market and up and down every street. That was the last time I saw my sister. She disappeared right in front of me."

"Wow." Dud sat back and shook his head as Kenzie fished a picture from her purse and passed it over the table "I don't know what to say. Kenzie, I'm so sorry."

The girl in the picture had Kenzie's eyes, but with her

hair pulled back and tied tight, her face seemed harder. The style seemed to lengthen her forehead.

"There's nothing to say. I know all about the police because they were as useful for me as they have been for you. I'm sure they looked for a while, but this is a busy island. Many people come and go. And there are many places where someone could be loaded onto a boat and shipped away. I'm also sure that Yanika wasn't on the island for long. That is why I offer you my help. If you know of your wife's whereabouts, you must move quickly. I just wanted you to see that I understand your pain and your frustration."

Dud passed back the picture. "Thank you. She's beautiful. Did they find no clues at all? Anything to indicate where she may have gone?"

Kenzie shook her head and picked at her food. "No. Nothing. She was there one second and gone the next. Now, I have taken enough of your time. You should go and do what you can."

"I'm waiting for back up to arrive," said Dud. "As soon as they get here, we'll head out. Some of the police are involved in this."

He considered Thomas and hoped that the cop had gathered his family and was leaving the island.

"They're as corrupt as it gets. The body of the driver that should have taken us out for our trip turned up outside town. Drug overdose. His employer swears he was a good kid and wouldn't touch drugs. Sounds to me like murder. It will be down to me and my friends to solve this. Well, I say friends, but they're more like family."

"So, you have family coming?"

"As near as makes no difference, yes. People I trust like family."

They ate in comfortable silence for a while and were finishing dessert when his phone rang. A familiar number flashed on-screen. "Here they are. Excuse me for a moment, Kenzie."

He ducked under the rail and answered the call. "Sarge. You made it. Where are you?"

Kenzie nodded as Dud relayed Sarge's directions. "My car is outside," she said. "Come on, I'll take you to collect your friends. It's time to put things right."

14

Ramirez adjusted his sunglasses as the large doors opened and Abigail walked in, shadowed by Marcia. The Jamaican guard towered over the white girl, a head taller, with raven black hair cascading over her shoulders. She was a good employee, loyal beyond fault for four years, and certainly attractive, although Ramirez preferred white women. Their pale skin made his tanned body appear to glow.

"How was your trip?"

Abigail dropped four bags loaded with shopping onto the marble floor and huffed. "It would be so much better if I could use a changing room without someone standing outside the door."

Marcia glanced at her, the whites of her eyes cutting like beams of light. Ramirez cringed. Abigail's voice had the quality of screeching brakes, and the temptation grew in him to waltz across the room and grab her by the throat. A few more sentences and Marcia might step in and do the job for him.

"And the stores are so limited," she continued. "Do you have any idea how hard it was to find these dresses? One of them will do, I'm sure, but good God, it was such a chore. By the way, you never said what the occasion was. What are we celebrating?"

Ramirez massaged his temples. "All in good time. For now, I'm sure you're exhausted." Marcia's rolled her eyes in his peripheral vision. "Why don't you run a bath? Pick out a dress and try it on while the water is running. I'll be up in a moment to see what you chose."

She'd know his statement was not a suggestion. He watched her bend to pick up the bags, marveling at her curves as she looped her fingers through the handles and lifted them. It was a shame this one hadn't worked out, but another day of her harpy voice scything through the open rooms and he'd be tempted to open his own wrists.

As she climbed the winding staircase, her sharp heels dug into the polished mahogany, and he chewed his knuckles until she padded across the thick carpet on the balcony above. Marcia caught his eye and smirked, then turned and left the room.

Ramirez ambled over to a drink cabinet, dropped a cube of ice into a glass, and watched it swirl as he poured Blanton's bourbon over it. Once the ice had stopped popping and cracking, he took the glass and crept up the stairs, grimacing at the semi-circles that shone in the wooden treads where her heels had sunk in.

Through the doorway, Abigail looked stunning in a backless black dress that hung below her shoulders. She angled her body from side to side to catch glimpses of herself as the mirror fogged up in the bathroom steam. Over dinner, a few months ago, he remembered her saying she thought of her bathroom as her 'safe place'.

The gilt-edged mirror took up a chunk of the wall space and reflected a porcelain tub that sat on a raised dais in the middle of the room. Twin chrome pipes, cut into the floor, rose and bent over the tub to connect to a solid brass faucet that matched the clawed feet that dug into thick carpet. She liked the way the carpet kept the room warm. He liked the way the thick mat dampened any sound.

She jumped as he spoke. "You look beautiful, darling."

Again, she forced a smile, a halfhearted attempt to please him. His nerves prickled. "Thank you. Do you like it?"

He placed his glass on the counter and ambled up to her. As she turned and spun to show off the dress, he rolled up his shirt sleeves. When she faced him, he grabbed her chin and stroked her cheekbones with a thumb. "It's such a shame," he said. "So pretty."

Confusion spread across her face before his fist crashed into her stomach. Air shot from her lungs as she doubled over, and he grabbed her by the hair and dragged her to the tub.

The carpeting masked the sounds of her toenails scratching for purchase as he dragged her level with the porcelain and smashed her head against it. It clanged as a red smear painted the surface before he lifted her and thrust her head beneath the water.

Its heat scalded the back of his hand as she thrashed. For a smaller woman, she had more strength than he expected, and he stepped up onto the dais to apply more weight. The water swallowed her body until only her calves broke the surface, kicking into nothing. He ignored her scrambling hands and held her down, growing angry and impatient that she fought so hard. Before long, her brain could no longer ignore the burning in her lungs. She'd have to take a breath, even though she would breathe in death.

Her body racked, then stiffened, as she inhaled and

filled her lungs with water. The lack of oxygen dulled her muscles and, after one more violent struggle, her hands slid off his and splashed into the water.

He turned the faucets off and dried himself with her towel. Even in death, she looked pretty. The dress had been an excellent choice, a nice contrast to the hair that floated around it.

Before he closed the door, he raised his glass. "To Abigail and to girlfriends past. I told you we'd be celebrating."

---

Kenzie followed the signs for Mosquito Cove, a location west of the hotel, then continued past the cove to a wooded area. To Dud, the scenery looked like the road that led to Nine Mile, the same trees and the same road surface, but it was a much easier drive. Her modest SUV held the road as well as the Jeep had, and she drove with a confidence that eased his tension a little. Still, she pointed out landmarks and places of interest, probably he thought, to distract and calm him. She must have sensed his anticipation as he fidgeted and played with his wedding ring. Evie was always on his mind. Every second that passed felt like an hour, and his insides crawled with frustration and a feeling of help-lessness.

"They'll be here somewhere, mon." she said as the road took a sharp turn to reveal more trees.

"How can you tell where we are? Everywhere looks the same," he asked.

"I know every inch of this island," she laughed. "Well, give or take a mile or two. There are places in the hills I don't want to know if you remember our earlier conversation."

"I remember it, although I hope to get acquainted with those areas soon enough. Just not for the right reasons."

"I'm sorry that my home has caused you so much pain, Mr. Dud. And I look forward to meeting your colleagues."

"It caused you the same pain, Kenzie. And yes, so am I."

The road leveled out and Dud spotted movement in a break in the trees ahead. It was hard to miss three large men all carrying weapons pouches. Hard to miss, that is, unless they wanted to be missed. Sarge signaled and gestured to an area of flat land across the road for the SUV to pull in to. Kenzie followed his directions and rolled the vehicle to a stop behind a row of bushes.

Dud slid out of the passenger seat and rushed over to the group. Sarge met him with an outstretched hand which he ignored, and he clasped the man in a hug and slapped his back.

"I'm so glad to see you, man. Thank you so much for coming."

Before Sarge could say a word, Dud spun and reached for Marbles. He laughed, partly in relief and partly because Marbles' glass eye now displayed a blazing sun.

"Very apt, my friend. The bugs might eat you alive, but at least they'll find your eye."

Finally, he turned to English. The man stood there for a moment, unsure of what to make of the open display of affection. Then he spread his arms and offered a grim smile. "Hello mate. Hate to meet again in these circumstances. In fact, it's bloody shit if you ask me."

Dud stepped forward and hugged the man like a life-long friend. "English, it takes a special kind of guy to drop everything and answer a call like this. It means more than you know."

"Nah, that's bollocks, mate," said English. "Reckon you'd do the same for me." He glanced over Dud's shoulder and whispered, "Who's the chick?"

Dud beckoned Kenzie to join them. "Guys, meet Kenzie. In the time I've known her, she's saved my life once and helped me out beyond measure. She knows exactly what's going on, she's a hell of a driver, and she knows almost every inch of this island."

As the girl joined them, he introduced the group. Each man respectfully shook her hand.

"So, come on," said Marbles. "Enough chat. Sit Rep."

With no effort, Dud slid into military mode. "Okay. Evie was taken in a white panel van, kidnapped by the bastard that posed as our tour guide. The proper guide turned up dead, so they're serious. There's a camp in the hills miles from here, manned by six soldiers, where she was held and..."

His phone rang.

"What the hell?" he said as he pulled it from his pocket. "Everyone's here."

He glanced at the screen and held it airborne. "Ah, Numbers. One sec guys... Numbers, it's okay, they all made it. We're just..."

Dud frowned as everyone looked on, then lowered the phone and pressed the icon to activate the speakerphone.

Numbers' familiar voice drifted up among the group. "... and I followed the red dot all the way along the coast road. It turned inland and moved on for a while, stopping and starting, and then I'm sorry pal...it vanished."

Dud froze as the words sunk in and registered. Then his face flushed red, and he looked through watering eyes at the group before he spoke. "Numbers, did you say the van disappeared?"

There was silence for a few seconds and then Numbers spoke as if the weight of the world rested on his shoulders. "Yeah. I'm really sorry, man. It was there one second and gone the next. I swear to God, I didn't take my eyes of it. It just blinked out, like someone flicked a switch."

Kenzie spoke up. "Do you know where it was when it disappeared?"

"I do," said Numbers. "I'm sorry English, I wrote on your monitor but I had to make a mark where I last saw it in case I couldn't get a hold of you guys and I lost the screen."

"No problem at all," said English. "I say we get back to the hotel and get in front of a computer so you can relay the coordinates to us."

Kenzie stood as part of the group and blazed with the determination to make a difference.

English continued. "And I suspect we have a new comrade who might offer an explanation."

"No kidding," she said, her eyes alight with the anticipation of action.

Dud blinked back tears and slumped in shocked silence as the group took over.

Kenzie stepped forward and placed a hand on his shoulder. "Show me where she was, and I'll show you how to get her back."

15

It took a few moments for a glimmer of light to reappear.

Evie gripped the side of the vinyl seat as the van bucked and bounced through the darkness. The lack of light meant that any abrupt motion resulted in the girls pitching forward or falling against each other while their other senses compensated for the blindness. Gasps of anxiety and moans of pain became the norm until the view turned to a murky gray. Small fluorescent lights fought to dispel the gloom from about ten feet off the ground. Smooth round curves of concrete faded into the distance as the van trundled through the tunnel.

Bit by bit, the intensity of the light grew. The girls rocked again as the van lurched and made a hard turn into a well-lit room that could have housed a football field. Through the small rear windows, the ceiling wasn't visible, but it bounced back the echo of shouting voices. Evie strained to listen but couldn't make out any of the conversations over the clang of heavy machinery.

Huge telescoping metal legs rose from the ground and

vanished out of sight. Outside the van looked like a scene from War of The Worlds.

The girls whimpered and clutched each other's hands as they jolted to a halt. Mumbled talking bled through the wooden panel as the driver spoke, before the sound of a heavy roller door sent vibrations through Evie's seat and the van rolled forward again. The whir of machinery and more voices filled the space until the rumbling began again as the door closed behind them with a thump.

Evie looked once more at her surroundings. The driver, or someone worse, would open the van doors soon. She stooped and felt beneath the seats for anything she could use as a weapon, or as a means to escape. Given the state of the other girls, if there was to be any struggle she would have to do it alone.

The tension inside the van was cloying. "Is everyone okay?" she whispered over the noise of squeaking seats, already knowing no one would respond. "Come on. We have to stick together and look for the right moment to escape." There was no 'try to escape'. She had to be positive. For all of them.

"No one escapes," said a young girl who leaned against the wooden partition. It was the first time she'd spoken since giving her name back at the camp. She fought back tears and clasped her shaking hands between her thighs. Shock had turned her dark skin ashen and sweaty. "People are taken all the time. They never come back."

"Yeah, well we're not regular people, okay? If we stick together, the right moment will come. These men are arrogant. I'm sure you're right, and they do this often and have no problems. But they've not met me before, and they've never met you. Don't give up. By all means, appear weak.

But inside you, believe that we will get out of this because I promise you, they will harm you over my dead body. Make them think they have us, but be ready to move. If I see a chance, I'm taking it. I hope you'll all help me."

The van rolled forward again. Something about the air outside didn't seem quite right. Small particles of pink dust gathered in the black rubber seals of the windows as they ambled onward.

Despite hearing voices, she'd seen no one. Set into the far wall, the huge metal door they'd come through now looked like a postage stamp. Still, in all the distance they'd covered, nothing moved. The tall metal legs rose at specific locations, all an equal distance apart, all looking as if they could support a building, but Evie couldn't see what was above them. Occasionally, the sound of gears and chains interrupted the constant whirring of machinery, as if a rollercoaster ride was being pulled to the top of a ramp before it hurtled forward into the unknown. Not for the first time, she wished she had the driver's view.

Another turn took them into different surroundings, the fluorescent light replaced by natural light. As the view unfolded behind her, Evie saw a huge opening. At first, it looked like the entrance to a plane hangar, with tall arches overhead and a wide gap for large vehicles to drive through. Then containers appeared along both sides. Massive boxes of ribbed metal, with double doors held closed by hand operated levers. Transport containers. The type used to move heavy goods across oceans on huge ships. Her stomach churned. Were they cargo?

The van stopped and rocked as a door opened and slammed closed. Someone whistled a UB40 song she recognized, something about a rat and a kitchen, before the girls jumped and screamed as a hand slammed against the metal side of the van.

He was still laughing when the doors swung open, and the leader, the guide, stood before them. Light glinted off his teeth, but Evie's attention centered on the gun he had leveled at them.

"Toilet break, ladies," he said. He motioned to the two nearest girls. "You two. Out. Now."

After a nervous pause, the two girls swung their legs around and clambered out of the van. The door slammed shut again.

Evie watched the girls until they walked out of sight around the side of the van and wondered if she'd see them again. Everything fell silent. No machinery outside. No whimpering inside. Nothing. Just silence. And waiting.

---

Lindsay watched the first girls climb out of the van. There was something about one of them that stirred his blood. Something about the way her curves moved, even though she was anxious. Terrified.

He smiled again. Maybe that was it. The terror.

Power was intoxicating and, if he left no marks, he could do whatever he liked with these girls. They weren't anything special, just merchandise like jewels or drugs. Another object in the chain that brought the money from the rich people to people like him.

Her skirt was dirty, but the dirt had stuck to where the shape of her rear pushed through. It accentuated everything and highlighted what was on offer. He guessed she was about eighteen years old. Old enough, but still fresh and new. Possibly untouched. He wanted to extinguish the innocence that burned in her eyes, to take that glimmer of hope and snuff it out while he took her and held her throat while she cried.

Then Mr. Ramirez's voice sounded inside his head. Do not touch the product.

"Move," he shouted, and beckoned them forward with his gun. They lumbered on until they reached a row of portable toilets. During the day, the men that worked here used them to relieve themselves. Later, as the sun set, they shied clear and used the wall at the front of the building. No one came back here.

He opened the door and pointed to the grimy toilet inside. "You. You go first."

The other girl, the one he had no interest in, moved into the tiny closet and he slammed the door behind her. He smiled again as she screamed at the sudden darkness until she must have realized that now was not her time to die. All she had to do was empty her bladder.

The girl before him squirmed as he ran his eyes up and down her body, as if she felt them burning through the fabric. He angled the gun barrel down, snagged the hem of her skirt, and lifted it slowly. The barrel dragged against her skin as her smooth thighs were revealed inch by inch. As it reached the curve of her rear, he dropped it and laughed.

"Think yourself lucky," he said. "I'm sure they'll have fun with you wherever you end up. But I? I would have destroyed you."

The door opened clumsily and the first girl stepped out.

"Now you," he said.

She rushed inside, no doubt grateful for the brief escape. When the door slammed behind her, she didn't make a sound.

It took fifteen minutes to get all the girls taken care of. Once they were back in the van, Lindsay tossed in a plastic bag filled with sandwiches and water.

"It's dinner time, ladies. I need you all fit and healthy. Don't worry. Soon this part will be over. Then, you will get to meet new people." He laughed as he closed the doors one by one. "If you think I'm bad, you have no idea."

He climbed back into the van. It was too soon to move them, but they'd be okay in the van for a few hours. All he had to do was keep them safe. Deaven would answer the hourly checks back at the camp, provided their intruder stayed away. And he had instructions to call if Mr. Ramirez asked for him.

The van chugged into life as he turned the key. The outside walls of the main complex were nothing but riveted seam metal. That would be the view for his guests for the foreseeable future. He made a three-point turn and drove forward and around to the back of the facility, then reversed the van until the rear windows were an inch away from the wall.

The Jamaican national team was kicking off in the soccer tournament in a few minutes. He switched off the engine, pocketed the keys, and walked to the mess hall It was time to relax.

---

The new arrivals clambered into the backseat while Dud sat upfront with Kenzie. After the initial back slapping, a cloud of tension hung in the vehicle while the men traded questions. Dud recounted the events up to his finding the bunker and listened as Sarge briefed him on their trip.

Kenzie sped through the roads with the confidence of a

race car driver and reached the hotel in half the time it took to drive out. She parked the SUV in a lot opposite the entrance gates while Dud and English checked through security and took over one of the lobby's computers. Sarge and Marbles followed Kenzie and carried their supplies inside. Dud and English logged in, contacted Numbers, and tapped the speaker icon.

"Dud, I'm truly sorry. I swear I followed that van with..."

Dud interrupted the trembling voice. "Numbers. You owe me no apology. I know you, man. There's a reason the van disappeared and we'll work it out. Not your fault. Now, let's get back to the map."

English relayed instructions and got the map on-screen as the others rejoined them. They formed a large semi-circle around the computer to keep random tourists from over-hearing the conversation. Kenzie marveled wide eyed at the detail while Dud followed the coast road with his finger and tapped the screen at the camp's location.

Numbers took over. "They left the camp and drove out to the main road, then turned east and traveled to here." The cursor slid across the screen and stopped over a fork in the road. "Then they drove inland to around here." The cursor moved again. "They stopped and started a bit at this point. Perhaps the road is treacherous, or they were drop-ping people off." The cursor moved once more and stopped in what appeared to be the middle of nowhere. There was silence for a moment, until Numbers said, "This is where the signal ended."

Dud stared at the screen and swallowed heavily. Numbers' choice of words sounded doom laden. This wasn't where the signal stopped. Or faded. Or even disap-peared. This was where it ended.

He snapped out of his morbid trance as his military mind kicked in. "Okay. So, that's where we need to be. Kenzie, would you mind if we used both vehicles? I doubt we'd fit in one and it looks like the boys brought an arsenal with them."

"Didn't you mention a toilet incident?" she said with a frown. "And anyway, wouldn't you prefer to stick together? You can take my SUV, mon. I can take the car."

"Would that be wise?" said Sarge. He tapped the screen where the camp was located. "Didn't you say there were more people here? Time is of the essence, I get that, but it's important to go in prepared. Since this is on the way, shouldn't we at least check it out and see if we can find anything? We could split up." He pointed to Dud. "You and English could drive up to where we lost the signal and recon that place while Marbles and I check out the camp. I don't doubt you, son, but you'd have been emotional and you might have missed something. It wouldn't take long for us to give it the once over and, by the time we reached you, you'd know what lay ahead. It goes without saying that you shouldn't push on without us. You spooked them. It may be they've relocated to another camp. What's not to say there aren't another half dozen men there, too?"

Dud glanced at the group. "What do you think guys? In my mind, we need to get up there as soon as possible. If they move again, we'll have lost her forever."

"We'll find her, mate," said English as he rested a hand on Dud's broad shoulder. "If it were me, I'd be going to the last position with all guns blazing. I also know doing that might get me killed. I'm prone to agree with Sarge. The more info we can get the better. And if you guys drive on ahead, we won't lose too much time, either. We can reconvene and see what's up there, armed with as much intel as we can get. Then we can formulate a plan."

Dud took a deep breath and exhaled. "We'll need to be in touch if we split up. That's vital."

"Got you covered," said English. "Sarge packed a few things, one among them being a phone each, all modified like yours, and all programmed and charged. Communication won't be an issue. Well, unless we find ourselves in a lead-lined room."

"Maybe that's what happened to the van," said Marbles. "They drove it into an area that blocked the signal."

"I don't know that area well," said Kenzie, "but if there was somewhere like that about, I'm sure someone in the tourist business would be aware of it. The only thing that might be around there would be bauxite mines. The conveyor runs over that area."

"We'll get up there and find out," said Dud. "Sarge, what about weaponry?"

"We've got plenty of toys, too," said Sarge. "I raided the basement. Pistols, scoped rifle, night sights, grenades..."

Kenzie let out a squeal. "You brought grenades? Why would you bring grenades? Can I see one?"

"Sometimes," said Sarge, "it's the only thing that'll do. And yes, young lady, of course you can see one."

Dud spoke into the phone. "Numbers, I need to get these guys cleaned up and fed and then we'll get to it. Are you okay, man?"

"I will be when this is over. Until we get Evie back, I'll be in this seat. Then I'll be okay. Go and do what you do best."

English leaned forward. "Get the wife to feed you, Numbers, she's a mean cook. Or there's left over beef and

Yorkshire pudding in the fridge. I'm not sure how it'll reheat but it's yours if you want it. We need to shower, get this salt water off us and then we'll hit the road. Call you when we get close."

"Copy that, guys. Numbers out."

16

Mr. Ramirez paid well, but sometimes the things he asked of her were painful to do.

Marcia smoothed out the plastic sheet across the bathroom floor and rolled up the sleeves of her white blouse. Abigail's long hair floated on the surface of the bathwater like seaweed, while her arms rested weightless by her side. Wisps of hair drifted over vivid black bruises that mottled her red neck. The tips of her fingers and soles of her feet had wrinkled and looked as if they were made from wax. From here she could have been someone's grandmother, not the thirty-something beauty Marcia had known.

She'd been the nicest one yet, and she'd lasted three years. The girl before her, Marcia struggled with her name, had become arrogant and pushy. He'd made a public display of her death as a message to everyone. Mr. Ramirez was in charge. Fall out of line and the punishment would be swift and deadly. Like something from a horror movie, he'd stood before them soaked in blood while her headless corpse stained the stones outside. A construction crew came from out of town to replace them. The body was lying in a concrete-filled tarp on the ocean floor miles off the coast. Marcia had no idea if her head was there, too.

Abigail's body was hard to grip. As it left the water it became a dead weight. Marcia had asked for help, but Mr. Ramirez had refused. No one was to know what had happened. Not this time. Abigail was going on a vacation she wouldn't return from.

Her employer insisted that all his guards maintained a strict fitness regime. Every tug at Abigail's body caused the sinews in Marcia's arms to ripple like waves, but rigor mortis had not set in yet and Abigail flopped around like a beached whale. She changed tactics, shifted the plastic sheet to the end of the tub, and rolled Abigail over. Her eyes stared, pleading and screaming for help. A spider web of red veins spread from her irises. Marcia leaned forward and brushed them shut with her palm, then grabbed her under the arms and slid the corpse up the sloping back of the tub. Her shoulders strained as the bends of Abigail's knees caught against the top of the tub. With one almighty pull, her heels clanged against the rim and then plopped with a squelch onto the plastic. Marcia let go and Abigail hit the floor like a wet cloth.

Before she rolled the body inside the sheeting, she took a moment to brush Abigail's hair. Someone had to show this woman respect, even if it was too late for her to realize. Her hair was beautiful, the way the light reflected off her highlights. Marcia's jet-black hair shined too, and she longed for some contrast. Maybe that was why Mr. Ramirez preferred white women.

Five minutes later, the body was wrapped tightly in the plastic and secured with tape. A large towel absorbed the water that rolled from Abigail's mouth as she rolled, and then Marcia used it with bleach to scrub the inside of the tub.

On the side of the sink lay hair clips, a brush and perfumes. The brush still had strands of blond hair sticking out from between its spines from the last time Abigail had brushed her own hair.

Marcia collected all the belongings and swept them into a gym bag. Beneath the sink were rows of perfume Abigail had worn to make Mr. Ramirez happy. They went into the bag, too.

The last thing she noticed was a pair of black heeled shoes that lay on their sides beside the toilet. Small stones glimmered from them in the bathroom light. Marcia smiled. Abigail had always liked diamonds. Maybe that was why women like her preferred people like Mr. Ramirez. At least when they had a choice.

She placed the shoes into the bag and zipped it closed. It would be an effort to drag Abigail down to the car. She dreaded listening to the dull thud as her head hit every dented step she'd walked up earlier. Still, Mr. Ramirez had moved the guards from this part of the property for one hour. Enough time to clean the bathroom, get Abigail in the trunk of the car, and empty the bedroom.

She checked the bathroom once more. It was spotless, the cabinet empty and ready for the next girl. Leaning down, she grabbed Abigail's ankles through the plastic and dragged her from the room.

---

Numbers sat at the long bench in English's basement. The chair rolled to one side on well-oiled wheels as he used another keyboard to Google 'transport in Jamaica'.

A screen sat beside him with the pen mark showing where the van had disappeared. More red dots moved around about a half mile above it, but trees still blanketed the entire area, rendering it hidden. Logic dictated that there must be a way to gain access to that part of the hills, either by road or train.

According to the internet, the government had dismantled most of Jamaica's rail system and only about a quarter of it remained, primarily to transport bauxite ore from the mines to the coast. However, due to congestion, old lines were being repaired and brought up to date so, in terms of stealthy movement, there were potential routes all over the place.

The map on screen showed a track that snaked past the area indicated by the pen mark, but it was still a distance away. There was no mention of railway stations or loading areas online, but that didn't mean they didn't exist. Many times, in his military past, Numbers had been surprised by the presence of buildings or establishments that were not publicly known. He had to be sure that when the guys reached the area, there would be no nasty surprises waiting for them.

The Google Earth shot of the area showed a blanket of green, broken now and then by a road or a cluster of buildings. A line ran down the middle of the image. Numbers zoomed in and followed the line from just outside a dock on the north coast to something hidden a mile or two inside the island. The image was useless in terms of giving away characteristics of the landmark, but it looked like a huge chute suspended on eleven towers. Geographically, the land rose and fell from the line's start to finish so, in theory, the towers would be different heights to lift it above the terrain it had to cover. The image was static, a snapshot in time, so there was no way to know if it was a stationary thing or something that had a purpose. Either way, it was close to where the guys would be heading.

He looked again at the thermal chart. Nothing stood out. Other than the regular routes ran by tourist vehicles up and down the coast roads, there were no clusters of red to indicate a crowd. The center of the island was lit up like a Christmas tree, but never in a way to show anything other than regular people going about their day.

It was business as usual in Jamaica.

---

The line for the shower was as impatient as a group of kids waiting to board the latest rollercoaster.

Sarge called dibs on the first jets of hot, clean water, citing experience and authority over the argument of age and good looks. He overrode the fact that this was Dud's room and never mentioned age, although the others bit their tongues as he closed the bathroom door with a smile. While he wallowed in luxury, the rest of the club broke down the pouches they'd brought and distributed the weapons.

Kenzie milled among them and watched the arsenal grow bigger on the mattress. "Is it okay if I touch one?"

"They won't explode," said English as he lifted the lid off an ice bucket that sat next to the TV. "Always assume everything is loaded, though. Don't point at something you don't want to shoot."

She lifted each weapon and seemed to marvel at them. Then she grabbed a Glock 9mm, ejected the clip, racked the slide to release the round in the chamber and caught it in midair. Then she field-stripped the gun and laid each part carefully on the bed.

The guys watched in amazement as she reassembled the pistol, thumbed the spare round back in the magazine and then slammed it into the hand grip. She racked the slide once more, applied the safety, and laid the gun back on the sheet.

"What the hell was that?" asked English as he smoothed out a plastic bag that had lined the ice bucket.

"Just a lesson, mon," she said. "Just cos I'm a lady, don't assume I know nothing about guns. If anyone tried to hijack my tour, I'd be ready for them.

If my bus broke down, I want to be sure I can defend myself. I told you, those hills are not the nicest place to be stranded."

"Lesson learned," said English with a smile. He picked up the TV remote, slid it inside the plastic bag, and turned on the TV.

"What are you doing?" asked Kenzie.

"What? This?" said English as he held up the plastic wrapped remote. "Can you imagine how many people have been in this room?"

"Plenty," she said. "I meet them every day."

"Exactly. And can you imagine what they do on that bed?"

"I'd prefer not to, mon."

"Exactly again. Now consider this. When the maid service comes in, they change the sheets and pillowcases. They disinfect the bathrooms and all the surfaces. But do you think they touch the remote control? Also, consider this. When the people have done whatever they do on that bed, and then they turn on the TV, do you think they get up to wash their hands first?"

"I'm never watching hotel TV again," said Marbles. He stepped toward the bed. "Come on, it's time to divvy up the supplies. If the old man is so concerned about his beauty, let him preen himself in the bathroom. While he's in there, I'm taking this."

He reached onto the blanket and lifted a Sig Sauer SP2022. Its ease of use and unerring accuracy had saved him a few times. The polymer grip felt like cheap plastic as he picked it up. But he knew better.

As he racked the pistol's cold metal slide, flashbacks of a time in dusty Kuwait clouded his mind; the movement from house to house; the wait for a barrage of gunfire to erupt from behind one of the kicked in doors. Each one opened onto the possibility of the enemy while, all the time, the snug fit of the Sig's grip in his hand brought comfort and security.

Marbles was luckier than most. He'd discharged his weapon plenty of times, but each round found the body of an enemy combatant, not an innocent civilian. No missed shots. A one-hundred percent record.

Some of his comrades had not been so lucky. They still sought counseling.

It was ironic that his worst time in Kuwait had been caused by a random game of soccer. Despite the security of the base he stayed in, insurgents tried to infiltrate the complex, even to cut through the metal fence at night and attempt to sneak past the sentries.

Marbles had his moment in the cold light of day.

A group of kids kicked about a soccer ball, crashing it from time to time against the wire fence that separated the U.S. troops from the Kuwaiti civilians. The dorms that held the sleeping members of the unit were feet away from the fence, and the relentless crash and clatter of cheap metal sang through the windows of the complex.

Marbles had stormed out of his dorm, uncharacteristically annoyed, and demanded that the kids stop, that they move away further into town. He stood among a group of guys as an older kid appeared. He placed a ball on the ground and kicked it, an effort any punter would be proud of.

It sailed over the fence and bounced in the forecourt of the barracks. Marbles picked it up and punted it back. The kid grinned, caught the ball and placed it on the ground a few feet closer.

He took the required steps backward to punt again. A few of the younger soldiers moved closer, ready to play the game in the name of public relations.

The kid ran forward again and, as he grew closer to the ball, reached into his pocket, pulled out a grenade and launched it over the fence.

One of the platoon recognized the shape as it sailed through the air. He stepped forward and kicked the thing on the volley. The metal object weighed more than the ball and flew back at a lower height. It clattered against the fence and detonated, sending shards of red hot metal in all directions. The blast tore through the kid and his friends, and a couple of the soldiers. A stray fragment somehow wormed its way past the multitude of bodies and embedded itself in Lucas Durrant's eye as he turned away.

He snapped out of his reverie and slid the pistol into his waistband, then slotted two spare clips into his back pockets. A tune drifted from the bathroom as Sarge whistled the theme to The Great Escape. Marbles retrieved his pouch and sifted through the glass eyeballs for something suitable for the occasion.

"That's all you're taking?" asked English.

"Never felt the need to carry loads of stuff," said Marbles. "How about you?"

English ran his eyes over the hardware that littered the pale red bed covers. It looked as if someone had dropped an arms factory onto an Ann Summers poster. "I prefer something that makes a statement," he said, and scooped up a gunmetal black AR-15.

Marbles smiled and pointed to the large firearm. "Are you compensating for something?"

English ran his hands over the semi-automatic and racked the slide to test its efficiency. "Mrs. English has never complained. She's moaned a few times, but she's never complained."

The way English cradled the AR, it looked like a third arm. Its metal blended into his body as he passed it between his hands and then held it like a child. "I never thought I'd see active duty again, but this is as good a cause as any I've fought."

Dud wrapped an arm around his shoulder. "Believe me brother, had the tables been turned, I'd have been there in a heartbeat too. I truly appreciate this."

"I know," said English. "That's why I'm here."

"That's why I'm blessed," said Dud as the bathroom door swung open and a rush of steam billowed into the room.

Sarge raised his eyebrows as he saw the scene before him. "If you ladies need a moment, I can go back in the bathroom. Otherwise, how about you clean up, we eat, and then we go and get ourselves some bad guys?"

17

A fine mist of dust, mixed with the sharp tang of metal made the air barely breathable. Lindsay slammed the van door closed and then hammered against the side of the vehicle with his palm to send vibrations and shock through its interior. The girls would hold each other, nervous and scared, wondering what would happen next.

The next part was easy. Two years of practice had ironed out any flaws. The system was as close to perfect as it could be. Get the girls to the mine. Move them to the dock. Load them up. Ship them overseas. Split the money. It was like selling ice cream in summer, with lines of potential buyers and a market fit to burst with product.

He remembered Mr. Ramirez's pitch all that time ago. Imagine a dam that held back millions of gallons of water. Make a single hole in the dam and a man will plug it and stop the leak. Now make two holes. The man might be able to block both holes. But make fifty holes, make a hundred, and the man would fail. The dam would breach and the water would come bursting through, cascading forward with unstoppable power. Lindsay was making the holes.

Every girl was another puncture in the dam wall. The police force was the man attempting, and failing, to stop it.

He spun and took in his surroundings. Despite extensive measures, a wispy pink shroud hung over everything. The dust from the bauxite ore was relentless in its spread. It covered everything, from the tops of the door frames to the ridges in the vents set high in the wall to channel the mildly toxic dust away. Nothing was one-hundred percent efficient. Except their operation.

This side of the facility was unmanned. Half a mile away, in the same building, ore was being sprayed and broken down ready for transport. The workers there wore white lab coats. They looked like doctors or scientists, not people trained to extract aluminum from stone.

They had no idea what happened at the other end of their facility. The ore left in large crates. As soon as it vanished from sight, they were done with it. No more face masks or breathing apparatus. At least until the next time. It left and moved down the line until it was miraculously transported over the tree line to the coast, where a huge conveyer would load it onto ships and send it to other countries. The other countries would pay handsomely for it, which would fund more mining, to dig up more ore to ship to the coast. And so the cycle continued.

Mr. Ramirez was smart. He'd spotted an opportunity years ago.

America was talking to Cuba again. Cuba's borders were becoming more lenient. Between Cuba and Columbia, the market for women was at an all-time high. With customs distracted by more and more tourists and imported product, getting the girls across their borders was so much easier.

Lindsay glanced at the van, its rear doors inches from

the wall. There was nothing for the girls to see and no way to open them. Sometimes, in moments of weakness, he felt a little sorry for them. Most of them had been shopping or walking home, thinking of how tough a night it would be with difficult homework or chores. Now they didn't need to worry about homework or chores. No more high school drama or concerns about which shoes matched which dress. That was the least of their worries.

When the feelings came, the sorrow or the pity, he reached into his pocket and squeezed the wad of bills packed into a roll; thousands of U.S. dollars, each one worth so much more than its Jamaican equivalent. The feelings were one thing. The wealth was something else, a different language, and one that Lindsay Anderson spoke fluently.

He thrust his hands into his pockets and whistled. Lyrics danced in his head as the tune echoed around the plant. A song from his favorite album, Exodus, by Bob Marley. Exodus, he thought, the movement of Jah people.

The people would move soon, even the white girl, although she'd be moving somewhere else.

She was earmarked for something special.

---

Evie dropped to her knees. The steel floor of the van was cold and the ribs in its design dug into her kneecaps. Now she had a consistent light that bounced off the wall outside the windows. She encouraged the other girls to stand and search once more for something, anything, they could use as a weapon to escape.

If the chance ever presented itself.

The seats squeaked and groaned as the girls stood. "Everyone," she said, "be careful not to rock the van. We don't want them thinking we're up to something. Carefully check around you. Look under your seat and feel behind it. Anything will do as long as it's sharp or heavy. I've not seen the other men from the camp, so this might be our only chance before more of them appear and we are outnumbered."

For a few moments, the mood in the claustrophobic space seemed to lighten. Evie spoke with a positive tone and tried to empower the others to help. They picked up on her attitude and weaved around the van, probing between folds of leather and tugging at chair supports.

The optimism was short lived, however. After a moment, one by one, they sat and resumed their resigned posture. Evie huffed and stood again. A seat squeaked as the final girl sat. Evie moved toward her.

"Please, would you stand again?"

The girl stood as Evie slid her hand beneath the seat. At first, she felt nothing but a sheet of coarse fabric, designed to cover the springs and supports that held the vinyl in place. Then something snagged at her fingers. A bump that poked through the fabric.

She rolled onto her back and pushed with her feet until her head and shoulders were underneath the seat. To one side, the thread had frayed, so she picked at it with her nails until a tiny flap of the fabric hung down. With a hard tug, she wrenched at the material and yanked it away. It left the seat with a loud tear that seemed to echo around the van. She stopped and held her breath for a moment. In the confines of the van, the tear had sounded like a huge sheet being torn down the middle. The girls held their collective breathes too, until Evie nodded and ripped the fabric cover from the seat.

The springs and supports looked like patchwork, all

interwoven to provide strength, but one support had broken free of its fastener. With the fabric gone, it hung like a knife, the broken edge hovering dangerously in midair.

Evie grabbed it and levered it back and forth until its other end grew weak enough to snap. Then she stood and inspected her work.

She held a piece of dull looking steel, about a foot in length, with blunt sides. The side she'd levered away was rough, but flat. The other side that had broken away ended with a jagged and uneven tip. It wasn't much, but applied properly, she now had a weapon to defend herself with.

"Not a word," she said with a finger over her lips. "We remain docile and let them think we're weak and vulnerable. As soon as those doors open, I'll get out first. If I don't see any extra men, I'll make my move and go for whoever is nearest. Please, I'm begging you all, do what you can to overpower anyone else. This trip won't end well and we may only have one chance to escape. Don't freeze because we have to take it."

The girls in the van stared back at her, scared expressions painted across their faces.

"I mean it. Are you with me?" She pointed to each girl until she received a verbal acknowledgment, then slid the metal into her waistband and took her seat.

---

Dud and English led the two-car convoy as it wound its way along the coast road. Dud steered through the turns like a pro as English marveled at the scenery. The pair had spent the first half hour of the trip trading war stories, sizing each other up, and discussing their colleagues.

"What's this thing I've gathered about Sarge not

wanting any more bloodshed?" asked English. "The profession we're in, that's the way of the world."

"Sarge found God," said Dud. "He went on one too many missions and got burned out. It happens to the best of us. Still, he had a rough tour and came home nursing a bottle of Jackie D and a pack of Camels. From what I can tell, he smoked and drank himself almost to death. One day, something happened, no idea what, and he turned himself around. I'll tell you, when I first met him his eyes could turn ice into ashes, he was stone cold. You wouldn't know him from the man he is now."

"And how did all of this come about?"

"No idea. I just remember, he started talking one time like he was at confession. It's weird what strong coffee, a bacon and egg McMuffin and a hash brown can do to you first thing in the morning. Anyway, he told me he almost lost it. He'd quit drinking. Quit smoking. Threw everything out; bottles, cigarettes, lighters. You name it. Said he did okay for a while, and then the stress got to him, so he tried yoga. Only position he said he could do was 'hair of the dog', so that didn't work. So, he bought a pack of scented candles, figured he'd light them and the scent would calm him down. Lavender, or some shit. Might have been vanilla? Whatever, he placed these candles all around his place, and he's already calmer. Then he comes to light them, and he finds he's thrown away all his matches. So basically, he's in a house full of lovely smelling candles, eating his fingers down to the knuckle with stress, and he's got nothing to light them with."

English smirked. There were dozens of tales like this from every front line. "So, what did he do?"

"He knee-mailed," said Dud.

"I'm sorry?"

"Yep. He said he got down on his knees and spoke to The Man Upstairs. This being the age of technology, he dropped to the floor and knee-mailed the main man."

English laughed. "He's a hell of a guy. Like the guy that binds it all together."

"Yep, I reckon Sarge is the glue."

The ice broken, both men relaxed into the mission. Dud described the camp and the men guarding it and vented his frustrations at losing his wife when he'd been so close. English did what any friend would do; consoled, empathized, and threatened to maim everyone involved.

As the road straightened, Dud glanced in the mirror. Sarge and Marbles kept a perfect three second gap behind them, taking the same turns and avoiding the same potholes and, all the while, maintaining an exact speed. Marbles had an instinctive ability to drive, fly or sail anything. Give him a couple of minutes and he would have it worked out. Despite being on the wrong side of the road, on the wrong side of the car, and driving a stick shift with his wrong hand, he drove as if this was his daily route to work.

English picked up on the same things that Dud had when he'd first taken this road. The way the opulence of the city center dwindled the further from town they drove. The large buildings perched in the hillside, with their elaborate balconies and brightly painted fences, that changed to small shacks of corrugated metal pinned to two by four frames partly hidden by foliage. The smooth glossy asphalt roads that changed to noisy stretches of pockmarked gravel that spat and pulled at the tires.

Goats and wild dogs roamed the side of the road, picking at litter and foraging for scraps.

"I've never seen so many goats," said English as they passed another animal tethered to a frayed rope.

"Don't get attached," said Dud. "They're not pets, they're food. Apparently, it's getting harder for the farmers here to compete against the cheap meat we're sending overseas, but goat is like chicken here. It's a common meal."

"So, Billy Burgers then, huh?"

Dud laughed. "Something like that. They taste quite gamey, and the bones are a pain in the ass, but goat curry is a fine meal. Maybe when we finish this mission, I'll take us all to a nice restaurant."

Another goat passed by as English pointed to it. "Look at goats. They're cute. Have you ever raised chickens? Chickens are mean. Those beady eyes and nasty claws. Why don't we have chicken? Chicken's good. Full of protein, too."

"Hate to break it to you, pal," said Dud, "but goat is also chock full of protein. And it doesn't flap as much when you break its neck."

English shuddered and looked out into the road again. "You're an evil man. Karma will get you. Probably with a goat bone to the throat."

Dud laughed again. He knew what was going on, the banter and joking, deflecting from the mission ahead. Both men knew there was a good chance of bloodshed. They also knew not all men made it back. There were always casualties, sometimes fatalities. That's what happened when desperate men faced off against other desperate men. The victors were normally the ones that would do anything, whatever it took, to get the job done. The ones that would step over the line of morality and not worry about any mental consequences.

The curve in the road, where the jeep had veered away and crashed against a tree, was a few hundred yards ahead. Dud noticed the whites of his knuckles and relaxed his grip on the steering wheel, took one more glance in the rear view, and eased off the accelerator. Images of Evie flashed through his mind and, as he pulled over to the side of the road, he slipped into full military mode.

He was getting his wife back and to Hell with the consequences.

The other vehicle rolled to a stop behind them. Sarge climbed out as Marbles opened the driver's door and rested his arms on top of it. Even at this distance, Dud could see he'd switched out his glass eye. A circular round face with a beaming grin had replaced the blazing sun.

"So, this is where we split up?" asked Sarge.

Dud pointed up the slight incline. "There's a smaller road that branches off to the right up there. The camp is just past a fork in the road. I assume it'll be empty now, but you know what happens when you assume, right?"

"Yeah, it makes an 'ass' out of 'u' and 'me', buddy. I know full well." He reached for his phone, dialed and hit the speakerphone icon. Numbers answered after the first ring. "Numbers, you still have us on that imaging thing?"

"Sure do, Sarge. I see the group of you at the side of the road."

"Okay. Do a sweep to the east of us. Check out that camp, would you? Just to be sure we're not gate crashing anyone's party."

"Will do, give me a sec."

The line went silent for a while as Dud marveled at Sarge's tenacity. In the heat of the moment, he'd have gone charging in blind, despite any planning. It was good to have the guys around.

"Well, we seem to have a solitary dot in that area," said Numbers. "Obviously, I can't tell you what it is. It might be a large animal, but I'd recommend caution."

"Advice taken," said Sarge. "Stay close, Numbers. I'm sure we'll be calling on you again."

"Be careful, everyone," said Dud. "These are some big guys, together with a couple of kids. If that's one of them, it could be a well-trained beast or a trigger-happy kid. Either one will get you killed."

"Copy that," said Sarge. "You guys go on ahead. Get to where the van disappeared and recon the area. Marbles and I will take care of business here and see what we can find. It goes without saying, keep your phones handy."

The men shook hands and back slapped, while Marbles gave an enthusiastic thumbs up from behind the rear vehicle, and then they split up again.

As the car pulled away, he leaned out through the window. "Good hunting!"

A few hundred yards behind them, just around the curve, Kenzie's SUV sat at the side of the road. She sat inside and watched and waited until the two vehicles pulled away.

Then she followed.

18

Now he was alone, the outside sounds from the woods bled through the cheap windows. Deaven tried to relax in a chair pushed up against one of them in the main cabin. He leaned into the wall and glanced occasionally at the sofa. It was a much more comfortable seat, but the sight of D'Andre's dried blood, spattered over it like a rash, was enough to put him off.

He was no stranger to blood. There were countless times when he'd left school with someone else's blood smeared across his knuckles. It wasn't the substance itself that bothered him; it was the reason for the marks. Lindsay would not tolerate failure. D'Andre had failed, and Deaven had watched the life being literally beaten out of him.

So far, Lindsay had been lenient with him. And, of course, there was the trust. Lindsay trusted him enough to stay here alone and man the radio. The radio was a vital part of the operation and, having had to bring the timetable forward, regular communication was vital to keep Mr. Ramirez happy. He couldn't know about the intruder.

As he shuffled and found a position that didn't dig into his bones, the radio squelched. Deaven jumped, cursed, and ambled over to the small table. The person at the other end never spoke, just keyed the handset and waited for a response.

"All is good," said Deaven.

That was it. Three little words that meant he would wake up again tomorrow and get to live another day. He hung the handset back onto its shiny clip and collapsed back onto the chair.

Final check-in was over. Now he could mount his bike and race up to the plant to join the others. Lindsay would be pleased to see him. If he turned up on time, everything had gone to plan. Mr. Ramirez would be none the wiser, and the girls would be moved as planned.

Deaven's stomach rumbled, and he jumped again as something moved outside the cabin. It sounded like a tree limb falling, a loud thud with a heavy bass sound that cut through the chatter of the relentless insects. With his gun, he moved to the door, and edged it open. There'd be no surprise attack this time, no rock to the forehead. He frowned and the congealed blood pulled against the wound.

The AK-47 felt good as it led the way outside. In a fluid motion, as Lindsay had shown him, he swung around the edge of the frame and leveled the gun ready to mow down any intruders. Nothing of substance moved. Tree limbs waved in the breeze, but that was it. For a few seconds more he held his breath, daring whatever it was to announce itself again. When his lungs could no longer hold the breath, he released it and retreated into the cabin and closed the door behind him.

Back in the chair, he squirmed against the wall again,

enjoying the last chance to relax for a while. Wild boar sometimes moved through here, much bigger and clumsier than the goats or packs of wild dogs that roamed. Still, he continued to glance through the window to pick out any movement against the dark backdrop of trees. Then he heard it again. A noise outside that was definitely not caused by the natural inhabitants of the woods. He checked the clip on the gun, more out of nerves than efficiency, and performed the same maneuver when he reached the door.

This time, as the door swung open, a man greeted him. If not for the light cast from the cabin, he'd be hidden. He looked to be older, but still trim and tall. And dressed for a vacation, his outfit topped off with a military-looking base-ball cap. He stood perfectly still with both hands raised in the air. Deaven frowned. Why would someone approach the cabin, this far off the road? He stepped out onto the first step. As if to answer his question, the man spoke.

"Hi. I wonder if you can help me." He pointed across the clearing toward the ocean. "I was driving along the coast road when my engine blew. My cellphone is dead, and I saw your lights. Do you have a phone I could use to call for help?"

At first, Deaven felt sorry for the man. He'd been in the same position. Then it occurred to him; the man didn't seem at all concerned that he was asking his questions to someone holding a gun. In fact, he seemed very relaxed, despite the situation.

Lindsay always said 'take no chances'. Something was wrong.

Deaven raised the gun and slid his finger inside the trigger guard. He eased the trigger back to the point where it grew taught, to where it tripped the hammer that released a stream of deadly lead, when another man appeared beside him.

The gun fired and bucked as the man dived into him. Deaven's finger slid from the trigger. He turned in time to see the strangest thing. The man had two different eyes. One blazed a cold steel blue, but the other smiled at him, like the figure at the end of a friendly text message.

He used the height advantage and curled the man's arm away until the barrel of the gun angled down. A couple more inches and it would be level with his face. He smiled and pushed his finger back inside the trigger guard.

Two loud cracks sounded. Deaven felt as if someone had punched him in the stomach. Warmth spread down the front of his pants as his gun clattered onto the steps. The man stepped aside as his body grew too heavy for his legs, and he tumbled down the remaining steps and crashed to the ground.

Then it went dark.

Marbles slid the pistol back into its holster. Years had passed since he'd taken a life. It never felt good.

He jumped when Sarge slapped him on the back.

"It was you or him, buddy. It upsets me that we've already had fatalities, but you had no choice. And you know I don't say that lightly."

Sarge stared at the body on the dirt floor as if it was one of his kids. He knelt, closed the staring eyes, and said a silent prayer.

Marbles wiped his eye with a shaking hand. "He was a kid, Sarge. That was someone's son."

"You know as well as I do, another few seconds and it'd

be you or me lying there. The kid had a choice, and he chose wrong. Nothing you could do." Sarge stood and reached into his pocket. He palmed his phone as if he was creating a distraction. "Numbers? You still got us on screen?"

"Sure do, Sarge," said Numbers. "Still got the three dots but, since they're all so close and you're talking to me, I guess the situation's under control."

"Afraid so. One of those dots will blink out soon, I'm sorry to say."

Numbers remained silent as the implications of Sarge's statement sunk in.

"Nothing else moving?" asked Sarge.

"Nothing near you, just regular movement on the road."

"Okay, buddy. Keep us in sight and call if that changes."

Sarge pocketed the phone. "Come on, Marbles. Let's look around and find out what happened here. Dud's relying on us to dig something up."

They entered the main cabin. Other than a radio and a sofa covered in blood, there wasn't much to report.

Outside the cabin, blood pooled beneath the kid's body.

"We can't leave him here," said Marbles.

"You read my mind," said Sarge. "Come on; let's see if we can find something to dig a grave."

They ambled over to the smaller cabin and pushed open the door. Sarge led the way.


"Presumably, the kid outside would have locked up when he left. If this wasn't stuck in the middle of a forest, I could stay somewhere like this for a few days. Off the grid, with nothing but me and nature."

"Don't you normally shoot at nature?" said Marbles.

"Don't get me wrong, I'm all for creating balance in the universe, but that hunting you do? That's not for me."

"Come on now, Marbles. The book of Genesis says animals were created for the benefit of man. It's not like a slaughter. Deer meat is very good. You've eaten my deer jerky."

Marbles pulled back the rug to expose the hatch Dud had mentioned. He pulled his pistol and lifted the door. Darkness faced him. "I ate it," he said as he flicked a switch to the side of the opening, "because I didn't know what it was. If you'd told me I was chewing Bambi, I'd have thrown up. You didn't tell me until days later. By then, whatever was left of Bambi, after going through me, was floating toward the ocean."

Nothing moved through the illuminated hatch. Marbles placed a foot on the first rung and stepped down into the bunker. Sarge stayed at the hatch and shouted through the opening. "Enjoyed it though, didn't you?"

"No comment." He looked around the room. Other than a row of beds pushed up against one side, the space was empty. The musky smell of old perfumes and sweat permeated the air. "There's nothing down here other than real basic beds. They remind me of the Middle East, except these look way comfier. Honestly, I dread to think of Evie being stuck down here."

"Come back up," said Sarge. "We don't have time to dig a grave barehanded. Let's get back to the others, and we can get Numbers to call this in. He can get the authorities out here to take care of the kid."

They placed the body on the sofa and walked away from the camp.

A tunnel of trees led away from the two buildings. The ground was packed dirt rutted with countless tire tracks.

Sarge disconnected a call to Numbers and pointed into the distance. "Numbers is calling the police. They'll make sure Junior gets a proper burial. What's that up there, a fork in the road? It seems odd that a camp as secretive as this would have another point of access so close."

Where the two roads met, the packed dirt had been scuffed and lifted.

"Looks like there's been activity here," said Marbles. "I vote we check this out. Dud mentioned something about bikes and trucks, but he didn't know where they were parked."

"I'm with you," said Sarge.

They followed the curve, moved across into the tree line for safety, and followed the dirt road until it opened onto a small clearing. A shack faced them, no more than fifteen feet square. Corrugated metal sheets sloped away from its side to create a small carport. Multiple tire tracks plowed the earth beneath it.

"So, this is vehicle storage," said Sarge. He pulled out the phone again. "Numbers, how many dots do you see?"

"To almost sing a song, just the two of you," said Numbers. "Unless there's something else underground, you're all alone."

They crept forward until they kicked open the door. This cabin didn't even have the luxuries of the first, with a table, chairs and a desk. There was no hatch, just rough-hewn planks.

Marbles moved toward the desk. "What do you reckon? A bad guy's taxi rank?"

"Looks that way," said Sarge.

Marbles slid open the small drawer at the front of the desk and stepped back in surprise. "Er, you might want to come and look at this."

Sarge stepped forward as Marbles reached into the drawer and pulled out a handful of Polaroid photos. He fanned them out and turned them toward his colleague.

"I'd say this was all planned," said Marbles. "Smile, Evie, you're on Candid Camera."

19

Fifty minutes after the two vehicles separated, Numbers instructed Dud to turn east into the center of the island.

English kept the mood of the drive as relaxed as he could. During the banter, he confessed to being impressed with the way Dud had earned his nickname.

"You'd have done the same thing if you'd been there," said Dud, as he steered the car around yet another tight turn. He kept his eyes on the road and followed the twin beams of his headlights. "It takes a callous bastard to toss a grenade into a room full of kids. To be honest, it made the rest of the campaign much easier. Not that it bothered me before, but after that, I had no issues firing on those people. And I use the term 'people' loosely. Don't get me wrong, there are some amazing folks over there; hospitable, eager for change, and very diplomatic. But those behind the black flags? They're not people, they're animals. It was our job to put them out of our misery. So, you'd have done the same thing, if only to thwart them."

"I don't know, mate. I suspect I'd have frozen in that situation."

"No, you wouldn't. Trust me, if push came to shove, you'd have done the same thing. I can't imagine being a parent and scraping bits of my kid off a classroom wall. I'll tell you this though, it changed me."

"What? Is that why there are no little Duds running around?"

"No, kids just never happened for me. It's probably too late now. No, for all the firefights I've been involved in, none of them changed me like dropping on that grenade. And I won't say I suffer from PTSD, but I suffer from something. Loud noises are not my friend, and I frigging hate Independence Day."

"That sucks, as you Americans say. Have you spoken to anyone about it?"

"Yeah. You. Just." Dud smiled.

English barked a humorless laugh. "It's okay to be nervous, mate. I can't imagine what you must be feeling right now."

Marbles had called a few minutes earlier to tell them about a Polaroid collection of Evie.

"You know we're all here though, right?" he continued. "We'll get this done."

For the first time, Dud took his eyes off the road and glanced at his passenger. Few people would have picked up on his mood so quickly, especially someone he'd just met. "I know. And it means the world." He indicated through the window. "Speaking of the team, call Numbers again. The turn he mentioned is up ahead. Let's see if we can get an idea of what's up there."

Numbers answered instantly and listened as English explained where they were. "I can get you about a mile down that road," he said, "and that's where the signal died. The road you're travelling down looks clear for the first mile. Then trees get in the way again. I did see a railway line that ran behind the area. Railway lines go somewhere, right? And there's a monorail, too. There's so much around there, there has to be something ahead of you."

"And how about on the thermal imaging view?" asked Dud.

"Hang on," said Numbers. He was quiet for a while. "Well, I thought I'd got the hang of this." The sound of key presses clattered down the line. "Oh, okay. There it is. I can see two heat signatures about a mile and a half ahead. After that, it's as if there's nothing there."

Dud turned onto the road and plowed forward. The black asphalt of the coast road changed to a crunching gravel that was stained pink. It grew deeper in color the further they drove until the road appeared to bleed.

"Is this road sponsored by a breast cancer charity?" said English. "What's with all the pink? I saw weird looking roads earlier along the main road."

"Yeah, it's bauxite dust. It's everywhere inland. Keeps the island's economy afloat. As well as tourism, of course."

"And rum. Don't forget rum."

"As if I could," said Dud as he pulled the car over to the side of the road. "Okay, let's travel the rest of the way on foot and see where that van went."

They stepped around to the rear of the vehicle and grabbed weaponry and supplies from the trunk.

The landscape on the left side of the road rose away from them in tall, rocky hills punctuated with trees. The other side dropped away, but not so severely that they couldn't use its brush and foliage as cover. Dud's palms still smarted from the splinters he'd gained from what seemed like days ago, so he balanced his weight and slid, one foot after the other, down the bank. English followed and rode the incline like a skateboard.

Dud raised his eyebrows. "Are you showing off?"

"Not at all, mate. Maybe it's a British thing. I'm used to sliding around in snow."

"You're showing off," said Dud under his breath, as he led the way and moved along the side of the road. "Limey bastard."

"I heard that," said English from a few feet behind him.

In no time, the road bent out of sight. As they rounded the curve, the built-up hills opposite solidified into solid rock and huge stone mound cut off the end of the road. A tunnel was carved into its face.

"Very Indiana Jones," said Dud. "That would explain why the van disappeared. What do you think it is?"

English shrugged. "The more important question might be, what would be out here in the middle of nowhere, with two armed guards posted outside?"

---

After rounding a curve in the road, Kenzie Anderson pulled to the side and beat her steering wheel in frustration.

In the time it took for the occupants of the first vehicle to disappear into the woods, Dud and the other guy had got a decent start on the road ahead of her. She'd driven erratically, at least for her, to catch up to them until she'd glimpsed the taillights of her own blue car in the distance. She wasn't sure how good a memory the American might have so she kept a decent distance between them. If he spotted the SUV, there'd be no way he'd allow her to tag along. Then, a goat wandered into the road and forced her to stop. It bided its time and seemed to check out every inch of the asphalt. By the time it trotted past her, the lead car had disappeared.

As she sat there, numbers rattled around in her head, ingrained from four years of painful research. Every year, over a thousand children, between the ages of thirteen and seventeen, went missing in Jamaica. Of those thousand, seventy-five percent were girls. Runaways made up a part of that figure; kids that reached the age where they figured they knew what was best for them and ventured out alone to find independence. Many of the missing were found, or returned home, but between two and three-hundred vanished, never to be seen again. No one knew what happened to them.

She was certain that her sister, Yanika, was not a runaway. Sure, they'd lived on just the right side of poverty, but they had the essentials; a roof, three meals a day, schooling, and family.

Yanika was already independent; she didn't need to go looking for it. Driven and bright, she excelled at school and had ambitions to train in medicine. Yanika wouldn't run away.

Dud's wife didn't fit the same profile. She was more than twice Yanika's age and, more tellingly, she was a white tourist. Outside countries gave their citizens warnings about the dangers in Jamaica and, so, the rate of incidents involving foreigners was minimal.

Still, she had been kidnapped. In the pictures Kenzie had seen, the woman was beautiful. Perhaps they'd been in the wrong place at the wrong time. Either way, she may have been taken by the same people that took Yanika. Kenzie wasn't naïve enough to believe she'd ever see her sister again. In four years, assuming she was still alive, she could be anywhere in the world by now. Getting her sister back never entered her mind, but the thought of avenging her burned like hot coals inside her. Both of her parents died with no closure. They passed away not knowing if their little girl was living somewhere against her will, or had been tortured and murdered. The loss ate away at them, a little at a time, until Kenzie returned home one night to find them holding hands in bed, with two empty pill bottles resting on the bedside cabinet.

Shaking her head, she thought back to the conversation at the hotel. The men took direction from another by phone. She'd seen the image on-screen, where he said the van had disappeared, and tried hard to picture it. She backtracked and realized that she'd gone too far. Due to her focus on the road ahead, and her straining her eyes in the moonlight to find the missing vehicle, she'd driven past the turn she needed.

The SUV screeched in the road as she executed a three-point turn and headed back to find the others.

Numbers had grown accustomed to living in a basement. Still, it was strange to be alone in someone else's home, especially someone he'd just met. Despite the level of trust shown to him, he still couldn't help but feel inadequate. As the others cut a swathe through Jamaica's countryside, he concentrated on the thermal images flashed across the computer screen, and researched the gangs and crime lords of Jamaica. English's wife had called in to keep him watered and fed. Warm tea, as opposed to the iced version, complimented with a splash of milk, seemed to be a relaxing drink. He'd eaten Shepherd's Pie (she assured him there were no shepherds involved in the ingredients), and he'd enjoyed a dish of Spotted Dick. He didn't dare ask about that, but the spiced cake was delicious served with a creamy custard. Now, he was left with a flask and instructions to raid the fridge.

The thermal dots that made up the two vehicles carrying his colleagues had followed the course he laid out. Other signatures moved around at random, but one caught his eye. For their entire trip along the coast road, the men had another vehicle trailing behind them.

As he picked up the phone to dial Dud's number, the vehicles stopped. The trailing dot stopped behind them and hovered on the screen as if it was waiting.

He watched and held his breath. Time stopped as he tried to visualize what was happening on the ground. After a couple of minutes, the lead vehicle pulled away. Its signature followed the curve of the road and moved north. The third vehicle, whoever it was, stayed put for a while. He watched again as Sarge and Marbles made their way through the trees toward the camp. Then the rear signature pulled away again and also moved north.

Phone in hand, he scrolled through the contacts until he found Dud's number. The first car drove past the fork in the road and continued onwards toward Nine Mile. It found the road that would take it to the position where Evie's van had disappeared and turned inland. As he was about to hit 'dial', the rear vehicle drove past them and continued along the road, past the turn and out of sight.

Numbers breathed a sigh of relief and repositioned the cursor to follow the men at the camp.

20

Mr. Ramirez sat alone, at the end of a long, polished mahogany dining table. Marcia had counted the settings many times; there were enough chairs to seat twenty people. She'd only ever seen two people eat there; Mr. Ramirez and his current woman.

A long, red velvet cloth stretched along the center of the table. It had been pulled closer to the far end as Mr. Ramirez used it as a place mat to rest a silver platter, piled high with food. A crystal glass of red wine shimmered beside it, flickering in the light coming from a solitary candle. The whole scene screamed loneliness to Marcia, but he seemed content as he sliced through thick cut chunks of steak.

She topped off his glass. "Will that be all, Sir?"

"Yes. I think so, Marcia."

The second she stepped back from the table, she shuddered as his eyes wandered up and down her body. In the four years she'd been here, she'd noticed his gaze, but he'd never stepped over the line and touched her. All the women she'd seen him with had been white. She was blessed with flawless skin and an athletic body, but her flawless skin was black as night. Not something she'd ever seen him touch. She edged away as casually as she could.

"Very well, Sir. I'll be outside if you need anything."

She turned on her heels and strode from the room, closing the heavy wooden door behind her. As she leaned against the wall, cool air from the overhead fan brushed across her face. It surprised her. A thin sheen of sweat dampened the back of her hand when she wiped her forehead. Hopefully, he hadn't seen her nerves. His eyes had been elsewhere, she was sure of that.

Her hand still trembled. It was all she could do to not clink the bottle against the crystal glass as she poured his wine. In her four years, she had no complaints over her treatment. If anything, he'd been an outstanding boss and generous to a fault. Over the past few months, however, a sense of unpredictability had crept in.

Two guards had disappeared. The word among the soldiers was that they'd helped themselves to more than their entitlement. Mr. Ramirez had no qualms about disciplining employees in public to make an example of them, but there was something more sinister and threatening about them vanishing with no word.

And then there was his asking her to 'take care' of Abigail's body. He knew the girls had forged a friendship. At the time, she'd kept her face as impassive as she could, and didn't think she'd telegraphed the wave of nausea that had washed through her. But the slightest doubt remained. He would not tolerate weakness. She had to remain strong.

Then his voice bled through the door. "Marcia? Come here."

She opened the door again and stepped into the room.

As the door closed, she rested her back against it and kept her distance.

"Come closer," he beckoned with a fork.

Stay strong, she thought, and strode with false confidence to the side of the table. He laid the fork across his plate. There was still a pile of food on it.

"Closer."

His eyes burned into her as she took a few more steps to the side of his chair. Each step was like walking through wet sand. Her stomach turned again, and she folded her hands behind her back so he wouldn't see them shaking.

"Yes, Sir?"

Goosebumps broke out all over her body as his fingertips brushed the fabric of her blouse where it rested against her hips. Every hair on her arms stood on end as his nails dragged across the fabric before his hand fell back to his side. She inhaled deeply through her nose to steady her breathing.

"I never asked you about earlier," he said.

"I'm sorry, Sir. Earlier?"

"That unfortunate business. Abigail." He waved a hand as if the mention of her name was an inconvenience. "I appreciate what you do for me." His hand rose again, moved toward her, then wrapped around his wine glass.

Marcia fought back the hint of tears, unsure whether they were from fear or regret. "Of course. Thank you, Sir. I took care of everything. The room is clean and ready for -" Her voice trailed off.

"For what? The next one?"

"No, Sir, I wasn't -"

He laughed and sipped the wine. The pupils of his eyes were so wide, they looked like deadly pools of tar. Marcia was careful not to fall into them.

"It's okay," he smiled. "I know I'm hard to please. You do a good job for me, and I wanted to mention it. Thank you."

Unsure of what to say, she stood and clasped her hands tighter. As the seconds ticked by, the silence grew heavier. "Thank you," she managed.

It took a few more uncomfortable seconds before he waved his hand again. "That will be all."

***

Another thump against the side of the van caused the girls to jump again.

"Damn that bastard," said Evie. She looked around at her fellow prisoners. "Remember what I said. If we want to escape, we'll get one chance. Don't waste it. Please."

She was met by a host of downcast eyes.

Hinges squeaked as a door up front opened. She couldn't tell if it was the driver's door, or the passenger's. As it closed, and the other opened, the subject became a moot point. There were two people at the front of the van. Based on that figure, she fancied the odds. Adrenaline coursed through her veins and increased her heart rate. The she remembered that they were at the probable midpoint of their journey. There might be more people waiting when the van reached its destination.

Only time would tell.

Light flooded the back of the van as it pulled away from the wall. The girls gripped the edge of their seats as Evie balanced at the rear and watched their surroundings emerge through the windows. Huge steel supports and lots of space rolled away into the background as the van ambled forward and then, like an illusion, the light changed.

The harsh fluorescent glare faded into a more natural glow. Taller lamps led the way as the van drove outside and turned to follow the perimeter of the facility. Train tracks ran parallel to the building behind a chain link fence. The weird chute hung above them. Rolling green countryside beckoned in the distance and, barely visible over the tree-tops, a paper-thin stretch of ocean sparkled and rippled.

Evie reached back and brushed her fingers against the metal she had pushed into her waistband. She thought of home, of her parents, and of the house she'd grown up in. She thought of her siblings, the people she'd laughed with on the phone a few days ago. And she thought about her husband. About the way he'd found her once, only to be thwarted. She knew he'd be back, she just had to stay alive long enough for him to find her again.

They lurched and swayed as the van moved alongside the building, and the scenery changed again. The wire fencing stopped running alongside and, instead, stretched back and out of sight while something else swung into view.

The train tracks stopped, but they didn't vanish. As the van turned and drove along a large concrete platform, they merged to join others.

They'd driven into a railway station.

As the van crawled along the platform, more of the station appeared in the rear windows. The tracks ran off into the distance and ended at a huge turntable. Other tracks ran into it from different directions, like octopus arms.

Everything was here, the stores, the ticket office, and the uncomfortable plastic seats. But it was all aged and dusty and didn't look as if anyone had boarded a train here in a long time.

Shoots of grass grew unhindered beside the thick metal

rails and even poked through the slats that separated the concrete sections of the platform from the buildings behind them.

They drove on until what appeared to be most of the station lay behind them. Then the van stopped. There were no sounds and no movement as the girls sat huddled together and waited.

Seconds ticked by. Evie reached behind her and withdrew the metal support. There was no proper way to grip it, but she took a moment to move it in her hands until she found something that offered a decent grip.

A door opened. Someone whistled another tune and dragged something down the side of the van as they walked toward the rear. The other door opened and someone else shouted, their voice echoing through the empty station.

Except the station wasn't empty. Another voice shouted back and drew closer until two men held a muffled conversation outside. A shadow crossed the windows as the first rear door opened.

Evie knew of at least three men. She also knew there were six desperate girls; two girls to attack each man. If the girls stepped up. A figure appeared in the door space and reached the other door. As he leaned to pull the handle, Evie leaped forward.

The man reacted, but not quickly enough. As he recoiled, she thrust the metal blade down toward the side of his neck and hit her target at the first attempt. Bile rose in her throat as the metal tore through an artery and his heart pumped arcs of bright red blood across the platform. He staggered backwards and clutched at the wound as his life pulsed free between his fingers.

Evie tumbled out of the van ready for her next target. Behind her, the girls moved. As she spun to look behind the van door, she saw her next target was too close. He swung an arm and his fist connected with her chin and sent her reeling. Clanging metal rang through her head as her teeth rattled and her vision dimmed enough for her to lose her footing. As her knees jarred against the concrete, the guy with the neck wound collapsed beside her, his skin pale, slashed with vivid red streaks. Blood still oozed from the wound and bubbled from his mouth as he tried in vain to stem the flow.

The other girls froze inside the van as her assailant loomed over her. Suddenly, he too was sent sprawling to the ground as the leader pushed him aside.

"Are you crazy, mon? You can't mark her. He'll kill you if you do."

Evie looked up, confused and scared. The big man leaned down toward her and held out a hand. His dread-locks hung like snakes and covered his face.

"Take my hand, you stupid bitch. Be grateful you are a high commodity, otherwise I'd tear you apart myself."

Evie ignored the offer and struggled to her feet. Her attacker rose and dusted himself off and stepped behind the leader. The other guy collapsed onto his side as gravity drew the rest of his life through the jagged hole in his neck and created a red pool beneath him. Overhead light sparkled in it like rubies.

The big guy hammered on the van's door. "Out! All of you. Get out, now!"

One by one, the girls clambered out of the van and lined up next to Evie. Now she could see the main guy's face. It seethed with anger. He ushered them all to the platform's edge and had them stand side by side with their backs to the track.

"Your journey is almost over," he said, pointing a finger

at each of them. "Any more tricks like that and there'll be more bloodshed. After my men have taken turns with you. Do you understand?"

A distant train whistled as he stood nose to nose with Evie. "You," he said, as he prodded her chest, "can count yourself very lucky. Had you been anyone else, you would be dead by now."

Between his words, the sound of a train chugging along the tracks grew louder. Evie dared a glance to her right to see the gleaming front of an engine in the distance. Behind it followed a convoy of carriages topped with red stone.

Lecia stood next to her, cringing and sobbing. Evie reached out, brushed the girl's fingers, and took her hand.

"I feel like I need to make an example," continued the big man. "As much as I applaud your determination, it would be weak to simply accept the loss of one of my men without punishment."

Evie jumped as the train blew its whistle again and entered the station. Brakes hissed, and it began to slow before it reached them.

The big man threw back his hair. "However, I cannot harm you," he said and pressed his face into Evie's. He nodded his head to the side. "So, I'll take her."

He reached out a hand and pushed hard against Lecia's chest. Evie felt the tug of the girls' small hand as she stumbled backwards. She gasped and spun to grab her. Lecia balanced on her heels at the edge of the platform before she stepped out into thin air. Her eyes met Evie's a second before she fell backwards, in silence, onto the track as the train plowed through. There was no fear in them, just relief.

The train's brakes screeched once more and, finally, it stopped.

Evie cried.

21

After a 'heads up' from Numbers, Dud studied the tree line until the foliage parted and his colleagues appeared, and waved. After backslapping and knuckle bumps, Marbles fanned out a small deck of Polaroids. Dud fought back tears at the images of Evie on the beach, walking down The Hip Strip, shopping, and even one of the two of them leaned against the bar at the hotel. He shook his head as if to shake out the anger and refocus on the mission ahead.

"God knows what this place is used for," he indicated with a thumb. "It's basically a tunnel in a mountain, which sounds easy enough to enter except there are two armed guards stationed outside it. The rifle could take them out at distance but who knows what else is in there. We don't want to attract attention. And Sarge, I know you're against taking life, but I don't think we'll get through this with gentle conversation and handshakes."

The old man grimaced. "I know, buddy. We've already had an incident back at that camp. It's time to be realistic, so don't worry, I'm on board. Did you come up with a plan?"

"The ground this side is flat. No cover, with a lot of open space to cross to reach the guards. The other side of the road climbs. I say we cross further back and get to higher ground, and then track behind them, distract them, and try a surprise jump."

"I've already had one surprise jump, out of that damned plane. One more won't hurt," said Marbles.

Sarge unslung the rifle from his shoulder. "I'll stay back and keep everyone and everything in my sights. If it looks like things might go south, I'll provide cover."

"English and I will do the jumping, if that's okay with you guys. I'm invested, and English is the young pup. Plus, he's already said he's itching for a fight. Ready to scratch that itch, pal?"

"Ready as I'll ever be," said English. "Come on, let's get this done."

Ten minutes later, the guards were fifteen feet below and slightly ahead of the group. Sarge lay fifty yards back, flat on his stomach, with the rifle's barrel edged out over the top of the rise.

Dud could imagine the two guards dancing in the crosshairs. Butterflies fluttered in his stomach. "I thought I'd be nervous but, truth be told, I'm shitting myself."

"Natural reaction," said Marbles. "And I'd be concerned if you weren't. Okay, you guys shimmy down the bank. I'll toss a stone into the trees just past the guards when you're about half way down. When they turn, rush them. Basic, but sometimes blunt and to the point is the way to go. Don't forget, Sarge is watching you. He's got the entrance covered, too, and I'll be right behind you."

Dud stepped out onto the grass bank. The packed earth took his weight, and he edged down toward the road in silence. He didn't look back; English would be right behind him. The guards were talking, something about a soccer game, when the rock sailed over their heads and hit the base of a tree with a muffled thump. Their heads turned toward the sound and they stared into the shadows. Dud paused and felt English's hand rest on his shoulder. The nearest guard raised his gun for cover as the other left the entrance and moved toward the trees.

Each time the guard stepped, Dud followed. As the guard reached the far edge of the road, Dud reached the near side. He turned and gestured to English; I'll get this guy, you rush the other. English nodded.

They moved like shadows as if they'd rehearsed the move for years. As English powered past him, Dud wrapped a hand around the first guys mouth. The second guard turned in time to take an elbow to the jawline. His head rocked back, and he staggered onto the grass as English crashed another punch into his temple. The guy dropped.

Dud choked his opponent, as he had with the kid back at the camp, but the guard was much stronger. The barrel of his gun swung around, almost in line with English's body. Dud grabbed it at either end and forced it up against the guards' throat. With a twist of his body, he pulled the guard backwards over his hip. The guy's feet left the ground, and he kicked and gurgled as the metal cut into his windpipe. Dud imagined his eyes, wide and panicked as scrambled and fought for air. With one strong wrench, he jerked the body higher off the ground. Gristle crunched as the barrel bit deeper, and the guard twitched and went limp.

Dud dragged the body to the side of the road while English zip-tied the other guard's ankles and wrists together and rolled him into the bushes.

Moments later, Marbles and Sarge joined them and peeked into the entrance. The road stretched back into a tall concrete tunnel and disappeared around a turn.

"That's where your signal disappeared," said Sarge. "Not exactly a lead-lined room, but just as effective."

Dud palmed his phone and dialed. "Numbers. You have us?"

"Sure do. You're right where I lost the last signal, so I guess you're on your own as soon as you walk in there. I'll keep the whole area on screen and text you any changes. At least you can pick them up when your signal returns."

"Copy that, Numbers. Dud out."

He turned to face the others. "Shall we?"

Sarge slung the rifle over his shoulder while the others drew pistols and led the way. Footsteps echoed in the tunnel as they advanced and hugged the wall. The road continued past the curve for a couple hundred yards and stopped at a huge entrance. They split into two groups, took one side each, and moved closer.

The tunnel ended at a room full of silos. Steel supports rose and broke through the ceiling but, otherwise, there was nothing but two large metal doors on rollers, one at each end of the room. Only one of them had pink tire tracks running up to it.

"Looks like we need door number two," said Marbles.

They jogged to the door and paused.

"Standard drill," said Sarge. "I'll pull on the door. English, you cover left. Dud, you take the right. Marbles, kneel between them and cover center. I can't hear shit in there, but who knows how thick this door is?"

Sarge grabbed the handle, braced his legs and leaned back. The others took position and leveled their pistols.

With his other hand, Sarge counted down, uncurling his fingers.

Three. Two. One.

The door glided on its rollers as he heaved it back. Pistols waved side to side as the guys swept the room.

It looked like the other, but smaller, with the same silos lining one wall and an opening at the far side that looked out onto a thick wire fence. The color of the tire tracks was deeper against a side wall, and a small glob of liquid pooled on the floor.

"Oil," said Marbles. "By the size and shape of these tracks, a van reversed back to the wall, stopped here for a while, then drove off outside."

Dud's phone vibrated.

"Movement on the other side of you," said the text.

He called Numbers.

The man spoke as soon as he answered the call. "Multiple signals close to you," said Numbers. "And a train just pulled up."

Dud frowned. "Say again?" He glanced around the corner and stepped out of the building into the open.

"Yes sir. A train. There are tracks running behind you. Did you just move? If not, there's a signal even closer to you."

The others stepped out.

"Now I see you," continued Numbers. "If you head north, you'll run into the tracks. There are buildings there too, so you're probably walking into a railway station. Lots of movement, too."

Dud strode down the side of the wall as the others followed. "Sounds like they're shipping them out. I bet that movement's the girls. Going to love you and leave you, Numbers. Work to do. Stay in touch."

"Gotcha. Numbers out."

---

Lindsay paced back and forth in front of the girls, hands clasped behind his back, chin held high. Two men climbed down from the front of the train. One wandered off to the restroom, the other sauntered over and stood beside him.

Power surged through him, posturing to these girls against the backdrop of a huge train that ferried thousands of tons of bauxite ore. And, soon, a more valuable cargo.

The convoy of red paneled metal carriages stretched down the track, each filled with a mound of ore stacked to form small mountains of red brick. All except one.

One carriage was different. Its ore peaked and matched the others, but it didn't fill the whole space. A false bottom was welded a couple of feet below its tip. The ore hovered over an empty carriage.

Lindsay felt along its side until his fingers brushed against a small hollow. He dug in and searched until something clicked. The side of the carriage swung back like a huge door.

"Hopefully, you now see the futility of your actions." He stared into the blond woman's eyes, before pacing the line again. His palm itched to feel the side of her face, but he held his anger in check. "No one is coming for you. No hero will sweep in to rescue you. For as long as you're with me, you're mine and, after that, you belong to whoever buys you." The white woman glared in defiance when he stopped in front of her again. "Except you. You have someone special waiting for you."

She held his gaze and spat in his face.

"Do that where you're going," he said, "and he'll put

that mouth to good use." Then he bellowed out a full-throated roar. "Who am I kidding? That mouth will be busy anyway, at least until the newness wears off."

He wiped his face and glanced at his watch. Deaven should have been here by now. He took his phone and dialed the kid. The tone burred, over and over. No answer, no voicemail.

Damn him. When Lindsay had found him, he showed so much promise, but it seemed events were going against him. His stomach clenched. What if the intruder had returned? A tiny seed of doubt blossomed within him. Perhaps he'd made a mistake, leaving someone so inexperienced alone. Still, the kid was replaceable, the camp was now useless, and the intruder would have no way of knowing where they'd driven to.

If something had happened to Deaven, that would mean he'd lost two men and one of the girls. Mr. Ramirez would be angry. The flight would give him enough time to come up with a better excuse than his temper to explain the loss of the girl. The Columbian was unpredictable and there would be repercussions. At best, it would mean another trip into town to recruit, and he'd have to increase the number of girls in the next shipment for the same money. At worst, this might be his last job, but that would be extreme. He had a good record.

A throaty roar rumbled around the station. His ride was coming. He wandered over to the open container. "Okay, all of you. Get inside. Now!"

The whimpering girls shuffled forward into the open carriage as Lindsay thrust his arm across the white woman's chest to block her. "Not you, white bitch. You're coming with me. We have executive travel."

Her eyes blazed again. Lindsay found her spirit attractive and, not for the first time, he imagined leaning her against the side of the van and taking her. He was in charge, and she needed to know that. But, Mr. Ramirez was also in charge. It was not worth the risk.

The rumbling grew louder as a blue sports car approached from the other end of the station. He indicated to one of the men. "Close it up. Let's get them moving."

Metal clanged as the side of the carriage slammed shut. Screams came from inside as the girls were plunged into complete darkness. Lindsay smiled, grabbed the woman by the hair, and dragged her forward. The car drew close, then performed a three-point-turn on the platform until it faced the way it came. The driver stepped out and left the door open.

"You have a choice," he said. "If you can behave, you can ride in the car with me, or," he said, and patted the trunk, "you can ride in here, out of the way. It's up to you."

"I'll ride in the car," she said.

"And you're sure you'll be no trouble?"

"I'm sure," she said. Her voice was quiet, timid, as if the fight had left her.

Lindsay couldn't help himself. "I'm sorry, I didn't quite catch that."

"I said I'm sure, you bastard," she shouted.

He laughed again. "There you are." She yelped as he twisted her hair tighter and yanked her toward the vehicle. "Come on, it's time to meet your new husband."

---

Dud reached the end of the wall and steeled a look around the corner. His stomach jumped and his heart pounded against his chest. Not a hundred yards away, a line of girls stood on the platform with their backs to a train. Evie was there and looked to be staring down the guide. The carriage behind her was wide open, a gaping black space with red brick stacked on top of it. Behind them, a blue car idled, its driver standing beside it. The white van sat to one side.

"They're here," whispered Dud. "Four men. All armed."

"One each," said English.

"Not so quick. There's also five girls, and the main guy has Evie. We can't go in guns blazing. At this range, it's too risky."

"We have the element of surprise, though," said Marbles. "Let Sarge get the main guy in his sights, and we turn the corner and pick a man each. No shooting. We tell them to drop their guns and round them up."

Dud jumped as Evie shouted something behind him. He looked around the corner again, to see the girls herded into the empty carriage. And one guy was missing. "Time's up. They're moving. Chances are, one of them climbed into the car, so be wary." He racked the slide on his pistol. "It's do or die, guys. Ready?"

They fanned out into a line and swung around the corner as Sarge knelt and sighted the guy next to Evie.

"Don't move!" shouted Dud.

The guide looked up and swore as his colleagues raised their arms. The team shuffled closer as a unit.

"Put your guns on the ground. And you, let go of my wife, you bastard. Hurt her and I swear I'll gut you like a fish."

The man smiled as he removed his hand from Evie's hair and widened his fingers as if they were exploding. He held onto his gun. "Seems I'm definitely a bastard today.

Can't say it's good to see you again, mon. Still, long time, no see, huh?"

"I should take you out right now," said Dud.

"Good for me you're not that type," said the guide. He looped an arm around Evie's neck, pulled her close, and stepped back a few paces until they grew level with the car's open door. "Because if our roles were reversed, you'd already be bleeding out."

Dud ignored the baiting and gestured to Sarge. "Move another inch and my man here takes the top of your head off. Okay guys, let's round them up."

Evie pointed to the side of the train. "There are girls in there."

Red stone filled every carriage, but Dud pointed to another guy. "Open it."

The guy looked at him, then at the guns pointed at him, walked to the train and pulled on a latch. The side of the carriage swung open. Five girls huddled against the back wall amongst coils of thick rope, toolboxes and work wear.

All the while, the guide hadn't budged. Something about the guy's confidence was unnerving, but then all the violent sociopaths Dud had come across seemed to be the same.

They moved forward a little more.

Dud beckoned to his wife. "Baby, come here. It's okay now."

He watched as Evie strained against the arm around her throat, then she stopped as the unmistakable sound of an AK-47 being racked echoed behind them. Then a voice spoke.

"How about we round you up?"

Dud turned. Another man stood before them, a beaming grin plastered across his face. Behind him, the restroom door swung shut. The barrel of his gun didn't waver as he indicated he turn back to face the train. The guide smiled a flash of gold.

"Oops," he laughed. "That didn't go according to plan, did it?"

22

Kenzie found the turn in the road on her second attempt and swung the SUV around to follow the track.

Despite covering hundreds of miles a week in the tour bus, this road was new to her. The coast road, and its commercial exits, were second nature. This was new ground. Plus, Jameson drove while she sat with her back to the windshield to describe the surroundings to a busload of eager tourists.

The road looked well-traveled, with the dirt packed down and coated in a generous layer of bauxite dust. She craned her neck to peer ahead, then cursed and slammed on the brakes when she rounded a curve to find a tunnel carved into the rock yards ahead.

Erring on the side of caution, she parked the SUV and reached beneath the driver's seat for her gun. The Jamaican hills were fraught with danger. Most of her fellow tour guides carried small, easily concealed 9mm pistols, or sawn-off shotguns. She wanted to make a statement and have a semblance of control if she needed it. Handguns were okay, but they had limited range and ammunition. Shotguns were great for close range, but who wanted to let their assailant get that close.

Her weapon of choice was a gunmetal black AR-15. She admired its low recoil and mean appearance; it looked like a machine gun to her. Despite being semi-automatic, one trigger pull fired one round. Not the rat-a-tat-tat of the guns on TV. One round of accurate fire, compared to a stream of unpredictable hot lead. She dragged it from beneath the seat, climbed out, and locked the door.

The ground rose on one side, offering cover, so she shuffled along beside it until she was yards from the entrance. Something on the other side of the road caught her eye, an unnatural shadow in the undergrowth. Nothing moved in the tunnel, so she sprinted across the road and approached the trees. Two men lay side by side, both unconscious. Both wore bruises, although one lay awkwardly. When she knelt toward him, she realized why. His head lolled and his ashen skin made the bruising across his throat look like thick purple rope. She'd seen a broken neck before, when one of her tour group had slipped climbing a waterfall and had landed on rocks below. This guy looked the same, just drier.

So, the boys had already passed through here.

She leveled the gun and moved into the tunnel. While her head told her to relax, knowing she followed the others, her gut and fast-beating heart kept her alert.

One turn followed another as she followed pale pink tire tracks until she reached the entrance to a station. A row of red carriages sat in the distance. Voices carried around the corner. Familiar voices.

She edged forward again, keeping her body snug against the curve of the wall. As she reached the platform, she poked her head around the corner and gasped. The old guys were kneeling and held at gunpoint, lined up with their weapons raised. The blond girl from the pictures was with a huge Jamaican. They stood by a car while he held her close by the hair. A single man, no more than five and a half feet tall, stood with his back to her and held a pistol over all of them.

These were the type of people that had taken Yanika; callous and cold, with no respect for life. Even from this distance, anger seethed in the Jamaican's eyes. A red mist washed over her. Heat rose in her face, and her already fast-beating heart kicked into overdrive. She swung around the corner and screamed at the top of her lungs, "Drop your guns, motherfuc..."

Then everything went crazy.

The guy with his back to her turned and lifted his gun. She squeezed the trigger of the AR instinctively, and a hollow point round sent him reeling backwards as the lead impacted and expanded in his chest. A group of girls ran out of one carriage and pounced on the man standing next to the Jamaican. He collapsed screaming to the ground under their weight as they pounded and scratched at him.

The English guy burst forward with surprising speed and tackled the man standing by the car. They flew airborne on contact and hit the platform. Even over the screams, she heard a sickening thud when the guy's head bounced off the concrete. The rest advanced on the tall guy. His dreadlocks swayed and slapped as he fought with the girl and dragged her toward the car.

Dud spoke. "You got a shot, Sarge?"

The older man had knelt and leveled a rifle. He shook his head. "Nothing. Evie's too close."

"Let her go, and we'll let you go," shouted Dud.

The tall man laughed and pulled the girl behind the false security of the opened car door. "Not a chance, mon. If

I leave here alone, I'm a dead man, anyway. I have nothing to lose, so I'll take my chances. Don't push me, or I'll kill her."

He crouched behind the door column and forced the woman into the driver's seat, then ducked and kept the gun trained on her. "Even think about shooting and I'll kill her through the glass. Either I get into this car and we leave, or we both die. Your choice."

The English guy stood, leaving his opponent unconscious on the platform. His hands worked in frustration as the Jamaican slid by him, not ten feet away, and climbed into the passenger side. The door slammed shut, and the taillights flared. Then, after a short pause, the car pulled away.

Dud screamed, the noise filled with pain and anger. "Somebody do something!"

The old man with the rifle stood and held it at his side. "I can't shoot the driver, buddy."

The English guy pulled out his phone. He pressed his finger onto the screen and held the phone to his ear.

"Numbers," he said, "we need you to start tracking again."

———

Dud stood with his arms held uselessly at his side, lifted his face to the moonlight, and screamed again.

For the second time in a day, he stood by and watched his wife suffer through the back window of an escaping vehicle. No amount of military training could ease this pain.

He flinched as a hand landed on his shoulder. "Come on, mate," said English. "Numbers is tracking them. Let's get back out there and take care of this, once and for all."

"Look around," said Dud. His voice broke as tears formed in his eyes. "We've got a train filled with stone, and a van. We'll never catch them."

"Snap out of it, son," said Sarge. "I know you're hurting, but you've got to shut that crap away for now. We'll catch them; we just need to think a little, weigh up our options." He glanced around the station. "Marbles could get the train moving, I'm sure, but it's on a fixed route. And I agree the van's too slow, but he doesn't know we're tracking him. He'll make stops, because Evie's smart and she'll do all she can to slow him down."

Marbles joined them. "I've called the police to pick up these girls. Hate to say it, but they're one short. There's a body on the tracks. Poor kid, she was just a schoolgirl. Let's make sure she's the only one who doesn't make it home tonight."

Sarge dropped his head and then snapped to attention. "Hang on; the train. It's on a fixed route. This is the end of the line in this direction and I can see the means to turn the engine around behind us. Which means the girls were headed back in the other direction."

He pulled out his phone and dialed.

"Numbers, follow the route this track takes," said Sarge. "See if there are any junctions or stops from where we are to where the other end terminates."

Numbers was silent for a moment, and then, through the speakerphone, "This is an easy answer. There are no junctions. The line ends at a dock on the north coast, parallel to a huge conveyor."

"I know it," said Dud. "I've driven past it." He walked over to the train and rapped his knuckles against the empty carriage. "I bet that's how they're moving the girls. From here, by train, to the dock, and from there, overseas to anywhere they like. As far as outside eyes are concerned, these are full of ore. Once they're on a ship, they'd get nothing but a cursory glance by customs or the harbor patrols. And this stuff is slightly toxic, so I doubt anyone would get too close."

"So, we ride the train," said Marbles. "Wouldn't take me long to get used to the controls."

"No offense Marbles, but still too long. And hardly stealthy," said Numbers. "How do you feel about unconventional travel?"

"Explain," said English.

"Look up and east of your position."

Past the roof of the station's buildings, the night was lit by the moon. Other than swaying treetops, the only other thing visible was the overhead chute they'd seen on the way into the facility.

"Seriously?" said English. "You want us to run along that? It travels for miles. Plus, it's about eighty feet in the air."

"One step ahead of you," said Numbers. "I've been doing some research while you've been driving. It's motorized, and it moves at a fair rate. And you can get to it from inside the building you've just left. It operates during the day and shuts down at night while the dock closes. And since it only transports washed ore, it shouldn't be anywhere near as dangerous as the stuff you're standing by now."

Each man, and Kenzie, took an unconscious step back and craned their necks to follow the chutes path.

English placed his hands on his hips and addressed the others. "What do you think? I've only got one concern. Well, other than how we get off at the other end. It can't be quiet. Won't it announce our arrival to the bad guys?"

"Still ahead of you," said Numbers. "It rises and falls with the land. There's a point, about half a mile from the dock, where it passes a water catchment. I don't know if you've seen them, they're..."

"I know them," said Dud. "Huge concrete slopes that trap rainfall. So we're supposed to jump off this thing, eighty feet in the air, onto a concrete slide?"

"Might be fun," said Marbles.

"It's not eighty feet by the catchment," said Numbers. "I'm not exact on the elevation, but it looks to be about twenty feet up."

"Still enough to break bones if we land wrong," said Dud.

Kenzie broke away from the group and walked toward the open carriage. "You all seem to be military types," she said, "so I assume you all trained for zip lining?"

The men glanced at each other and nodded as Kenzie walked into the carriage and returned with coils of thick rope and a few pairs of leather palmed work gloves.

"So we zip line. Get close, and then use these ropes to drop to a decent height, and slide down the rest of the way. The beady eyed man is right. It could be fun."

Sarge spoke into the phone. "Sit rep, Numbers."

"They're moving along the coast road, nice and steady. Probably don't want to attract attention and seem like reckless night-time drivers."

"Okay," said Sarge. "We're out of options, so who wants to ride the rollercoaster with me?"

They each grabbed ropes and jogged back to the building.

Marbles took up the rear and gritted his teeth. "I frigging hate rollercoasters."

23

Ramirez paced his office, back and forth, from the huge windows that overlooked the harbor, to the back wall which opened onto the expansive tiled foyer.

A few hours earlier, he'd watched Marcia drag Abigail's body across the smooth tiles. From his position behind the door frame, he was as good as invisible to her. Her eyes had appeared pained as if the act had caused her grief. He had no idea if Marcia ever formed a bond with the girls. She was always their chaperone.

There had been three of them during her stay. So far, at least.

First, there'd been Bridgett, a young English girl with cute freckles, long blond hair and endless legs. For the first few months, her sparkling eyes and dimpled cheeks made him feel young again. Then, the sparkle faded and, in the rare times she laughed, the sound pierced his ears and caused him to wince. Despite the Columbian heat, she covered her legs with thick clothing. It was as if, just by being in her company, he'd somehow broken her.

Bridgett was somewhere in Somalia now. The

diamonds he got in exchange for her paid for the land-scaping that dropped away from the property, almost sixty feet, to meet the shimmering harbor out front.

Then Daniela stayed for a while. Her skin was the same color as his, but much smoother, and glowed in the sunlight. Daniela was a fellow Columbian. She knew his reputation and reveled in the danger of it all. Again, for the first year, she laughed and flashed her perfect smile and, for a while, he laughed along with her. As she grew more comfortable, her respect for his reputation dwindled. She talked back, challenged his opinions and requests, and demanded her own gun. None of the girls could touch any of the weapons. Women were not to be trusted, especially the fiery Columbian women. His Mother always said that, behind closed doors, Columbian women were of a strong disposition.

Over dinner, at the table he'd spoken to Marcia earlier, Daniela overstepped her boundaries. Beside them, artists were sculpting a new fireplace from solid marble as she stood from her seat and looked down on him. His anger flared inside him like an underground explosion, but he allowed her to speak and redeem herself. She continued in the same manner, so he reached for a sculptors' hammer and smashed in her perfect smile, swinging over and over until she was quiet again. Chips of red-flecked white spattered across the marble as the men backed away. When her voice still screamed in his head, he caved in her skull.

Marcia cleaned up the mess. And the men, all missing now, finished the fireplace.

Marcia also cleaned up Abigail. He'd cringed as her head thumped against each step on its way down the stair-case. The outline of her body distorted through the folds of the clear film. Abigail had a lovely body. As it slid across the foyer, her still-damp hair dragged outside the plastic sheet and left a snail trail from the staircase to the exit.

Ramirez clenched and unclenched his fists, eager to get into the room with a cloth to mop up the mess. Could the girl not see the telltale line that led from where he'd created a fresh start, to where evidence of the past would lie?

Marcia was getting sloppy. Maybe it was time for a lesson.

He checked his watch and then stopped to gaze through the windows. Beyond the patio, the ground fell away in stepped lawns surrounded by white concrete balusters, until it reached the harbor. About half way down, a gardener tended to flowers in a planter, while guards strolled back and forth above him. Any girl should be grateful to live in such gorgeous surroundings.

Lindsay would be driving toward the ocean now. Despite his shortcomings, the final check-in had been completed. In two days, a container would arrive with fresh girls for his buyers, and his new woman would arrive. The first few days would be troubling, but once she understood the futility of running, she'd settle in and become accustomed to her new lifestyle. They always did. Perhaps this would be a final test for Marcia. This time, he would watch them closely for any developing relationship.

In the empty harbor, moonlight danced against the waves, and glinted back a barrage of sparkling winks.

Ramirez smiled. Could this girl be the one? It would be nice to have a blond in the house again.

---

While Kenzie made an anonymous call to the police, the club ran back inside the facility. In the second silo room, a ramp led from a side wall, up to a large loading bay. On the first pass through, the doors were closed. Now, Dud, Sarge and English stood shoulder to shoulder in the open doorway, while Marbles looked over a control panel positioned beneath them.

The edge of the platform finished an inch away from a huge metal conveyor. Dud leaned out and looked along the length of it. For as far as he could see, it rose and fell with the landscape until it vanished in the distance. Moonlight bounced off its sturdy aluminum cover at various points where it raised and pushed up toward the sky. Two thick steel cables followed its curves and disappeared in the opposite direction around the back of the facility. Dud pushed against the metal. Nothing moved.

"Reminds me of a bobsled course."

"Yeah," said English, "except this is high in the air. At least, on a bobsled, you have ground beneath you." He peered over the edge. "One slip and it's all over."

Sarge slapped his back. "Don't slip then."

Marbles shouted from beneath them. "I think I've got it. Take a step back and I'll get it started."

The three men trained guns on the doors into the room as a precaution while gears whined and the chute moved. It trundled at first, like a smooth escalator. Marbles increased its speed and jogged up the ramp to join the others.

"That was easy enough. I've been looking for a power source, but I won't find one in here. This whole set up is self-powered." He pointed to the two cables. One of them wound out toward the chute while the other traced back behind the building. "The belt's movement creates its own power, like an alternator. As long as it's running, it's recharging itself."

"I appreciate the lesson," said Dud, "but Evie's in motion. We should be too."

Kenzie climbed the ramp and joined them. "This looks like fun, mon. What are y'all waiting for, a ticket collector?" She tightened her gun strap around her shoulder, then jostled through the men to the front of the platform. "Last one on is a big girl's blouse. Come on."

She looped a hand over the moving cable and gracefully swung her legs up as it pulled her forward. Her feet planted onto the aluminum cover with a dull thud and she rode away.

"I like her style," said Dud. He tossed the ropes onto the chute, followed her lead, and then crab walked along the cover until he caught up with her. The movement along the tracks was surprisingly quiet, and he heard the others follow right behind him. "If it's this quiet for the entire trip, we could get off at the dock and save time."

"It's quiet because the power source is behind the plant," said Marbles. The building was already a couple hundred yards behind them. "The only time this might make a noise is if any of the track is corroded, but I still think we should jump early and make the rest of the trip on foot."

"I agree," said Sarge. "Numbers can check the lay of the land before we get there, but I'd prefer to sneak closer and get a proper look. Avoid any nasty surprises and come up with a plan."

They knelt on the cover and let the chute carry them across the landscape. Dud looked out across the canopy. The moon cast just enough light to highlight the different trees that made up the forest below, the green only broken by the odd building.

"It's going to be okay," said Sarge. "I can tell that you're struggling to keep it together, buddy. We're all here for you, and we'll get her back or die trying."

Dud smiled grimly. "I know, Sarge. This'll make a hell of a story to share in McDonald's."

"Yes, it will, son. And we're still writing it."

As the chute climbed, the whole group leaned and placed a steadying hand on the cover. The tree line rose ahead of them as it grew up the side of a tall hill. The conveyor rose with it, maintaining a perfect distance above the obstacles below. As it crested the rise, the ocean filled the horizon. Tiny lights drifted in the distance as ships and cruisers traveled their lanes.

English balanced like a surfer and pointed ahead. "Guys, look. Follow the cables and you can see a pale circle inland. I bet that's the water catchment."

Dud nodded. "That's it. I've driven past it. Okay, let's split the ropes and get ready to disembark."

He tightened his belt to hold the pistol snug in the small of his back and stepped forward to take the lead. Despite its thickness, the rope was light and easy to handle. He tossed one end over the moving cable, caught it, and pulled the two ends level. The others followed suit.

English looped a rope for Kenzie. "I know we're all trained," he said. "I haven't rappelled in years, but I remember the basics. How about you? Will you be okay with this?"

She looked back through defiant eyes. "Don't you worry about me. I've done it plenty of times in the waterfalls around here. You just make sure you land and get out of my way. I don't want to land on you and put you out of commission. I saw how you handled yourself. We'll need you in one piece, mon."

"What's with the 'we' part, Kenzie? I appreciate what

you've done, I'm sure we all do, but this isn't your fight. You should stay back and let us take care of this."

"Of course," she nodded, "because that worked out so well for you last time. As I said to Mr. Dud; this fight might not have my name on it, but it involves my home. And it involves people that are destroying our way of life. It might only be one group, and I'm sure there are many, but you must start somewhere. I'm starting here. And anyway, you need me. All men need a woman to keep things straight. Now shut up and get ready."

Dud watched English take a breath and then do as he was told. The ride dipped again as the chute cleared the hill top, while the team stood with feet braced, holding onto ropes like they were riding the subway.

The coast road was visible now. Random vehicles followed its curves with their headlights blazing like cat's eyes. He strained his eyes and tracked each car. There was a strong probability that one of them carried his wife, but they were all too far away to see clearly. Instead, he followed the road until he found the dock. Silhouetted against the sparkling sea, its long arm reached out but, other than that, the whole area was shrouded in darkness.

Moments later, the water catchment appeared through the trees. He slipped on the work gloves, threaded the rope between his legs, and looped it over his shoulder. With the rope's end wrapped around his hand, he stepped closer to the edge of the chute and jumped.

24

Numbers poured hot tea from a flask and followed the team as they wound their way over the treetops toward the coast. Staring at thermal images for hour after hour took it out on the retinas and his eyes grew heavy.

When they'd jumped onto the chute, he'd switched the view from thermal to aerial to offer a different picture, but he couldn't maintain a steady view of his colleagues with the image zoomed in. They moved too quickly for him to follow.

His wife didn't seem too concerned about him, happy that he was still in the country, locked away in someone's basement. A ten-minute call earlier appeased any worries she had. He didn't mention spotted dick.

The guys, and Kenzie, were on their way to their final destination. The car containing Evie moved along the coast road and, by his calculations, the team would arrive at the dock just a few minutes after her.

He'd worked out how to access the Jamaican police force's radio to monitor the chatter. Everything seemed quiet on the north coast although that didn't come as much of a surprise. Any crooked cops weren't likely to advertise it over their radios. And there were enough trivial disturbances in the main town to keep them busy without stretching their resources. Numbers was counting on there being help he could summon if the guys ran into trouble, as risky as it might be.

He kicked off his shoes and stretched back into the computer chair. At its current rate, the team on the chute would reach the water catchment in ten minutes. As he watched the car ride along the coast, a thud sounded upstairs. Other than the whir of fans cooling down the hard-working computer motherboards, the basement was silent. The house had been silent too, but for the usual cracks and pops that came from a structure cooling down for the night. He strained his ears and heard nothing. Then, something scuffed the floor.

Numbers picked up the phone, retrieved English's voice commands, and pressed an icon. The strange accent said 'Lights', and the basement dimmed, lit only by the screens on the wall.

He listened again. A dull thump broke the silence. And another.

Footsteps.

He almost called out, then remembered that English's wife had been wearing heels that made a distinctive sound as she'd crossed the floor earlier. These footsteps were heavier but made with flat shoes. Given the lack of clatter, soft soled tennis shoes. The footsteps beat double time. Two sets.

Numbers glanced around the room until his eyes settled on the pool table and the rack on the wall behind it. He took his socks off, tiptoed to the table, then grabbed the phone, moved to the side of the staircase, and pressed another icon. English's voice said 'Camera', and the monitors blinked out.

The basement plunged into darkness.

Whispers sounded outside the door at the top of the stairs, mainly mumbling, but he caught "saw her leave alone" and "what if the guy's not here?". The footsteps padded away as the intruders presumably searched the upstairs level. After a few minutes, they returned and the latch on the basement door clicked. A circle of light danced across the stairs as the door opened. Numbers slunk back against the wall. His heart pounded and the sock in his hand absorbed the sweat from his palm. He silently cursed anyone listening; the guys had gone to Jamaica, and he was holed up in Kentucky, defending a strange basement from two intruders.

Wood creaked as weight pushed against the steps. A flashlight lit up the bank of monitors on the back wall and skimmed across his socks and shoes.

"Well would you look at that," said a confident voice. There was something strange about the accent. "Looks like we've found the right place."

More steps sounded as the intruders came down the stairs.

When the silhouette of a head appeared, Numbers stepped out and swung his sock. The pool balls inside it clattered against one another as the improvised club smashed against its target. A voice cried out as he pulled back and swung again, this time to the sound of crunching bone, and the first assailant fell forward onto the floor. A flashlight rolled from his hand and its beam of light performed small circles as it rocked against the carpet. The beam didn't light up the second intruder.

The last thing Numbers saw was a big fist before it

crashed into his jaw and sent him flying backwards. His head hit the floor, and all the lights went out.

———

Lindsay swung the car off the coast road, past the railway tracks, and under the giant loading arm that spanned the dock and hovered over the ocean. The place was deserted, but he continued to drive, past huge steel storage containers like the ones he'd left behind at the station. There would be repercussions regarding the missing girls, but at least the main part of the shipment was still intact.

During the drive, she'd done nothing but berate and taunt him. The woman had a death wish. At one point, he'd almost shot her with the pistol that rested in his lap, but that would mess up the car. Where the road dropped off sharply, he'd applied pressure on the brake with a mind to pull over, kick her over the edge, and drive away. There were other countries he could flee to and seek refuge. This type of work was available everywhere. But then, the logistics of getting a false passport and leaving the airport unseen dawned on him. He released the brake and continued the trip. The white bitch didn't even notice she'd been moments away from death. He took comfort knowing that, based on what had gone before, she was destined for something worse than death.

The car rolled to a stop alongside a portable office at the back end of the dock. Once headlights died, the place was lit only by the moon. The bay stretched out before him, open and waiting for transport. The forced exit from the station had placed him here thirty minutes early.

"Get out," he said.

Terror flashed across her face and he smiled. At last, a chink in that armor.

"What are you going to do with me?" she asked.

"Finally. After all this time, you ask what this is all about."

"I get it, you dumb bastard. I know I'm being sold. But what makes me so different from the other girls? Why leave them behind, but take me?"

"I'm thirsty. Get out and we can talk inside."

Lindsay closed the car door and walked toward the office. The girl paused for a moment, still inside the car.

He rapped the pistol against the car window. "If you're weighing up your options, I'll spell them out for you. Either get out of the car and sit in this office with me while we wait, or I'll lock you in the trunk and relax alone. Makes no difference to me. One way or another, we're leaving this island in thirty minutes. Leave filled with alcohol, or leave with cramps. I get paid either way."

The girl opened the car door as if she was defusing a bomb and then sauntered toward him. Her eyes still had that blaze burning in them

"When my husband gets hold of you..."

He grabbed her hair and yanked her around until their noses almost touched. Then he traced a line with his tongue, from the side of her mouth, up inside her ear, and across her forehead. Her skin was salty, and he enjoyed the taste until she recoiled. "And what do you think your husband will do when he gets hold of me? Do you think he will save you? Will he come swooping in like a superhero to rescue you? Or do you think he will watch you leaving again when he gets here a second too late?"

She strained against his grip and tried to stamp on his

feet, but he sidestepped her efforts and laughed. "Your husband is miles away. You need to forget him. Consider yourself divorced because you have a new husband waiting for you. That is what makes you different. Someone with a lot of money wants you." He breathed in deeply and let out a long, slow sigh. "Still, look on the bright side, you could have ended up a used whore, addicted to hard drugs. I hear heroin is the favorite. Lying on a mattress in a slum with other girls, while fat, sweaty men pay money to do what they like with you. At least Mr. Ramirez will treat you with respect."

Her eyes widened at the mention of a name. "Mr. Ramirez? Who is he?"

"Oops, me and my big mouth. When I say respect, what I mean is that, if you behave and become the woman he wants, he won't torture and kill you. Maybe close, but not quite the same."

He tucked the pistol into his waistband and climbed the wooden steps to the office. She shuffled behind as he fumbled for a key, unlocked the thin door and held it open for her. A waft of fear and sweat washed over him as he flipped the light switch and she swept past him.

The office was basic; plastic wall panels tacked onto an aluminum shell, with plastic strips hiding the joints. The ceiling was the same, while wafer thin Berber carpet covered the floor. One end of the space held a simple desk and a row of filing cabinets. The other had a cluster of small sofas, a water cooler, and a cabinet with a two-pot coffee machine sitting on it.

A search of the cabinet revealed nothing but Styrofoam cups, sachets of cheap coffee, and cartons of sugar and powdered creamer.

"Sorry,' said Lindsay, "no alcohol. How about coffee?"

She said nothing, just glared and took a seat on one of

the sofas. He moved alongside her and glanced through the plastic window into darkness. The bay was still empty although he'd hear their transport arrive way before it turned up outside.

"Coffee it is."

He took an empty pot from the coffee maker, held it under the water cooler, and depressed the lever as she spoke.

"Aren't you worried about the lights? We're in the middle of nowhere, it's pitch black, and you've lit us up like a beacon."

"I appreciate your concern for our wellbeing," he said as he emptied coffee grounds into a filter and poured the water, "but you answered your own question. We're in the middle of nowhere. This room is hidden from the road, and no one knows we're here."

The machine gurgled as it heated the water to boiling point and dripped it through the coffee grounds into the pot.

"You might as well relax and enjoy the ride," he continued, "Seriously, and I'm being nice now, when you get to where you're going, it's beautiful. If you can do as you're told, you'll live a good life." Then he laughed. "At least for a while."

She stood and moved to the wall behind him. Aware of the gun snug against his back, he turned to face her. Too many things had already gone wrong today.

"Why do you do this?" she said. "Does it pay so well you'd shun regular contact? And you must have a family. Can't you imagine how the families of the girls you take must feel?"

The fire had gone from her eyes. Was she playing mind games, or had she accepted her fate? "It pays better than you'd think," he said. She was close enough that her breath warmed his face. "And I know exactly how they feel. Why do you think I do this? I had a family once. At least this way, I'm at the top of the pile, not groveling on the floor for scraps. And don't think I don't have what you call regular contact. I have contact whenever I like."

As she took a step closer, he swung one arm behind him to maintain the slightest contact with the pistol. When she spoke, her voice was softer, almost seductive.

"What about contact with me? Have you ever been with a woman you've captured? You know, willingly? As a final farewell?"

This new mood intrigued him. There was something about this woman. Ramirez had good taste, but she differed from the others. Her spirit was like an inferno trapped in a jar and, for a moment, he considered the pleasure of taking this woman before his employer. And she seemed to be a willing participant. As he considered kissing her, a voice deep in his mind shouted a warning. He took a firm step back and turned to the coffee machine.

"Good try," he said, "but you should sit down before you get hurt." As he poured the steaming coffee into a cup, a droning noise shook the office. He turned to the woman again and smiled. "They're early. I like that. It's time to get off this island... and we're taking the scenic route to your new home."

25

The last time Dud rappelled had been at an indoor fun area that had climbing walls and scuba tanks. It must have been over ten years ago, someone's birthday party. This time was for real.

As his feet left the chute, wind tugged at his swinging body while the cable still pulled him along. He loosened his grip, and the rope slid through his palms. The friction as it ran between his legs caused him to gulp and, halfway down, he thought of Kenzie, grateful that she was wearing pants.

The water catchment was beneath him when he gripped the rope to halt his descent and looked up at the chute. Once the others jumped after him he relaxed his grip again and continued to fall. Rope zipped between his thighs and over his shoulder as the concrete rose to meet him. A few feet from land, he opened his legs to free the rope, released his grip, and dropped the remaining distance. He was just able to grab one end of the rope and pull it from the cable before it was swept away.

The concrete was slicker than he expected. As soon as his soles hit the ground, his weight carried him down the incline. He held out his arms for balance and rode the slope like a skier. The base of the catchment was dark, but one section seemed darker than the rest. Assuming it was a solid section, he aimed for that.

At six feet away, the darkness cleared and the solid section became a gaping hole, a sheer drop off the concrete and underneath the catchment. The rest of the base had some sort of filter to catch debris and channel the water. He wind-milled his arms furiously and twisted his legs so that his slide erred to one side. The air flew out of him as he hit the bottom edge of the catchment with a heavy thud, his feet inches from the inky black of open air.

Kenzie came next. She landed with a grace of a ballerina. As soon as her feet planted, she yanked at the rope and coiled it behind her as she slid down the bank until she glided to a stop beside him.

Sarge didn't have such an easy time. The rifle slung over his back caused balance issues, and he finished the slide at Dud's feet, sour faced and on his ass.

Marbles landed with his usual exuberance and punched the air as his feet hit solid ground. His punching caused him to miss his rope, and it flailed away from him. He waved goodbye to it in mid-slide and hunched himself down as he approached. With a smaller form, he offered less wind resistance, and he bulleted down the ramp, eyes wide, before he threw out his arms for help. Dud's fingers brushed his jacket, but he crashed through the middle of the group and fell through the gap into the underside of the catchment.

Kenzie was a blur of action. As the team stared down through the gap, she passed one end of her rope out for each man to hold, and dropped the other through the opening.

She leaned over and shouted, "Can you hear me?"

A muffled voice echoed back. "I'm okay. There's a ledge

I was fortunate to land on, but it's pitch black. I can't see a thing down here."

"Hang on, mon," said Kenzie. She reached into her pocket and held her phone against the edge of the rope, then illuminated the screen. "Can you see the light?"

"For fuck's sake, I'm not dying," shouted Marbles. "Tell me to walk to the light and I'll drag you down here with me. Of course I can see it. It's just dark down here. Lower it another couple of feet and swing it away from you."

A few minutes later, a bashful Marbles rejoined the group. Dud led the way as they climbed over the concrete wall at the base and moved off into the hillside.

The dock was visible in the distance. The loading arm that stretched over the entrance looked like a giant reaching out into the night. A tall building rose beside it, with antennae bustling on its roof, and row after row of steel storage containers nestled beneath it to line the yard. The place was shrouded in darkness.

They marched in silence, cutting through the foliage and, ten minutes later, met the road that ran past the dock. Hidden behind the last row of bushes, Dud pulled out his phone. "It's time to get an idea of what we're facing. It's all quiet, so hopefully we've beaten them here and we'll have time to get in place and set an ambush. I'll check in with Numbers and get a head count."

He pressed the dial icon, and the phone rang. And rang. And rang.

Dud disconnected the call. "Something's up with Numbers."

Marbles shook his head. "There's no way he'd fall asleep on the job. I'd trust him with my life. What time would it be back home?"

Dud glanced at the phone. "There's only an hour difference from here to there, but it's already been a long night."

"No way, he knows what this means. Something's wrong. You don't think his battery died?"

"There's more than enough technology there for him to recharge his phone," said English. "Give me a sec, I'll call the wife. She's at the mother-in-laws, but it's only a couple of miles away."

Dud walked toward the dock. "Let's multi-task guys, we can walk and talk." He pointed to the loaded arm that spanned the dock as the others followed. English paused and waited for his phone call to connect. "I say we climb up there and hang out until trouble arrives. It'll give us time to get the lay of the land and come up with a plan."

They jogged across the road and ducked into the shadows, then edged around the side of the dock until they came to the underside of the loading arm. The railway track ended to one side, next to a conveyor that sloped up to the arm. A crane was anchored at the other end of the dock, its metal hook dangling above row after row of storage containers.

Sarge pointed across to it. "So that's how they get the girls out; lift the whole crate onto a ship and sail away to wherever. I still don't see a ship though. Even without the other girls, he's still taking Evie somewhere. Where's the transport?"

"He's right," said Kenzie. "Those transport ships are huge. It takes a while for them to pull into dock. If they were working to a schedule, there'd be something here by now." She paused, and then her eyes widened. "Unless, they store the girls here until the ship arrives. What if there are girls already here, in one of these containers?"

As Dud shrugged, English caught up with them. "The

wife's on her way to the house. She's pretty security conscious, so I'm sure the house is okay, but she'll call when she gets to the driveway. I'll bet Numbers dozed off, and I don't mean that as an insult. It's surprisingly tiring to stare at screens for any length of time, so I wouldn't blame him in the slightest. So, while we wait, what's the plan?"

Dud pointed upwards. "Let's get some height, for observation. And Kenzie? We don't have time to check every container, but we can alert the police once we're done here. Fair?"

She nodded and led the way, searching out ledges and dips in the loading arm to lift herself. In no time, she was halfway up the structure. The men followed her lead.

The view from the top was spectacular. Behind them, the water catchment glowed in the moonlight. Ahead of them, the ocean glittered and shimmered. Dud slid to the far edge of the arm on his stomach and looked down at the yard. As he looked out from the ledge, a faint rumble seemed to bounce across the water. Then, a pinpoint of light swept out from the distance and headed toward him.

Marbles shuffled up beside him. "That's how they're moving her. Where's the thing going to land though?"

As the plane grew closer, a vibration sounded behind them. English scooted backwards on his rear to answer his phone.

Slowly, the dot grew until the shape materialized and dropped toward the ocean.

"Now I see it," said Dud. "Look at the undercarriage. It's got floats attached. It's a seaplane, they can land anywhere. We have to get down there."

Sarge had scooted to the farthest edge of the arm. He leaned back and called over his shoulder. "Dud, come and check this out, buddy."

The storage containers were stacked two high and, from the previous position, had hidden the far side of the dock. From this side of the arm, more was visible over the top of them. A portable office sat on concrete blocks. Light beaming through the window lit up a blue car parked out front, and shapes moved inside the small building.

"Shit," said Dud. "They've been here all along. We need a plan, and right now, but we need Numbers."

---

Jenny Watson killed the Audi's lights as the car turned into her driveway. Her husband's voice had sounded concerned, and she followed his advice to exercise caution. Being married to a military man had its challenges, but it had its perks too.

One of them lay on the passenger seat beside her. Keith, 'English' to his friends, had recommended the revolver as a compromise after a few hours at the gun range. The serious recoil from his bigger guns jarred her wrists, but she understood the need for 'stopping power', as he'd called it. The Taurus Judge offered both. She liked that the first and third chambers contained what he had called 'buckshot' rounds; a .410 shot shell that contained individual pellets that would disable an opponent, hopefully without killing them. Chambers two, four and five held .45 cartridges. If the buckshot didn't work, and they still kept coming, the .45s would finish the job.

She didn't know if she had it in her to kill someone, even if they presented a threat. Still, the big truck she didn't recognize, parked at the side of the house, helped the argument along. She pushed in the clutch and rolled the Audi up to the side of the house, wincing as the tires crunched across the gravel.

Fearful of light, she pulled on the parking brake to stop the car an inch from the front of the truck, grabbed the revolver, and climbed out onto the driveway. The house was dark, but that was no surprise. English's friend was in the basement, helping with a very important assignment, and none of his activity would be seen from up here.

She dialed her husband. "Honey? There's a black pickup outside the house. We don't know anyone with a black pickup, do we?"

"No," said English, "although it could be one of Numbers' friends, babe. It might be prudent to call the police before you go in."

"Are you sure the police won't mind you operating that equipment out of the basement?"

There was silence for a moment, and then, "Okay, good point. It's not illegal, but what we're doing here might take some explaining. Got the Judge with you?"

"Of course."

"We need Numbers, babe. Urgently. I'm sure everything is fine, but be careful just the same, okay?"

"You taught me better than that, Keith Watson. I'll be careful. Call you soon. Love you."

"Love you too, baby."

With the gun held in shaking hands, she sprinted to the front door. The darkness from inside the house peeked out through a one-inch gap, so she toed the door open further, leveled the gun, and nervously entered her own house.

Years of living here had taught her where all the floor's creaks and groans were and she skirted each one while she checked the upstairs level. Each room was as she'd left it, apart from the bedroom where the closet door was open, and items from her lingerie draw littered the floor like graffiti. In your dreams, she thought, and moved to the top of the basement stairs.

The door was open. A faint noise drifted up the staircase. Someone was in the darkness below. She heard no voices, just the rustle of movement.

The third, ninth and tenth step squeaked. She knew this from creeping downstairs to surprise Keith. When he'd set up the basement room, she wasn't sure of his intentions. A grown man, ex-military, possibly not used to commitment, and living a new life on the other side of the world. Surely, he was setting up a porn den. Over time, she discovered that hard trained habits die hard. He spent hours in isolation, pouring over maps, data, images, you name it. He absorbed it all. When she'd asked why he did it, his eyes watered and he replied simply, "I never want to lose it."

He was an amazing husband, and she'd give her life to protect him. This was his space, and someone uninvited was in it.

As she went to cock the hammer of the revolver, she remembered his words. Just point and shoot. Simple as that.

A beam of light danced in the basement. She leveled the Judge and began her decent. First and second steps, feet center. Third step, move to the edges to avoid stressing the floor board. Down to the eighth step, and then center again.

At the eighth step, her eyes grew accustomed to the dark. A man, dressed in black, lay out cold on the floor at the bottom of the staircase. The light flickered some more and lit up another figure sitting on the sofa, head lolling like a puppet. The baseball cap gave him away. It was Numbers.

She scolded herself. She didn't even know his real name.

Whoever held the flashlight was talking to himself. The

guy on the floor must have been his partner, and this raid wasn't going according to plan. One long stride over steps nine and ten placed her confidently on eleven, and she jumped the last few to land beside the prone guy. As her feet planted, she turned to face the light. In her imagination, when they'd been at the range shooting paper targets of bad guys, all kinds of cool lines came to mind. This time, in the heat of the moment, faced with a live opponent and a shoot to kill possibility, her imagination failed her.

She shouted, "Drop it, bitch!"

Everything after that happened in slow motion. The figure on the sofa jolted awake. The one on the floor remained stationary as the guy with the flashlight spun to face her. Given the situation, there was a high probability he was armed. Scenarios flashed through her mind. Either way, he was a threat. Her range experience had taught her that the first shell to leave the Judge would spread out like a shotgun round.

She ran forward and closed the gap to a few feet as the flashlight lifted even higher. It lit her thighs and traveled across her stomach before she pulled the trigger. In the confines of the basement, the shot boomed like a cannon. Her hands shot back as the gun discharged, and the flashlight fell to the ground, followed by the guy holding it. A groan sounded as she leaped back to the stairwell and shouted "lights!".

Numbers stood from the sofa and moved toward her, his eyes squinting. His hands were tied behind his back, and a trickle of blood ran from his nose but, otherwise, he looked okay. The guy at the foot of the stairs didn't look so good. His face was a mask of blood, but his chest still rose and fell.

The guy with the flashlight writhed on the floor. A red semi-circle painted his shoulder where the buckshot had peppered him. Somehow, her shot had missed his face and neck and had just incapacitated him.

He struggled to sit upright. "Wait, we just..."

She remembered an episode of Charlie's Angels, where the Angels were attacked and their assailant had recovered enough to attack again. A full-forced kick in the face rendered him unconscious.

When she turned to face Numbers, he stood looking at the two unconscious intruders, mouth agape. Finally, he spoke.

"Er, do you think we should call your husband?"

---

By the time English's phone vibrated, the team and Kenzie had climbed down the loading arm, leaving Sarge still spread-eagled at the top with the scoped rifle.

The plane's pilot had anchored the plane and waited in the cockpit while his co-pilot entered the small office. Shadows still danced in the light through the window.

Dud wrung his hands and checked his pistol again as English sidled up to him. "Everything's okay. Tonight, of all nights, some idiots broke into my house."

"Shit, man," said Dud. "Is everyone okay?"

"Everyone we care about is. The two guys didn't get off so lightly. They're still out cold, trussed up and gagged in the closet until we resolve this."

"And Numbers?"

"They had him tied up. Jenny took care of business."

"Remind me not to piss off your wife."

Despite the situation, English smiled, then passed his phone to Dud.

"Numbers, you there?"

"I'm here, pal," said the old man with a nasal whine.

"You sound different, you sure you're okay?"

"Yeah. Took a smack to the nose. Nothing some tissue won't solve."

"Cool," said Dud. "Okay, down to business. How's it looking where we are?"

"The screens are just coming back up. I had to shut them down." He paused for a moment. "Give me a sec to find you. Okay, I see you guys. And I see, I think, three or four bodies a few hundred feet from you. Can't be certain, because they're all clumped together. I'm getting a big heat signal off the water, too."

"Yeah, they've got a seaplane. Nothing else around, though? Just us and what you can see close by?"

"That's it, brother, other than regular traffic in the shipping lanes. I guess you already took care of the rest."

"Yeah, well we're about to take care of these, too. No prisoners, Numbers. These people don't deserve to leave the scene."

"Well, let's see what Sarge thinks of that. Just be careful, buddy. I'm here if you need me."

"Copy that. Sarge is a distance away, so he'll do what he does. No one messes with my wife like this. He's paying. Dud out."

He turned to the team and dialed Sarge's phone so he could listen in. "There are three people in that office. We know one of them is Evie, and one came from that plane. So, other than the newcomers, the big guy is on his own. I say we flank the office and wait until they exit. Sarge, if you get a shot at any of them, take it. Outside that circle of light by their window, it's pitch black. They won't have a clue what's going on." He paused, almost for effect, but mainly to compose himself, then continued. "The big guy? He's mine. This is personal."

"As long as you've got it," said Marbles. "But if it looks like he might get the upper hand..."

Dud nodded.

"You good, Sarge?" he said.

"Go get em, buddy," said Sarge. "I'll cover you."

They ducked into the shadows at the back of the dock and crept along toward the office. Kenzie subconsciously took the rear as the trained men moved along in silence and approached the right side of the building.

Once there, Marbles and English broke off and moved around its rear to the left. Dud and Kenzie squatted in position on the right.

Dud looked up at the loading arm. Sarge was nowhere to be seen, but he was there, focused, steeled and ready.

Now they just had to wait.

26

When the rumble began outside, the whole office shook. Evie shivered as the vibration traveled from the thin floor, through her feet, and up her legs into her body. Most of all, she felt it in her heart.

This was it. The moment of truth. No one was coming to save her. Lindsay, her tormentor, had said she was promised to someone else; a new husband.

Tears fought for release as she thought about her real husband; Dan 'Dud' Wilkerson. The man who'd thrown himself onto a grenade and, years later, thrown himself into her arms.

Selfless, both times.

The man who'd brought her tea and toast in bed, even though he hated tea, and detested the crumbs between the sheets. The man that massaged her shoulders after a long day even though he'd had a full day of his own.

Her tears won the fight and rolled down her cheeks, and she turned away to face the wall.

"That's right," he said. "Our ride is here."

She flinched when her captor placed his hand on her

shoulder, and she walked away before she turned to punch him.

"I take no pleasure in this," he continued. "Now, when I get paid, there will be much pleasure, but this... I'm sorry it has to be you. I like your spirit, and you remind me of my sister, although I think your life will be much better than hers."

He took her arm and spun her around. "Do you even like Bob Marley?"

Evie shuddered and stepped back away from his touch as she thought about that morning trip up the coast that seemed like a lifetime ago. "What kind of psycho question is that, you chickenshit?"

"He was a wise man, full of prophecy and intellect. You know his song 'One Love'?"

Despite her best efforts, the melody crept into her head. Evie had heard Dud sing it at the top of his lungs in the shower many times. It was one of his favorite Marley tunes, but she wouldn't give this bastard the pleasure of knowing that.

"There's a line," he said, "that goes 'Have pity on those who's chances grow thinner, there ain't no hiding place from the Father of Creation'. I know my station, lady. I'm the sinner here, and my chances are beyond thin. I won't make excuses, they're for weak people. We all walk the path. It's up to us to face the right direction. I didn't do that. And on the day of reckoning, I'll be judged fairly and I'll be cast down, because he's right. Marley is right. There is no hiding place from the Father of Creation. I'm a sinner, and life has made me this way. So, I'm going to embrace it, because it's all I have left. Unfortunately, it is at your expense and, for that, I am truly sorry."

The rumbling sputtered and died and, moments later,

the door opened and a man walked in. He was tall, but thin, not built like the guide. A baseball cap sat at an angle on his head, and wisps of gray, wiry hair sprung from beneath it and spiraled against his jet-black skin.

He nodded. "Hey mon, I'm ready when you are. You know it makes me nervous if we hang around."

"I hear you," said the guide.

He looked at Evie. Guilt flashed across his eyes. Then, as quickly as it had appeared, it vanished. "Time to go."

The knot in Evie's stomach tightened even further until it felt like she'd garrote herself from the inside. The guide walked toward the door as the other guy walked toward her and reached out an arm. She pulled back and retreated to the far corner of the office.

"What?" he said, "You don't like what you see?"

He smiled, showing a row of tobacco stained teeth.

"If you touch me, he'll kill you," said Evie. "Ramirez? He'll kill you."

The guide frowned. "Hector. This is not the time for that."

The man advanced, still smiling. "As if he'd believe you over me."

As he moved into her space, Evie looked around and grabbed the first thing she could. He reached out a hand that brushed across her breast, just as her fingers curled around the handle of the coffee pot. The heat from the liquid warmed the side of her hand as she lifted the pot and swung it.

The thin glass crashed against his cheekbone and boiling liquid splashed across his face. He screamed through the steam and clutched at his skin while Evie bolted for the relative safety of the door. The guy staggered, blinded by the liquid, and stumbled backward toward the window.

As she reached the guide, the window imploded. The guy's head disintegrated in a hail of blood and bone.

Evie screamed, and the guide flung his arm around her neck, pulled her close, and dragged her through the door.

As they clambered down the stairs outside, she looked over his shoulder, and saw nothing but darkness. Despite her scream, she already knew what had happened. Dud was an expert marksman, but he'd said his friends were even better. A long-distance rifle round had ended that guy's life. He never knew what hit him.

Her husband and his friends were out there somewhere. She just had to survive for a few minutes longer.

---

Sarge watched the scene from his perch on the loading arm. The spray of crimson that blossomed behind the window signaled an accurate shot. He felt guilt at the loss of life, but he had to take the shot. The movement in the building had been slow and fluid for a while, but then the shadows moved much quicker and erratically, signaling a confrontation or fight.

Right after the shot, the door swung open and the tall guy from the station appeared with Evie. Sarge slid the rifle around and focused on him through the sight, but there was too much movement to take another shot. Evie struggled with him despite his tight grip around her throat and the pistol pressed to her temple. He was streetwise, too, and kept his head and body tucked well behind hers. Eyes dancing wildly, he sought out his enemy, but he had no idea where the shot had come from.

The crack of the rifle had acted like a starting pistol to the pilot who leaned out of the plane and pulled up the anchor.

Marbles and English crouched to the left of the office, waiting for the main guy to step forward. Dud did the same to the right and held Kenzie back to stop her giving away his position. Her lack of training had shown. She was champing at the bit and ready to fight.

Step by step, the guy dragged Evie along the front of the office. He was more than streetwise, he was good. Even though he couldn't see the shooter, he'd worked out where the shot came from. The direction the guy's head flew in would have indicated a shot from directly in front of the building, and he took no chances. He switched his stance and alternated his head position, back and forth, between her left and right shoulder. Evie still struggled as he edged closer to the corner of the building. Marbles sat on his haunches, waiting for the right moment to pounce, while English was right behind him in the shadow, prepared to back him up.

The guy was no more than two feet from the side of the building when Marbles raised himself and edged forward. For a moment, the circle of light around the front flashed across his face. He ducked back, but not before a shout echoed across the dock.

Sarge swung the rifle around to the plane. The pilot had finished pulling up the anchor. It was stowed, and he watched the movement from the plane.

"To your right!" he shouted.

The big guy spun Evie around so quickly, her feet left the ground. He kept her facing out front, but stepped sideways two large steps, carrying her with him, and flew past the corner. Marbles balanced on the balls of his feet as

English appeared behind him and held an assault rifle over his comrade's shoulder. If he fired, Marbles would probably sustain hearing damage. Both men waited to see what the guy would do.

To the right of the office, Dud and Kenzie had vanished. Sarge guessed they'd either gone behind the building to join the others, or had crawled beneath it, between the blocks, to mount a surprise attack.

Neither option mattered as the guy pulled Evie back and dragged her away from the office, toward the pier that stretched out into the bay.

"Move and I'll kill her," he shouted and backed along the pier.

Sarge swung the rifle around to the plane again. A dead pilot meant no escape, but he was nowhere to be seen. The next best option would be to puncture the fuel tank. If this was anything like the small planes he'd seen, the tank sat at the front, beneath the cockpit. He sighted below the front windows and fired. As he re-sighted for another shot, pistol fire cracked from below and he instinctively ducked as three shots rang out. When the firing stopped, he peered over the edge. The big guy was almost at the plane, looking back and forth between the building and his position. Dud had edged along the pier, his hands held high to show he was no threat.

Sarge fired, this time a little lower, and ducked again as more shots rang out and then stopped abruptly. He looked back to see the big guy toss his pistol aside. He was out of ammunition.

Dud bolted along the pier as the guy passed Evie to the pilot. Yet again, too much movement prevented a shot. Evie's feet disappeared as the pilot dragged her into the plane, just as Dud reached the end of the pier and threw himself forward.

Both men fell backwards as Dud swung a long cross toward the guy's head, then ducked and pummeled against his ribs. The guy buckled, his face contorted with pain but, as Dud lifted his head, rose and crashed a head butt into his face. Dud staggered back, dazed. The others ran along the pier as the pilot appeared and shot at them from behind the door. They dropped to the wooden boards and lay flat as the two men by the plane crashed together again and fell into the plane's doorway.

Sarge pivoted the rifle's scope and tried to get a clear shot into the plane when the pilot appeared with a red cylinder. Dud had the big guy pinned to the door frame. He raised his fist as the pilot leaned out and smashed him across the back of the head with a fire extinguisher. His body went limp and slid to the deck.

Sarge looked out from the scope to see the whole scene as the pilot handed out a pistol. He dragged Dud into the plane and disappeared again. The big guy fired a couple of shots across the pier, and then clambered into the plane, too. Before Sarge could re-sight the scope, the door closed.

The rest of the team ran along the pier as the plane circled. The pilot appeared in the cockpit window, but without knowing where Evie was, it was too risky to fire.

Sarge sat, useless and deflated, as the engines powered up and the plane skimmed across the water before lifting into the night sky.

27

The seaplane's light winked out in the distance as Marbles turned to the others. Lined up along the side of the pier, they looked like a group of redundant fishermen.

"Shit! Now what do we do?"

Kenzie ran back toward the office and shouted over her shoulder. "I'll check in here to see if they left any clues."

The men followed her lead. By the time they reached the office, she was already inside. Sarge rejoined them moments later.

"They could go anywhere," he said. "Do those things even file flight plans? I imagine they'd be easy to fly under the radar; it's not as if you have to worry about water landings. And what's in that direction, anyway?"

"The way they turned," said English, "they're probably heading for Columbia, although there's land mass past it. I'm not sure how far one of those planes can travel on a tank of gas. Not that it's hard to land and refuel."

Kenzie stepped out of the office, her face ashen. "Nothing, mon. And if you want coffee, you're out of luck. There's a dead guy and a messy room, but that's about it."

"There must be something we can do," said English. "We've come this far to rescue one of the family, and now we're down by two."

"First things first," said Marbles. "Assuming we work out where they're going, we'll need a plane to follow them. Doesn't matter what kind, I'll work out how to fly it."

Kenzie's eyes lit up. "There's a tourist service about a mile down the road. I'm not sure what type of plane they have, but there's one they use to fly visitors over the island."

Minutes later, Marbles had hot-wired the car that had carried Evie and they raced along the coast road. As they neared the tourist center, English piped up from the back seat.

"I've got it. Well, if luck is on our side, I have. I know how we can track them."

He dialed Numbers and, after a brief explanation, had him open another program.

"There's a list of our phone numbers on the desk," he said. "Key Dud's number into the search engine and hit enter. If his phone is still powered, or wasn't tossed into the ocean, you should pick up its location."

They waited in silence. English put the phone on speaker while Numbers tapped away at the keyboard. After a few moments, he came back.

"That's incredible. Does the Government know you've got this stuff? Anyway, this screen isn't as clear as the other program, but I've got something here. If it's Dud's phone, it's flying across the Caribbean Ocean. It's not too far ahead of you."

"I don't think those seaplanes travel as fast as regular planes," said Kenzie. The car slowed and swung into the tourist center entrance. "Hopefully, we can find something with enough speed to catch them."

The entrance was a pair of wide, wire metal gates, held shut with a thick chain and a padlock. The wire continued around the entire place.

"Can anyone pick that lock?" asked English.

"Of course," said Marbles. "I've got this." He looked up and down the road, reversed the car back as far as he could, and turned it so the rear faced the gates.

"Might want to hold on to something, folks," he said, and then floored the accelerator. Tires screeched and the car shot backwards across the road, bounced over a pothole, and crashed against the center of the metal gates. They slowed the car for a moment as the tension in the chains caught, and then it snapped and they flew backwards, clattering against the fence. Marbles slammed on the brakes while spinning the steering wheel. The vehicle skidded in a perfect one-eighty to face the other way, and he drove forward as if nothing had happened.

While Sarge and English sat in silence with their mouths agape, Kenzie shook her head and smiled. "Beady eye man, you need to speak to my driver, Jameson. He could use skills like that."

"Hire me and pay me in rum," said Marbles.

The plane sat alone at the rear of the lot like a cast off. Its body was fluorescent yellow, with the words 'See Jamaica from the air' daubed along its side in red paint.

"Damn," said Sarge. "Looks like someone murdered a big banana. You think it'll will work?"

Marbles shouldered past him and ducked under the wing. "It's going to have to."

He yanked open the door. "Give me a sec. Let me check the fuel level and get this thing started before you all climb aboard. Do we have everything we need?"

Sarge had a rifle slung over his shoulder, and who knew

what else concealed on his person. English hugged the AR as if it was his child. Kenzie had the same gun, a blue metal version compared to English's gunmetal black. And he had the trusty Sig pushed into his waistband, along with a few clips of spare ammo.

Sarge grinned, although there was no humor in his expression, just determination. "If we need more than we have, we'll get it from someone else when we get there. Let's get going."

Marbles climbed into the cockpit, levered off a panel, and combined wires to start the plane. The single propeller sputtered a stubborn refusal at first, but was soon coaxed into a smooth pattern. As the blades spun and blurred, the others boarded and fastened themselves in for the ride. While English clipped himself into the co-pilot seat, Marbles checked the dials. "You folks can all relax. It looks like they fueled this baby before they called it a night. Wherever we're going, we'll either get there on a full tank of gas, or we'll plummet into the ocean and die in a huge and spectacular fireball."

"Is that supposed to be reassuring?" said English. "Honestly, mate, it's a good job you're not a doctor. Your bedside manner's shit."

Marbles taxied the plane to a short runway and lined it up against the dials until they pointed in the right direction and parallel to the fence. He powered the engines and the plane shot along the concrete as he shouted an announcement.

"Okay folks, stow away all belongings, except those with any serious firepower. And please disable all portable electronic devices, except any which communicate with an old guy in a basement back home. The smoking section is located on the left wing. And most of all, please enjoy the flight. Thanks for flying Air Marbles."

The plane rose into the air, cleared the wire fence with yards to spare, and banked right, headed for Columbia.

---

Ramirez disconnected the call and placed the cell phone face down on his desk.

Regardless of how many times he'd done this, the hours before a delivery were always fraught with nerves. So many things could go wrong; one reason deliveries were made at night. Less conspicuous.

More guards were on site, too, upping the employee count from ten to eighteen. Separate rooms were prepared for the girls. It was important to split them before they developed camaraderie. It also made selling them easier. Prospective buyers could visit each room to test the goods personally. Each room needed its own guard to make sure the buyers had privacy and, most importantly, a comfortable experience.

Whenever he imagined a worst-case scenario, the interception of a boat or plane always came to mind. The passage from Jamaica, through international waters, was the traveling equivalent of walking through a minefield in oversized boots. With more borders dropping, so many patrols buzzed around the ocean now, and it was harder to miss them than to find them. The ships he used were always legitimate transport vessels, but one random check by an overzealous customs official might derail a delivery and lose valuable product.

Lindsay's call proved he was wrong. Interception wasn't the worst-case scenario, after all. Losing a container was.

And there was no cause to worry about a ship interception. This time, there would be no ship.

His rising anger prevented him from finishing the conversation, and he disconnected the call before he scared the man so much that he might not deliver the one thing he got right. A group of misfits had sabotaged the delivery and freed his girls. And Lindsay had called and instructed the ship to change course. No one made decisions without his approval. If not for the fact that Lindsay had the blond woman with him, he would have instructed the pilot to throw him from the plane. Still, once he arrived, Ramirez would use him as an example. It had been a while.

Through the windows, the moon hung full in the sky, making the concrete railing that lined each level look like a white slash against the sloped landscaping. The ocean rippled and lapped calmly up to the base of the property. It would be disturbed soon enough.

He opened the large French doors and stepped out onto the patio. Flowers stood to attention in an expensive Chinese vase that sat on the table, surrounded by a porcelain tea set prepared for his new wife. Ahead of the table was a patch of false grass with a rubber golf tee secured in its center. He picked up a three iron that rested against the door frame and hefted the club to test its balance, before he raised it over his head and smashed it against the table. The flowers exploded in a shower of blooms as he swung through the vase, sending ceramic shards flying into the air. The guards on the next level jumped and tensed, then continued their watch as he screamed to vent his rage and repeatedly hammered the table, demolishing the tea set.

Seconds later, he carefully placed the club against the door frame and ran his fingers through his hair. He pulled against his jacket to straighten it, breathed in the scent of the broken flowers, and walked back into the house. Once the doors clicked shut, he poured a drink from the decanter, took a seat at the desk, and waited for the plane.

---

Marcia sat on her balcony and cringed as the golf club smashed into the table.

Her bedroom was directly above Mr. Ramirez's sound-proofed office. No one knew what went on in there once the heavy doors closed. She'd lain awake at night on many occasions while business deals were hammered out beneath her and had never heard a single word spoken. There was no such luxury with the patio below. Men had died beneath her window and she'd seen or heard the pleas and screams of every one of them.

Over the four years of her stay, Mr. Ramirez had changed. The stone-cold killer was still there, but he'd gone from ruthless and calculated to ruthless and unpredictable. The display just now emphasized how much he'd lost control of his emotions. Previously, he would have retreated to his office to brood over an issue. Every side would have been considered; every angle, every reason and every outcome. Now, there was only one angle and one reason. And always, only one outcome. Violence.

The nerves that shook her in the dining room earlier returned. For a moment, as brief as it seemed, she thought he was about to take her. The way his eyes seared through her clothing, and the way his hands brushed against her. She'd been vulnerable and powerless, not something she was used to. In her thirty-two years, she'd beaten down many a man who'd belittled her or made her feel anything less than what she was. A strong woman. Independent. In control of her life and destiny.

Except now, she didn't feel that way. Not entirely. He'd undermined her, playing her off against the women he brought here. And there was another one coming. That's why she was in her room, while he prowled and strutted beneath her. Get some rest, he'd said. I'll need you at the top of your game when she arrives. The first few days were always the hardest until they realized it was useless to resist.

Even now, hours later, the sound that Abigail's head had made played in her mind. The dull thud that had echoed through the foyer as it slapped against each step of the staircase when she dragged the corpse behind her. It sounded similar to someone hitting a heavy table. With a golf club.

Marcia lay on her bed. She pulled her knees up to her stomach and wrapped her arms around them to pull them even tighter, and then she closed her eyes.

She didn't set an alarm. The plane would wake her.

28

Dud woke to the sound of a single prop engine and the smell of plane fuel. The steady sound of airflow rushed beneath him while he kept his eyes closed, feigned unconsciousness, and tried to work out who was with him. Occasional chatter in broken English drifted from behind him; the guide and at least one crew member.

He opened his eyes just wide enough to reveal a sliver of the plane's interior. Pins and needles pricked his arms, and he wiggled his fingers to coax blood flow past the tight plastic tie that held his hands behind him. He gritted his teeth and tolerated the discomfort until the time came to do something about it.

As he took in his surroundings, his vision settled on a pair of tennis shoes and his stomach lurched. He'd seen those shoes in the closet many times.

Evie sat a few feet away.

She'd be scared but, hopefully, unharmed. The care the big guy had taken at the station showed that he needed her for something.

Dud wanted to get up and hug her, to tell her everything would be okay.

Except he couldn't.

When they met, he'd promised to never lie, and to always tell her what was on his mind. He couldn't tell her they were in deep trouble, even though she'd know that. Or that the person here would kill him without blinking, just to make an example of him. Or that they were on their own, unarmed and outnumbered.

Once he removed the ties, he could still hug her. He attempted to lift his head, but pain shot down his neck and spread through his shoulders. Spots danced behind his eyes. Evie gasped and whispered over the background noise.

"Babe. Don't move."

The sound of her voice sent ripples of emotion through him. Even now, in this situation, she was exercising common sense.

"I'm okay. There are two of them behind you, the guide and a pilot. We're over the ocean, flying to Columbia. I've looked..."

She stopped speaking and Dud closed his eyes as something prodded him.

"Still sleeps like a baby, huh?" said the guide. "I didn't think I hit him that hard. Maybe this husband is a pussy," he laughed. "Don't worry, your new husband isn't."

"What do you want with him?" said Evie. "You obviously want me, so why do you have him?"

"Would you prefer I throw him out?" said the guide as he laughed again. "He's cost me a lot. I must smooth things out with my employer, so I'm taking him as a peace offering. It won't be too peaceful for him," he said and jabbed Dud in the ribs again, "but at least I'll be able to show that the problem is taken care of. And anyway, my employer will find his own way to make your husband pay for what he's done, and I'm sure he'll be happy to carry out your divorce. And I'm sure he'll make it long winded and painful."

"I'll die before anyone lays a finger on me," said Evie. "Do your worst."

"Well, you wouldn't be the first," said the guide. "Won't be the last either."

Even from his fetal position on the floor, Dud sensed the atmosphere darken even further. He opened his eyes again in time to see Evie wipe her face. At least her hands weren't tied, but they shook uncontrollably. He rolled forward until his knees were beneath him, then lifted his head from the floor and uncurled his body.

"It lives," said the guide. "Welcome back, mon. Take a seat next to your wife and enjoy some time together."

Dud struggled to his feet and dropped onto the seat and leaned into Evie. He yearned to hold her while their bodies touched. "Sure you're okay?"

"Yes, babe, they've treated me okay. I can't say the same about the other girls." She raised her voice. "He murdered a poor girl who would have been celebrating her sixteenth birthday next week. She did nothing wrong, and he treated her like a piece of meat."

The guide spun in his seat. His eyes glistened with fury. "Be grateful I can't reach you right now. And remember, she paid for your actions."

Tears rolled down Evie's cheeks again. She rested her head against Dud's shoulder and sobbed as he looked around the plane. They were the only things in the cabin not fastened down. Nothing looked capable of cutting through his ties, and even the seams of the fuselage were smooth.

"Babe, stay strong," he whispered. "There's nothing

here we can work with, so be patient and wait for the right moment."

Evie turned in her seat to face him. Her hands cupped his face as she leaned in closer to him. "There's something I need to tell you."

"It can wait, baby," said Dud. "Tell me when this is all over."

"Damn you and your confidence, Dan Wilkerson. Listen to me. If it ever gets to where they might force me to be with someone else, I want..."

"Don't talk like that," said Dud. "We're not done yet."

"Listen. I want you to put me out of my misery if you can."

As she spoke, the tears came again. Dud watched them roll and fought his own that pushed against the corners of his eyes until they won the battle and coursed down his face. He leaned forward and nestled his head against his wife's neck.

"We'll get out of this Evie, I swear. I don't know how or when, but we'll get out of this."

Evie pulled away and gazed into his eyes. "And if we don't?"

Dud leaned forward again and brushed the tip of his nose against hers. Their tears mingled as they kissed. When he finally pulled away, their eyes met. Every ounce of training, of survival skills, and of the wish to stay alive to see out the rest of his life with this woman flooded his system. Love for her awoke every sense in him and empowered him with a solid reluctance to give up.

"Babe, we either get out of this with a hell of a story and we live a good life, or we go out together. And if we do, we take as many of these bastards with us as we can."

———

Numbers watched the two moving signals with a concentration that bordered on fanatical. Jenny, English's wife, placed a mug of coffee on the desk and pulled up a chair beside him. Her own mug had 'Married to a Brit and proud' painted around its side. A silver colored revolver sat in her lap as she watched him watching them.

Muffled noises came from the closet at the other side of the basement. The two thieves were both conscious, but a whole roll of duct tape ensured they were going nowhere until the club finished its mission.

Jenny had insisted they cut a hole in the mouth section of one of the bindings. One guy had trouble breathing through his nose where Numbers' sock sling had broken it and flattened it against his face. Numbers had no sympathy, but Jenny put up a convincing argument involving suffocation and murder charges. Numbers cut the opening himself and ignored the attempts at conversation.

The planes flew over the open ocean with no land mass visible on screen. The trajectory of the lead plane would take it to Columbia and, based on what Dud had told him, it made perfect sense. Venezuela, Ecuador, Peru and Brazil all bordered Columbia, and all had dubious reputations concerning sex trafficking and prostitution. Once there, the cargo could be moved to whichever country was paying.

All he had to do was make sure that, this time, he didn't lose the signal and, since it was hard for a plane to fly through a tunnel, he bristled with confidence that he could finally be of use to the team.

English's wife placed her coffee cup on the desk top and faced him.

"So, is this what you guys talk about when you're in

McDonald's? You know? Old war stories, and tactics and surveillance? Keith won't invite me, and I've always been curious."

Numbers sat for a moment and measured the situation. The woman was sitting on the edge of her seat. Her nails were chewed to the quick, and the thoughts and emotions that came with shooting another person would be racing through her.

"Ma'am, you'd be amazed at the topics of conversation we get through. But there is one subject that divides us the most, one that separates the men from the boys."

Jenny leaned forward, drawn into the conversation.

He smiled. "Why the hell would you go into McDonald's and order a breakfast muffin with egg whites and low-fat cheese? You're in McDonald's. Grow a pair and eat the damned stuff the way it's meant to be eaten."

Her face froze in confusion for a second, and then she exploded into laughter. Numbers smiled with her, grateful for the change in mood. After a long and stressful day, it felt good to break the ice. It was also reassuring to have another set of eyes beside him as, despite the caffeine, his own were growing heavy.

"To be honest, it's more like a support group. We've all seen and done things that no one should. Don't get me wrong, anything done was in the service of our countries. But that doesn't make it feel any better." He glanced at the screen. The two dots were still playing chase across the ocean. "I haven't got to know your husband that well yet, but he seems like a good man. Sarge is an excellent judge of character and he let him eat at our table. That's good enough for me."

"Even if it is full-fat fast food?" said Jenny.

Numbers chuckled. "Especially if it's full-fat."

"I doubt he told you," she said, "given his male ego and all that, but I didn't just go to my mother's just because he left. I stormed out pissed because he upped and left to fly into danger again for a virtual stranger, but I suppose that part of him will never change. The military man. He'll always be there for his brothers, won't he?"

"Yes, and I can't argue that fact. If it wasn't for this old body, I'd be alongside them. This is my contribution because I need to do something. Don't blame him for going, though. Another thing we discussed, and all agreed on, was that we missed parts of military life. Not the fighting, or even the adrenaline rush that came with it for some of us, but the fact that you were part of something. A unit or a team, a group of fellow men that would check on you. And there was a system, so you always knew where to be and what to do. We've all been fortunate enough to adapt to civilian life and we love it, but some of those things are ingrained."

Numbers reached for his coffee and took a sip. "Don't worry, your husband is with good people. His back is well and truly covered."

"I'm glad I got to talk to you," said Jenny. She smiled. "And save your ass, of course. But when Keith gets home, I'm still going to kick his."

Numbers glanced at the screen. It was hard to be sure, but it looked like Marbles had closed the gap a little.

Jenny followed his gaze. "How long have they been flying?"

Numbers glanced at his watch. Despite the technology in the room, old habits still died hard. "Just over an hour and a half, I think."

With a jerk, he sat bolt upright in the chair and reached for the mouse. The two dots were still moving over the ocean. There was still no land mass anywhere on the screen. A shift of the mouse zoomed out the view to reveal more of the area.

Still two dots. Still nothing but ocean.

He wound it back even further until the south coast of Jamaica appeared at the top of the screen, and the north coast of Columbia appeared at the bottom.

The two dots weren't even halfway across the ocean, and there was nothing between the two coasts but cold, unforgiving, almost bottomless water.

"Shit. We have a problem. A big problem."

"What?" asked Jenny. "What is it?"

"How could we have missed it? The planes might have had full tanks when they took off, but it's still not enough fuel. They won't have enough to reach Columbia. They're going to pitch into the sea."

29

"I just fly the frigging thing," shouted Marbles. "I figured a full tank and a similar plane... how could we not match them in terms of distance? And I was joking when I mentioned crashing in a huge and spectacular fireball."

English sat in the co-pilot seat, his knuckles white as he gripped his phone. Everyone in the plane heard the conversation over the speaker and Marbles was the only one of them able to make a sound.

"What?" he said, "You want to take this seat? You think that'll double the fuel supply? Coax a few more miles out of vapor?"

English raised a hand. "Stay cool mate, no one's having a go. We're all in this together. I didn't get a good look at that seaplane, but I didn't see rows of fuel tanks on it, either. I get why they're using it, it can fly low to the ocean and miss all kinds of inconvenience, but it still looked like a regular plane."

"Could it refuel in mid-air?" asked Sarge.

"Seems excessive," said Marbles. "That's not something everyone can do, it requires quite a bit of skill. Not that I doubt their pilot, but I'd sooner say they're meeting a boat. Maybe they'll land in the middle of nowhere and switch to a small boat. Then they can beach anywhere on the coast and not have to worry about entering the country through the regular channels."

"In which case we're screwed," said Kenzie. "Shit, mon, we got so close."

Marbles checked the dials again. The needle hovered at just over a quarter of a tank. "We're not done yet. Don't give up, guys. While we're flying, anything can happen, and I don't mean swimming with the fishes. Numbers, what's the status of the lead plane?"

"Same speed, same heading," said Numbers through the speaker. "So far they've been very consistent, which strikes me as odd since they're not exactly following the rules. If it was me, I'd make a dash for it. You know, head down and run for the finish line."

"Yeah, but they think they're alone," said Sarge. "If they knew we were up their ass, they might have bolted for it."

Marbles shook his head. "No, consistent speed is essential for good fuel consumption. It's like they knew they had so many miles to travel, and only so much fuel. And then there's the wind factor, too. Tailwinds help, headwinds hinder. They'd have to take that into account. No, I'm more and more inclined to believe they'll rendezvous with a ship or a boat, and finish the journey by water."

English rocked in his seat as Kenzie pushed against it from behind him. "Hey, I get your frustration, but taking it out on my seat won't help."

"Sometimes there are life vests underneath the seats. I don't want to drown, mon, I'd sooner take my chances with the sharks. Do a 'punch them on the nose and swim like crazy' sort of thing."

"I'll land the plane," said Marbles. "We'll keep after them and we'll work something out. We have so far, I see no reason to change now."

"Well unless you've learned to walk on water, we need to start..."

"Guys, wait up." Numbers' voice chirped through the speaker. "Marbles, I need you to circle the plane for a while."

"Numbers, have you lost the plot? We're already short of fuel, and you want me to burn more by circling?"

"I need to find out what's happening with the other plane."

"Come on, mate," said English. "You're talking bollocks. What's going on with the other plane?"

"Well," said Numbers, and then he paused. "I've only got this reading to go off, but based on what I can see here... it's stopped."

No one spoke for a while, then Marbles broke the silence. "Stopped? Numbers, unless it's a Harrier fighter plane, it can't just stop. Last time I checked, with few exceptions, planes don't stop. Or hover. And especially not seaplanes. You sure it didn't land? Did my theory pan out, and it's met up with a ship?"

"No other signatures close," said Numbers. "One minute it's flying, same heading and same speed, next minute it's stopped. I can't explain it, but I'll try different views and see if I can work out what's going on."

"Look into it, Numbers. I think I'll circle."

---

Lindsay marveled through the front window at the expanse of blue beneath them. Even at this height, coral and sand berms moved and created belts of deeper blue in the water. Despite the evil in the world, there were still areas of natural beauty.

The breathtaking views normally made the flight exciting, but this time his stomach knotted and churned. Bile had made a home at the base of his throat, and its acidity burned. He was under no illusions, he added to the evil in the world and now karma was calling.

Ramirez gave nothing away on the phone, his voice the same steady tone it always was but, as soon as the call disconnected, his employer would be thinking of ways to make him pay. The only blessing, as small as it was, was that he had the cause of the troubles with him. If he could convince Ramirez it was not incompetence, but the skills of the man tied behind him that had caused the day's losses, he might escape with minimal punishment. And the blond woman; she was attractive, unharmed and she would be delivered on time. That had to count for something.

The pilot turned to him. "A few minutes and we'll be there." He gestured over his shoulder. "Are they okay? I mean, will they be any trouble? Especially the woman. Should we restrain her?"

"No. Mr. Ramirez would be angry if she turned up damaged." Lindsay turned in his seat until he faced the people behind him. "I don't want to have to restrain you," he said to the girl. "Can we come to a compromise instead?"

Despite the hopelessness of her situation, the girl's eyes met his with something resembling a glimmer of hope alive in them. It was admirable she could still seem to be so strong against such overwhelming odds, but it was time to snuff that out. There could be no more complications. He met her gaze and gestured to the husband.

"I suggest," he continued, "that if either of you cause

any trouble, I will put my gun to the back of his knee and blow out his kneecap."

The girl flinched, which was the response he hoped for.

"A shattered kneecap is one of the most painful things a man can experience. Add the wish to run, basic human nature, and you'll be screaming louder than anything you've ever heard. You'll have to run, because if you don't, you'll die. But you won't be able to. And I'll be sure you watch when I put another bullet between his eyes. Are we clear?"

Tears ran down her face as her husband glared. If not for his ties he might have dived forward to fight. The struggle in her mind was painted all over her face until, finally, she nodded.

"Fine, you vicious bastard. For now."

He laughed, softly at first, until the full extent of the situation hit home and he doubled over and belly laughed. "For now. It's a shame you're promised to someone else. I'd like to strip you and spend days taking you apart, piece by piece."

Again, she met his gaze. "Really?" The roof of the fuselage brushed her head as she shuffled upright in the seat. "Let me tell you something. Without a doubt, I'd dive head-first through a window before I let you lay a finger on me. Or anyone else, for that matter. When the time comes, that I'm able to kill you, I won't bat an eyelid. I'll do it without thinking, and I'll do the world a favor."

"I wish you luck. As for diving through windows, you can get that out of your head. Where you're going, it's been tried before. Everything has. The windows are reinforced and do not open."

Lindsay blinked as the pilot nudged him. "We're here. I'll take us in."

Even now, after many flights, the spectacle ahead still

amazed him. Below them, the moonlight lit up a tiny blot of green that sat like a pinhead in the vast expanse of blue. As the seaplane closed in, details came into focus. The land mass was barely large enough to call an island. The color of the ocean faded from a deep midnight blue to a pale royal blue as the sea reached the shore. Ripples lapped onto white sand that ran back and vanished into dense palm trees.

It wasn't until the plane was almost over the island that the pier came into view. It stretched back to a clearing in the trees and out into the ocean, a brown finger pointing back to Jamaica. A red box hung off its side.

The pilot guided the plane until it ran parallel to the pier and then cut the engines and glided the craft closer until it splashed into the water and floated alongside the wooden structure.

Lindsay turned in his seat. "Here we are, a little taste of paradise. I'll let you stretch your legs if you stay on the pier while we refuel. You could run but, as you can see, there's nowhere to run to. And it would be a shame to hurt you."

The couple glanced at one another, probably weighing up their chances. The guy must have been either lucky or smart to have found the camp. From his stance and posture he was ex-military and had that assured and confident presence about him. It was impressive how, despite being alone, he always seemed to be a step behind them. His wallet and phone were in a bag beside the pilot's seat and the girl had been searched back at the camp but, still, it wouldn't pay to underestimate either of them.

The pilot opened his door, stepped onto the float beneath it and pulled himself up onto the pier. He tied off the boat against a thick wooden beam and then opened the rear door. Lindsay shuffled across and climbed out as the others joined him.

"Can I at least use my arms while we're docked?" asked the man. "I've lost all feeling in my hands."

Lindsay peered behind him. "Maybe those ties are too tight." He walked back to the plane as the pilot pulled out a pistol. "Don't let it be said I'm a bad man. I'll give you some relief. One moment, mon."

The pilot held the gun to the woman's head while Lindsay cut the man's ties, gave him a minute to massage life back into his hands, then retied them at the front. "Don't make me regret my moment of kindness," he said. "You may walk back to the clearing. Disappear and we will hunt you down like animals. Understood?"

The man nodded once, and they set off together along the pier. Lindsay leaned down to the red pump, keyed in a code to release the pump's nozzle, and passed it to the pilot to refuel.

"It's the start of another beautiful day. Call me when we're ready to leave," he said, then wandered off along the pier whistling a reggae tune.

30

English glanced at the dashboard through the corner of his eye and tried to read the dials.

"I see what you're doing," said Marbles. "Don't forget, my right eye works. If you want information, ask me. And if you want to sit here, I'll switch with pleasure."

"Shit. Sorry mate, you're doing a stellar job. I wondered how much fuel we had left."

Marbles tapped the dial with a fingertip. The needle hovered over the red marker that screamed 'empty'. "Not much. A few more minutes and we're running on fumes. I've piloted a glider before, but it was a lot lighter than this, more like a..."

"A glider?" finished English.

"Well, yeah. They're more streamlined and with less weight."

English sat forward and turned to face his colleague. "Could this plane glide if it needed to? You know, if we get desperate?"

"Oh yeah, it could glide, no problem."

English let out a breath and relaxed back into his seat.

"Until we hit the water." said Marbles. "Then the surface tension would shatter us into a million pieces."

"Bloody hell, mate, you could at least say it with a bit less honesty."

"Sorry," said Marbles. "A hundred pieces."

English swiped his phone's screen and dialed. Numbers answered on the first ring.

"Still no change, guys. I've tried the satellite view, but every time I zoom in, all I can find is ocean. It might just be me because I can't seem to focus on where the signal paused. I can see the heat signature, but when I try to scan the area, there's nothing. It's as if I can't get close enough. How are you all doing?"

"In a few minutes, we'll have to start pedaling," said Marbles. "And then, pretty soon, it makes no difference one way or the other. We have to know what's beneath us before we fall out of the air."

"Okay, I'll text you the exact coordinates where their plane stopped. I guess you could key them into your GPS and see if you can eyeball anything. No offense, Marbles."

"None taken, brother."

"Just because I can't see anything with the satellites doesn't mean you can't buzz over the area and check it out."

"Send 'em," said Marbles. "What's the worst that could happen?"

"A fall from the air, a fiery ball and a million pieces?" said English. "Talk about seeing Jamaica from the air, I'd welcome solid ground right about now."

The phone beeped as the text arrived. "We'll call you back, Numbers," said English. "English out."

Marbles keyed in the coordinates and pulled on the yoke to guide the plane. The needle hovered over the red area on the dial, and the GPS estimated their flight time at ten minutes.

"We gonna make it, buddy?" asked Sarge from the rear of the plane.

"Honest answer?"

"Yep."

"No chance. Unless this plane differs from every other one I've flown. These smaller planes aren't known for their reserve fuel tanks. That's what flight plans are for. Planning."

"Appreciate your honesty, son."

"I don't," said English. "Pedal faster."

English jumped when the phone rang in his hand.

"You won't believe this," said Numbers, "but we've got movement. Whatever happened, they're moving again. Same heading, right for Columbia."

The minutes ticked by. Marbles steered the plane as directly as he could and flew it to draw every inch of distance from every drop of fuel. Time and again, he wiped his sweaty palms against his shirt, and kept his good eye on the relentless blue canvas before them. A couple of times, the moonlight glinted off something on the surface to cause his heart to race but each time, when they reached it, they found nothing but deep glassy ocean.

Then English pointed through the cockpit windows. "What's that?"

Marbles scanned the area ahead until his eye settled on a blemish in the water. The GPS was almost centered.

"No idea. Let's take a closer..."

The single propeller stuttered, and the plane lurched. Kenzie shrieked behind him. "Is that it? Are we out of fuel?"

"No. I'm sure we've..."

It sputtered again. Ahead, a tiny patch of green punctuated the blue like a comma. Marbles gripped the yoke and angled the plane for a controlled dive.

"We're out of fuel, aren't we?" said Kenzie. "Oh, mon, I didn't want to check out like this."

"We're not checking out, Kenzie," said Marbles.

The propeller continued to spin, and the plane continued to move forward.

"Is that an island?" said English.

Marbles peered over the console to look closer. A tiny patch of white stood out against the green like a smile, with a wooden platform stretching into it.

"And is that a pier?"

"I believe it is," said Marbles. "I have a plan. Tighten your belts. It's about to get interesting."

Sarge put a hand on Marbles' shoulder. "Interesting how, buddy?"

"What do you reckon the wheel track is on this plane?"

The tiny island loomed closer as the engine coughed and sputtered.

"The wheel track? What's that? Tanks have tracks," said Sarge.

"No, the wheel track. The distance from wheel to wheel on the landing gear."

"How the bloody hell would we know that?" shouted English.

Marbles looked at English. "When I say the word, split the wires I joined to start the plane."

English gulped. "But won't that...?"

"Yes, it'll kill the engine. I need a controlled descent and I don't have time to explain, but years ago, I landed a plane on a dime in the desert. Did it in a few yards, from landing to dead stop."

"Don't say 'dead'," said Sarge.

"Guys, come on. This is our only chance unless you fancy swimming. English, the wires are between my legs."

"You're making no friends here, pal. Just saying." English leaned over and fumbled around until he found the cluster of wires under the console. "Okay, got them."

Marbles angled the plane toward the pier. "I'm sure the wheel track of this plane is narrow. Hopefully, narrow enough that they'll not fall off the pier."

"Hang on, mon," said Kenzie. "You're telling me you're landing the plane on a fucking pier?"

"I'm going to try," said Marbles. The plane dipped lower as the engine protested. "English. Now."

English pulled apart the wires, and the propeller gave a couple of final spins and completed quarter turns. Kenzie and Sarge groaned as the plane dropped. For a moment, the plane glided and then Marbles spoke again.

"Connect, English."

With the wires rejoined, the propeller completed a few turns. The plane moved forward, but still dropped in height.

The pier was ahead as the plane reached the height of the trees that covered the tiny piece of land. Marbles adjusted the yoke and lined up the plane as its lights lit up the front edge of the walkway.

"Split!"

English pulled apart the wires.

They dropped again. The wheels were feet above the height of the pier. Marbles adjusted the flaps to compensate for the loss of power.

"Connect!"

The propeller spun again, half-heartedly, and the front wheel of the plane touched down on the pier. Then the rear wheels landed with a bump. Wood cracked and splintered over the drone of the engine.

Marbles pulled back the power to idle and applied the brakes. The flaps on each wing stood upright as the plane rumbled along the pier and crept toward the tree line. His arms rippled and shook as he held the yoke, until the plane slowed to a trundle, reached the end of the pier and rolled onto white sand. As the wheels dug in, the plane leaned forward and almost toppled, until the right wing nudged up against a tree. Palm fronds dropped onto the cockpit window.

"And split," said Marbles. He ran his fingers through his hair, let out a deep sigh and turned in his seat. "Ladies and gentlemen, we have reached our destination. Thank you for flying Air Marbles."

---

Sarge rolled out of his seat and fell, feet first, out of the plane. Sand puffed up as his shoes landed with a soft thud. The pier stretched back behind him toward the moon's reflection, which danced on the waves far in the distance. Two parallel lines ran along the pier's boards, about three inches on either side from falling off the edge and into the water.

The old man adjusted his cap. "That was some impressive flying, buddy."

"All in a day's work," said Marbles. "The good news is, there's a fuel pump back there. We need to spin the plane to face the other way and get it close enough for the hose to reach."

"There are footprints over here. The breeze would

settle the sand after a time, so they were here, and not that long ago."

"Agreed. Come on, without fuel this plane should be quite maneuverable. Whip it around so we can push it along the pier and closer to the pump."

Ten minutes later, the plane faced the ocean. The sand in the clearing looked like a newly furrowed field and, even in the early morning air, all four people were red faced and wore damp patches under their arms.

After another five minutes, and even deeper tracks in the sand, the rear wheels of the plane bumped onto the pier.

"That's close enough," said Marbles. "I need as much runway as possible. Now we can refuel and be on our way again."

While English called Numbers, Marbles, Sarge and Kenzie walked along the pier to the fuel pump. Its red top peeked over the top of the wooden sidewalk like an old-fashioned bubble gum machine. The arm of its hose rested leisurely against its metal side. When they reached it, Sarge cursed.

"What the eff, you, see, kay is that?"

Kenzie stifled a nervous laugh. "Old man, we can all spell. Even us Jamaicans. Still, that looks like a challenge to me."

"I'm trying to behave," said Sarge. "English, tell me I'm wrong. Is that thing password protected?"

English leaned over the side of the pier and inspected the fuel pump. It looked like a gas station pump, but the hand grip of the nozzle was locked to the body by a thick metal clasp with a small 0-9 figured keyboard attached to it. "Shit. There are ten thousand combinations on a four-digit lock. God knows how many are on that."

"You know some useless crap, English. Step aside, son" said Sarge, "we don't have time for messing around." He lifted the flap of his jacket and withdrew a blade from a holster attached to his belt. His four fingers slid through the holes in the grip as the serrated blade shined in the moonlight. "I've got this."

He gripped the hose in his other hand. "Marbles, get the fuel port, or whatever you call it, ready. I assume, as long as fuel is flowing, the delivery system doesn't matter?"

Marbles looked nervous, but nodded anyway. "Well, as long as the stuff flows, it'll work."

"Okay, then get ready. I'm down with the new lingo. I'm about to get medieval on this hose."

"In the history of our language," said English, "that line will never be uttered again outside of a porn film."

Marbles held out his hand to receive the hose as Sarge gripped it and began to saw through its casing.

The plastic outer cover offered no resistance, but the woven metal core proved to be more of a challenge. The team flinched as, occasionally, the blade hit the metal pump itself, and produced sparks that lit up the small bay.

After some heavy back and forth, fuel seeped through a small cut. Sarge continued slicing through the material, oblivious to the risk of fire, his elbow flying to and from his body, until the hose fell free. The nozzle remained clipped to the pump as plane fuel spewed through the end of the hose.

Sarge passed it to Marbles, who fed it into the plane. "I don't know how much we'll need until we're fully fuelled."

"Why don't you pump it until fuel runs back out?" said Sarge. "Once it's full, it'll overflow. We don't know what the next leg entails, so let's make sure we approach it with a full tank."

"I'm with you," said Marbles. He held the end of the hose firmly as it pulsed between his fingers. "All I have to do now is take off... with a pier as my runway."

31

La Ciénaga is a road that runs through California, somewhere near Hollywood in America. A boulevard, if his memory was right. Lindsay smiled at the recollection. A tall woman, with long brunette hair, a model's legs, and that annoying accent that seemed to speak down to everyone, had lived there. She lived in South America now, in a town he'd never heard of. He didn't really care; she'd fetched a great price.

Every time the plane approached the Columbian north coast, he thought about her. Ciénaga was a town that lay to the east of their destination, but it sounded so romantic he couldn't help but be swept up by it every time it flashed up on the GPS. It had a town called Paris, too. It wasn't just the Americans that stole all the best names.

Santa Marta was no slouch either. It was more of a tourist trap, with large boats moored in slips along its coast, while inland, swamps flowed all the way to Ciénega that were great places to dump unsaleable product. No one found the bodies they dumped there. Local wildlife took care of that.

And Santa Marta had the mansion that Mr. Ramirez owned.

Properties sat on the beach, lifted above the water level with elaborate landscaping that kept them away from the corrosive effect of the ebb and flow of salt water. The pilot mentioned they were a few minutes away.

Lindsay's stomach churned again. Behind him, the American couple sat in silence. The woman had calmed down since the man appeared. And he seemed to be too cautious to try anything as if he feared the repercussions.

The missing container of girls gnawed at him. Each one would have fetched a decent price. As well as the missing revenue, Lindsay had never failed to deliver, and that ate at him more than the money. Mr. Ramirez trusted him and relied on him to get the job done. The transport ship wouldn't miss one container, but Mr. Ramirez would.

He glanced behind him. The woman's eyes burned with hatred, while the guy twirled his wedding ring and stared back at him.

"Almost there. It is a lovely place. You won't have much privacy, but you might enjoy it," he said to the girl. Then he turned to the guy. "You, not so much. I'm not sure what Mr. Ramirez will do with you but, since you've cost him a lot of money, I doubt it will be very nice."

The guy ground his teeth. "Go screw yourself. I've faced worse than you and lived."

"I'm sure you have, but were you alone? And I know you Americans, all brave when you're in groups. You think you can police the world. Well, there are no police now. I've seen bigger men than you beg for their lives."

Lindsay felt anger build inside him as the man sneered and looked away through the window. The lights of Santa Marta twinkled in the distance as the plane skimmed the ocean and tipped a wing to face the harbor. As if on cue, two rows of flashing runway lights appeared in the water.

The pilot corrected his course to line up with their center and then guided the plane lower. The cabin jolted as the twin floats hit the water and rocked while the engine slowed and the plane taxied forward to the harbor's edge.

---

Dud craned his neck to look through the small side window. From a distance, the mansion had seemed impressive but now, as he sat beneath it, it was intimidating. Moonlight reflected off tall windows that rose like cathedral arches to break up the stone cladding. He thought he saw movement in one of them but, when his eyes adjusted, only the glass shone back.

The ground level was hidden by landscaping that climbed in sections. Each looked to be around chest height and eight feet deep, lined with white concrete railing. A matching stone staircase wound its way from the edge of the sand to the top of the rise.

At each level, two guards stood at attention by the stairs, guns held across their chests.

Four levels. Eight guards. No chance of overpowering them, at least not yet. He resigned himself to be pulled from the plane and pushed along the beach until he reached the bottom of the staircase. Evie stumbled up beside him, followed by the guide and the pilot.

Dud spoke under his breath. "This isn't over as long as I'm breathing, babe."

Evie offered a forced smiled. She believed in him, and he knew he'd do whatever it took to free them.

"Sit tight, and cooperate as much as you can," he continued. "When the chance comes, I'll be ready. I love you baby."

"I love you, too," she whispered.

A hard prod in the back forced him forward. "Climb," said the guide. "Let's say hello to your host. He's been waiting for you."

As they passed between each set of guards, Dud studied and memorized the surroundings. Halfway up the staircase, he turned. The sea stretched back in an unbroken carpet of blue. Without Marbles to pilot the plane, there was nowhere to go in that direction. Another prod sent him forward.

At the top of the last rise, a set of huge double doors swung outward and a mid-sized man in a pristine blue suit stepped forward. A tidy goatee gave him an Egyptian appearance, emphasized by olive skin and a lean physique. He gestured to a patio table littered with smashed ceramic pieces and broken flowers.

"Please, my honored guests, take a seat. Apologies for the mess; a vase paid the price for my frustration, but I feel much better now."

The man took the seat that faced the ocean, locked his fingers together, and rested his hands on the table. For the first time, Dud saw confusion in the guides' eyes. The destruction that covered the table was for his benefit. After a pause, the guide stepped forward, pulled out a chair next to the man and motioned for Evie to sit. She brushed her hand against Dud's arm as she walked around the table to sit. The guide pulled out the seat opposite Evie and waited for Dud to move. When he sat, the guide took the seat that put his back to the ocean, the furthest away from the man.

Behind Evie, the landscaping swept back and around a corner out of sight. The white concrete railing that isolated each section also ran around the edge of the grounds. It was impossible to see if the sides of the property tapered down in stages like the front, or if it was a sheer drop. Dud looked to his left to see if the building itself offered any hope of escape, but the doors had swung silently shut.

The man rapped his hands against the table top and the ceramic shards bounced with each thump. "At last," he said. "I have to say, this has been a long time coming." He laughed. "I'm not known for my patience, but still, it's been worth the wait."

He leaned forward and held out a hand. "I'm Ramirez," he said. "And you are?"

Dud remained seated, with his tied hands resting in his lap.

"Ha. Forgive me. Lindsay, don't be such a barbarian. Untie the man's hands."

The guide frowned at first, then produced a knife which sliced through the plastic ties with one easy swipe. Dud massaged his wrists, ignored the offered hand, and resumed his original position.

"I see," said Ramirez. "It's going to be like that. Fair enough." When he turned to face Evie, Dud leaned against the table. The guide tensed and Dud heard movement. An armed guard strode into view and took up position behind him.

"Please, don't get any stupid ideas. I'll be honest; things don't look good for you, but at least be man enough to take your punishment away from this beautiful woman." He cupped Evie's chin in his hand. "She doesn't want to see you suffer, and I doubt she wants to suffer herself."

Evie pulled her head free. "Keep your hands off me, you bastard. You have no idea who you're dealing with."

Ramirez shrugged, stood and walked to the doors. "On the contrary," he said. "Give me a moment."

He pushed open the doors and returned moments later with a handful of cards. He sat and cleared a space on the table, then fanned them out and laid them flat.

There must have been fifteen to twenty of them. Polaroids of Evie walking around the island, sunbathing, or swimming in the sea. The time stamp on them stretched from the start of their vacation to the day before they were run off the road.

"It seems I do know who I'm dealing with. I've been watching you for a while. I know all about you. Your favorite drink, how you lie when you relax and, who knows, maybe I have pictures of you sleeping, of how you lie at night. It might take a while for you to get used to lying next to someone new."

Dud snapped. His heart thrashed blood around his body and his head pounded as he stood and lunged over the table. The chair shot backwards with a screech and he was inches away from grabbing the man's lapel when a blow to the back of the head stunned him. Lights danced in his vision as he pitched forward onto the table. Broken china cut into him and he slid across the table and onto the patio. Strong hands cupped under his arms and lifted him to his feet. The chair slammed into the back of his legs and the same hands forced him to sit.

Ramirez was on his feet as Evie sobbed beside him. A piece of the broken vase created a white dimple against her soft skin where he held it against her throat. "Now that will get you into a lot of trouble; and you're already in enough. We don't like it when people stand up against us. Makes us feel threatened and we don't respond well to threats. Consider yourself fortunate I have other plans for this girl."

Dud's eyes refocused in time see Ramirez nod his head. "Take him and put him somewhere safe until later. He's earned a little quality time with me."

As the guy behind Dud lifted him to his feet, Ramirez held out a hand. Evie glanced at it, then looked up at him. Dud shivered at the fear in her eyes.

"And you, my lady, will come with me. I'm sure you're exhausted after your flight. There's a beautiful bathroom waiting for you. Let's get you cleaned up."

---

The evening breeze cooled the sweat that ran down Evie's back. As a guard pushed Dud around the corner, she fought back more tears and rubbed the side of her neck as if the tip of the broken vase still pushed against it.

Ramirez held out his hand again. She ignored it again. "Get used to me," he said, "otherwise you'll have a short and uncomfortable stay. Why don't we start with your name?"

"Seriously? You have pictures of me sleeping, and you don't even know my name?"

"I could find out, but don't you think that would ruin the fun? Half the pleasure is us learning one another."

Evie flinched away as he guided her toward the double doors. "You'll never get to know me, you son of a bitch. I'll die first."

"I'd hate for us to start on the wrong foot but, in that case, you would die second. He would die first. And you would watch."

She stifled a sob as they passed through the doors into a huge foyer. Despite appearing outwardly terrified, Evie remained strong inside. This man was one of many, but he still had to be stopped. She thought of Lecia's face as she'd fallen backward onto the railway tracks, and the relief she'd had. Lecia had probably heard stories of human trafficking that had fed her fear. Evie had no such hang up and, for as long as she and Dud were alive, there was always a chance to stop this. For Lecia, and for the girls before her. And for the girls still to come.

"My name's Evie."

"Evie," he smiled. "I like that. We'll keep it."

To her left, a wide arch led out to a large room that contained sofas and throw rugs. The doors to the right opened onto an office. Ahead, a winding wooden staircase climbed to the upper level.

A strikingly athletic woman strode through the arch toward them. She was easily six feet tall, even in flat shoes, with hair pulled back to reveal a flawless face of dark skin. Her eyes swam like pools of chocolate. They met Evie's. Evie struggled to read the emotion in them.

"Evie," he said, "I'd like you to meet Marcia. She will be your assistant, your chaperone, and your friend. You will spend a lot of time together."

The woman held out a hand. Evie grasped it and flinched at the firmness of the shake. "Welcome, Evie. It will be my pleasure to help you in any way I can."

Ramirez continued. "The rooms at the top of the stairs are yours. Sunrise looks beautiful from the patio, and we have about an hour, so go and bathe. You have an amazing bathroom with a luxurious tub. Take a long, hot bath. There are clothes in the closet for you. Pick out something suitable and join me in an hour."

He grabbed her elbow, spun her until she faced him, and leaned forward to kiss her. As she turned her head to avoid his lips, he whispered in her ear.

"Please, I beg you, don't think of running. Assuming you get past the guards, there is nowhere to run to."

Marcia stepped between them as Evie wrenched her elbow free. "Come," said the tall girl, "let me show you to your room. It really is quite beautiful."

Evie followed her up the staircase.

32

"Everyone ready?" said Marbles.

"You're sure you can do this?" asked English. "That's not a lot of runway. In fact, I've seen bigger patios!"

"Sure. I did something like it in the military. Still, I'd buckle up and hold on to something."

He checked the GPS once more. Numbers had texted the coordinates of the other plane, and it seemed to have resumed its original course. The engine hummed while the craft strained against the brakes.

"Okay. Excuse me while I talk to myself, guys. It's all in the technique. Flaps at ten percent. Check. Power up until markers are in the green."

The engine's hum grew to a shriek as power increased and then, with a jolt, they hurtled forward along the pier. Marbles ignored the gasps behind him and concentrated on keeping the plane straight. Wooden boards rumbled beneath the wheels and the end of the pier hurtled toward them as he eased back the yoke. Kenzie clapped as the front of the plane lifted and screamed as the left wheel dropped off the pier. The plane lurched to one side before wind caught the wings and lifted it clear.

"And pitch slowly," said Marbles to himself. "No stalling."

The plane climbed for a while and then leveled out.

"I'm not known for profanity," said Sarge, "but shit, that was nerve-racking. Good job, Marbles."

"I had no choice," said Marbles. "My old man always told me that, if I was going into danger, I should wear clean underwear. You know, in case of toilet accidents. I doubt any of us brought a change with us. I certainly didn't."

"Way more information than I needed," said English.

For just over an hour, they flew in a silence broken with idle chatter. Then English's phone chirped. He hit the speaker. "Hi Numbers, what's up?"

"I'm going to send you fresh coordinates. They've landed. It's still too dark to get a decent image, but they're on the Columbian coast."

"That's great news, buddy," said Sarge. "Now we can come up with a plan."

"That's the good news," said Numbers. "The bad news, if the heat signatures are correct, is that there's about a dozen people in there. And the way they're spaced, they're regimented. This isn't a sleazy drug den you're going into, it's a well-protected fortress. These guys are organized."

"I've dealt with plenty worse, buddy. You're able to keep an eye on things until we get there?"

"Yep, everything seems stable. Well, other than the kidnapping and impending gunfight, that is. You guys just get there, and I'll be on the other end of the line when you do. Jenny's keeping me awake with very strong tea."

"Is she still there?" asked English. His voice cracked with emotion. "Can I speak to my wife?"

"I'm here, babe," said Jenny through the speaker. "Please be careful. I miss you."

"Miss you too, baby," said English. "Everything good where you are?"

"It's all good here. It's very important that you come home though, okay?"

"I get it, Jen. I remember what we talked about, the babies and stuff? That was between me and you, okay? Love you."

"Babe, we're on speakerphone but yeah, definitely the babies and stuff, but also there's a shit ton of blood spatter on the wall up the stairwell. It'll need redecorating and you know how I hate painting. Oh, and I love you too."

English smiled. "That's my girl. I'll be home soon. Keep my side of the bed warm."

Thirty minutes later, the lights of Santa Marta twinkled against the changing sky. To their right, a glow shimmered on the horizon.

"Will we get there before sunrise?" asked Kenzie. "I figured you guys might work better in the dark."

"We've not worked anywhere together," said Sarge, "in any light. But I'll tell you this; we're all vets and we all have experience. Don't worry about what shade of day it is. Whatever it is, we'll get our guys back or we'll die trying." He turned to Marbles. "Speaking of dying, have you worked out where we're going to land?"

"Yep," said Marbles. He pointed through the cockpit window. "Right there."

Sarge unclipped his seat belt and leaned forward. "Where? I don't see anything."

"Correct. You might want to refasten your seat belt. There's no easy end to our trip, I've been checking the landscape. It's too built up. This'll be our last landing, because

I'm sure the wheels will be torn from the fuselage when we hit the water. Still, look on the bright side. Either we'll get a hero's ride out of here..."

"Or it won't matter," said Sarge. "Fair enough. Salt water's no good for the equipment so get as close as you can."

Marbles maneuvered the plane so that the propeller followed the GPS to the inch. As the harbor grew closer, he lowered the plane until the wheels skimmed the ocean.

"I'll do my best but, unless you're a duck, water landings are never good. I'd hold onto something solid, because this is going to get bumpy."

As the curve of the bay loomed into view, he turned off the plane's lights and eased back the throttle. The engine calmed down to a steady purr as he floated the plane into the harbor. Ahead of them over the sand, the landscaping rose to underline a huge mansion. A few of the windows were lit, but they were too far away to make out any movement. Marbles steered to the right, to a small cove.

"Hold on folks," he said. "Here goes."

He wrenched back on the yoke as much as he could to lift the plane and slow up its contact with the ocean.

The wheels cut through the water's surface and sent shockwaves through the cabin. Kenzie gripped Sarge's thigh while the metal panels of the plane creaked and groaned against one another. English ducked his head between his legs and covered it with his arms as rivers of salt water washed over the cockpit windows. Marbles shook in his seat and fought the controls to steer the craft forward. The wipers flapped across the windows like frantic arms while the fuselage surfed toward the beach.

As their momentum slowed, Kenzie relaxed and English sat back in his seat.

Sarge looked at him. "Did you reach Him?"

"Say again," asked English.

"The main man," said Sarge. "They always say, in a crisis, you should stick your head between your legs and pray. I've been trying for a while, so I wondered if you reached him."

"Hate to break it to you, mate," said English, "but in my life, I always heard that you put your head between your legs and kiss your arse goodbye."

As the ocean lapped over the wings, Sarge sat back. "Oh. Okay. So, did you reach it?"

The crew lurched forward as the nose of the plane beached against the sand before settling back into their seats. Marbles climbed over them and opened the cabin door. "Grab your things, guys and gals, I don't know how long this thing will float and I'd rather not find out. Let's go save our buddies."

---

As the girl climbed the wooden staircase, one stuttering step at a time, Marcia glanced back at the patio. There was no sign of Lindsay or Ramirez. He'd done enough chest puffing and posturing for now and had left the girls to take care of themselves.

"So," said Marcia, "your name is Evie. Is that your real name?"

The girl stopped on the stairs, turned and frowned. She was three steps higher than Marcia and towered over her, but Marcia felt no threat.

"Yes, my name is Evie. And you're Marcia. Is that your real name?"

Marcia held out her hand. "My name isn't important. What's important is that you survive."

The girl shook her hand. The grip was firm, but also yielding, as if there was already an element of trust. "Why do you say it's important that I survive? How many have been before me?"

"That doesn't matter. All that matters is that I can't get to know someone else, only to have them taken away. I can't see another one gone. Please, do as he says."

Evie gulped as they reached the top of the staircase. Marcia pointed. "That door leads to your bedroom. Mr. Ramirez will visit you most nights. If you cooperate, it will be much easier. And you have a closet full of clothes. Dress to make him happy."

The girl looked at the door as if it held back the answer to life itself. "Why should I make him happy? He's going to keep me here against my will. Where I come from that's not a good thing."

"You have no idea. Please, remember than I'm here for you. Let's work through this together, okay?"

Marcia pushed open the bathroom door and saw the ghost of Abigail's lifeless head against the back of the tub. She swallowed heavily. "Please, take a bath. Prepare yourself as a willing woman to him. Whatever you're thinking about escape, it's hopeless. Forget it. Clean up, and we'll live this new life together."

Evie stepped into the bathroom and looked around. "I'm not staying here. The first chance I get, I'll run. I'm sorry if you have to shoot me or whatever, but that's the way it is. And please, don't feel bad about it. I can tell you hate this too, but I'm nobody's slave. I'd rather die."

She swept her hand around the edge of the tub. As she

raised her hand, the light glistened off a strand of long blond hair between her fingers.

"I don't imagine there are many blondes here, so who's hair is this?"

Marcia gazed at the toes of her black shoes and then stepped forward. She pulled the lever to drop the plug, gripped the hot water faucet and turned it.

"There is bubble bath in the cabinet. Get the water really hot, fill it with bubbles, and relax. We have about an hour before breakfast. I suggest you bathe and then dress in something comfortable. It's going to be a steep learning curve but, like I said, I'll be here for you."

33

Sarge tucked the plastic pouch that had protected his rifle under a large rock and took in the surroundings. The mansion that held Dud and Evie rose from the next cove and reached into the brightening sky like a monolith. Even from this view, partially hidden by rock formations and set back half a mile, it still towered like a giant hand ready to crush them.

To the east, the beach swept away, its arm winding around the Columbian coast to hold it tight. To the west, the jagged rocks continued, broken only by a lighthouse, whose light pulsed every few seconds and seemed to beckon in the sunrise. Kenzie held her hand flat over her eyes and gazed out over the ocean.

"So, what's the plan?" said Sarge.

English palmed his phone. "Numbers. Sit rep."

The old man didn't miss a beat and replied right away. "Still just the two guys in the closet. They're getting noisy, but I find that if I kick the door and shout, they shut up. Mrs. Watson is in the kitchen making bacon and black pudding. What the hell is black pudding? And should I be excited or scared?"

"Excited," said English. "It's oatmeal and pork blood. Once it's fried, you'll love it, but that's not what I meant. What are we up against?"

Numbers sounded nauseous. "Pork blood? Can't I just have cereal? Er, nothing's changed. Guards posted in standard formation. Same amount. Same configuration. Same drill. I can see where you beached now, you're not too far away. Sarge, do you still have the rifle?"

Sarge adjusted his cap and leaned into the phone. "Sure do. You got something for me to do?"

"Well, there's a lighthouse close by. You're a crack shot, so why don't you get to the top of it and provide cover? English and Marbles, I can guide you closer step by step. Having said that, that'll make noise, so forget that. Am I seeing this right? It looks like the front of the building rises in stages. The rear and sides are walled off, so there's no other way in but to climb the front."

Sarge slid his hands up and down the rifle for reassurance and then looked at the others. "What do you think?"

"I think it's perfect," said Marbles. "The bad guys don't have an infra-red Numbers, so we'll have their positions, but we're still outnumbered. It's been a while since any of us saw active service, too, so I say stick to our strengths. You can take out more bad guys from a couple hundred yards away than I could face to face."

"Yeah, but..."

"I get it," said English, "loss of life and all that. I'm with you, Sarge." He stepped forward and placed a hand on Sarge's shoulder. "I don't like it any more than you do, but it's time to realize that not everyone follows the same moral compass. There are good guys and bad guys, all over the world. I went through the Middle East, and I followed and trusted the barrel of my gun before anything else. But you know what? I met a Saudi mechanic who could fix anything. Lovely bloke, who was teaching himself English by watching television. And a Kuwaiti girl who cooked the meanest pie you've ever tasted. What I'm trying to say is there's good and bad everywhere. It's working out which is which."

Sarge nodded as English continued. "In this instance, we have the luxury of knowing. The guy we saw at the station is a heartless bastard, and I'm sure he'll report to someone worse than him. And, these people are holding Evie. Now, I haven't known Dud for long, but from what I gather, he'd lay his life on the line for a comrade. That's why I'm here, to help a fellow man in the fight against evil. I signed up for that years ago, and I'll die doing the same thing. Sarge, there's no guilt in this. These are evil men. The world will be a better place without them."

Sarge curled his fingers around the rifle. "I know you're right."

English nodded.

"And son?" said Sarge. "Your story about the Epi-Pen was good enough to get you in, but seriously, welcome to the club."

English flushed and lifted his phone. "Numbers, you ready?"

"I was born that way," came the reply.

"Okay. Sarge, there's a lighthouse waiting for you. Marbles, Kenzie, you ready to get our friends back?"

"As ready as I'll ever be," said Marbles. "Let's go."

Kenzie nodded and slung the rope over her shoulder. "For my sister."

They split. There were no words spoken, no commands, but Sarge broke one way and jogged toward the lighthouse, as the others moved along the beach. The ocean lapped against the sand and filled the impressions made by their footprints.

English looked back at Marbles. "Did you leave a will?"

"What?"

"In case anything happens. Did you leave a will or instructions on what to do if you die?"

"Are you kidding me? You think I'm going to die?"

English pulled up. "Well, not right now, but..."

"But nothing. Take that shit out of your head." Marbles thumbed over his shoulder toward the house. "Dud's back there. And Evie. Two of the nicest people I've ever met. Believe me, if I have to die it won't be while watching the Wheel of fucking Fortune with a lap full of popcorn, or dragging a crap ton of groceries back from Wal-Mart. It'll be doing something like this, something I believe in. We're getting our friends back, or I'll die trying."

"I get you," said English. Kenzie stood behind them wide eyed. "And for the record? You swear a lot when you're passionate."

"I know," said Marbles. "That's why I'm married."

They rounded the curve of the bay and knelt beneath the outcrop of rock. Ten minutes later, Sarge checked in.

"I'm in position. Had a little trouble with the lock, but nothing I couldn't handle. The view from up here is spectacular. There's no movement in the house, I checked every window through the scope. You've got four guys out front, which means some of them moved inside. I think you can get to the first two without the others seeing you; the rise in the property should cover you if you can do it quietly. I'll follow you in my sights. If it looks like it might go tits up, I'll help out. Last resort though. Once I get that first shot off, the place'll erupt."

English glanced up at the lighthouse. Every time the light spun around, a tiny black speck appeared. It was impressive how quickly Sarge had reached the landmark and climbed its staircase.

"Sounds like a solid plan, mate. Numbers, how's the interior looking?"

"I've got two close together, just through the main door although I can't tell you which floor they're on. There's one alone in the middle of the house, and then a group of them together at the other end. I'm going to guess they're eating breakfast. That room is lit up like a flare, so it's toasty in there."

"Now's the time then," said English. They rounded the curve and ducked at the base of the landscaping. "I'll get to the other side of the property and get behind the guy there. Marbles, you get behind the other and we'll take them out together. Sound like a plan?"

"Works for me, bud. How will I know when you're ready?"

"Kenzie. You get central and stay down. You should be able to see us both moving. We'll each give you the thumbs up when we're ready. You give the signal to move and we'll go. Once the first two are down, we'll move up together and work on the next two. Okay?"

Kenzie nodded. "Good luck, mon. Be careful."

"Okay, everyone," said Marbles. "Radio silence."

The two men shook hands, then English crouched and made his way along the front of the property. His shoes slopped against the wet sand as he ran, the sound bouncing back off the cobbled brick wall that ran the length of the building. For the entire time, he sensed Sarge's scope tracking him, and imagined Numbers following his every step. It was a reassurance he'd not felt before, in any previous mission. They had to succeed; he wanted to get to know these men he'd fallen in with.

The end of the wall curved upward like a skate ramp and wrapped around the building. English reached up, curled his fingers over the top of the brick, and hoisted himself up. Well-manicured grass stretched away, bisected by a chalk white concrete path that rose from the lowest level, all the way to the top of the landscaping. Marbles hugged the wall of the first rise at the opposite end of the lawn. Above his head, white painted concrete railing traced the front edge of the next level, broken only where wide steps rose.

English stood to peer over the top. A guard stood fifteen feet away, looking up at the house. Another stood on the other side of the path, pointing at something in one of the upstairs windows.

Marbles waved and indicated that he was moving closer, then edged inwards along the lawn beneath the wall until he was a few feet from the path. English followed until they almost met in the middle. At the base of the landscaping, Kenzie looked over the house once more and gave the thumbs up.

As one, the men rose and hoisted themselves up. They landed behind the two guards. English unslung his gun and raised it as Marbles clamped his hand around his enemy's mouth. He wrapped an arm around the guy's throat and squeezed as English slammed the butt of his rifle into the back of the closest guy's head. He dropped like a stone as Marbles dropped to his knees, dragging his man with him. After a brief struggle, the guard's arms dropped to his sides.

"Now what do we do with them?" asked English.

"Guys," hissed Kenzie. She lifted the rope and beckoned for the two men to move toward her.

The limp bodies made a dull thud as they rolled over the edge of the first wall. English and Marbles followed them and rolled them again until they splashed onto the wet sand.

"Keep going," she said. "I'll drag them around the corner and tie them up. I'm sure I can find something to use as a gag. Maybe my socks if they're really lucky."

Marbles shook his head. "If I wasn't already married..."

"You couldn't handle me, mon." Kenzie waved them off. "Go on. Get going."

They climbed up to the lawn, then crept around the railing and up the staircase, until the voices of the other guards broke through the faint sound of the lapping ocean. English looked back to the sea and cursed.

"We don't have Kenzie to tell us when the coast is clear," he whispered. "Now what do we do?"

"Don't see that we have a choice," said Marbles. "Go back to the phones."

English nodded and turned his body to reach into his pocket. As his hand brushed the tip of it, his rifle dragged across the wall behind him. The sound of metal on stone grated. Both men froze.

An accented voice said, "Did you hear something?"

34

Sarge kept his left eye closed while the other pushed against the rifle scope. Despite the precaution, the light from the huge bulb behind him turned his vision red as the brightness seared through his eyelid.

He'd smiled as Kenzie dragged, first one man, and then the other, around the corner into the next bay. She'd be an asset to any team. He smiled even more when she removed her shoes and used her saltwater soaked socks as gags. Those guys would be better off if they remained unconscious.

Marbles and English climbed the front of the property again and paused beneath the last level. He scanned the windows for movement and centered on the two guards posted in front of impressive looking French doors. His heart raced when both their heads snapped around and stared toward the ocean. As he moved the scope to see his colleagues, Marbles pulled his pistol while English cradled the AR. Then they waited.

The guards edged forward and approached the wall.

Marbles and English waited.

The guards moved closer, only a couple of feet away from them.

Stand, thought Sarge. Stand and shoot.

Marbles and English still waited.

Sarge wrapped his finger around the trigger and steadied the scope until the crosshairs centered on the guard above Marbles.

They moved as Sarge squeezed and released a round. As the rifle cracked, the guard on the right vanished from sight in a puff of pink mist. By the time he re-sighted the scope, English was upright with his gun pointed forward. The report from the AR echoed off the building as the other guard staggered backward. A volley of bullets peppered his torso and sent him dancing wildly until he collapsed onto the patio.

Seconds later, the downstairs windows erupted in a flurry of movement. The figures moved too quickly to pin down, so he fired two shots through the windows to give Marbles and English a chance to find cover. They ducked behind the wall as Kenzie sprinted up the steps to join them.

---

Evie lay back in the hot water and looked around the room again. There was nothing in here to use as a weapon unless she improvised a garrote with the belt of the thick bathrobe that hung on the back of the door.

A million different thoughts whirred through her mind. Option after option came and went. For the time being, escape was impossible, and the thought of angering the man downstairs filled her with dread. Fresh tears ran when she thought of Dud. She had to get to him, which meant toeing the line and waiting for an opportunity. Annoying Ramirez would put him at grave risk.

She reached for a sponge when a sharp crack sounded outside the door. Then a barrage of noise broke out. Water cascaded over the sides of the tub as she slid upright. Footsteps thudded along the hall until someone hammered on the door.

"Evie. Get out. Now!" shouted Marcia. "I have to get you to safety. Move. Now."

Evie climbed out of the water and dragged the robe over her wet skin. When she opened the door, Marcia grabbed her wrist and pulled her along the hallway. "Come with me. You must stay in your room and lock the door."

Evie jumped as two more shots rang out and glass shattered downstairs. "What's happening. Are we under attack?"

"Yes. Please, stay here. I have to go and help."

"Who is it? Do you know? Is it my husband?"

"I have no idea," said Marcia. She pushed Evie into the bedroom. "Promise me you'll stay here."

"Okay, I promise," said Evie. She looked into the pretty face of the woman assigned to protect her and saw the closest thing she had to a friend. "Marcia, please be careful."

"Don't worry about me, I've been through worse. Lock the door and stay away from the windows."

She turned and ran along the hall. Evie stood in the doorway as Marcia's steps clattered down the staircase and faded, leaving her alone. The hallway beckoned like an escape tunnel. It would take seconds to cross it and run for front door. She took a cautious step forward and stopped. Dud was somewhere in the house. This is not over while I'm still breathing, he'd said. And hadn't Marcia said there was nowhere to run to? Assuming the people firing the guns meant her no harm, and she was able to get past them, she still couldn't go anywhere. Not without her husband.

She stepped back into the room, locked the door, and sat on the bed.

---

At the sound of the first gunshot, Ramirez leaped up from the sofa and grabbed his pistol. By the time he reached the archway that led to the foyer, three guards and Lindsay had already run past him. More shots rang out and the windows in the hallway shattered and crashed against the tile floor.

He slid to a stop and peered around the edge of a jagged window frame. The body of one guard was bleeding out a few feet away on the patio and, by the door lay the almost headless body of another. It was hard to tell who it was, the bloodied mass above the shoulders resembled crushed watermelon. Other than that, there was nothing to see. No boat in the harbor, just the seaplane. No men lined up ready to assault the building. Nothing but the two bodies.

"Who is it?" he screamed. "Show yourselves, you fucking cowards."

Lindsay and a guard took up positions beneath the windows and two more sprinted past the door and did the same thing on the other side of the house. Ramirez swung his pistol around as footsteps clattered around the corner, then lowered it as Marcia appeared. She slid up to the wall and turned to him.

"What's going on? Is it the police?"

"I don't know," said Ramirez. "The girl. Is she safe?"

"Yes, she's upstairs in her room."

"Good," he nodded. "Thank you, Marcia."

Other than an occasional tinkle as a piece of glass fell,

the only sound was the ocean. The first hints of orange glowed on the horizon as the sun raised its head.

Ramirez shouted through the arch across the hallway. "Vasquez. Go to an upstairs window. Look toward the harbor and see if our attackers are hiding in the landscaping. Radio back anything you find."

A tall man slid out from beneath the window, sprinted across the foyer and bounded up the stairs, two at a time. Ramirez heard footsteps cross the balcony and enter the room above them as he pulled a radio from his pocket. "Come on," he said under his breath. "Those shots were too rapid to be long range rifle fire, they have to be close. I still don't understand how anyone knows we're here. We're so cautious, no one of threat to us knows about this..."

A single shot interrupted his words. The crack echoed around the outside of the house. As it faded, small slivers of glass fell outside the window and shattered on the patio. A dull thump sounded above him.

"Fuck." He keyed the radio. "Vasquez. Vasquez, answer me."

The radio remained silent. Plastic flew in all directions as he launched it down the hallway. He turned to the remaining three men and Marcia.

"They want something from us, there's no other reason to come here with guns blazing. The only thing that's changed is the arrival of the girl. So, we will wait them out. If they want her, they'll have to come into the house to get her. There is no access to the back of the house, so we have to watch the front and the side doors." He pointed to the lone man on the other side of the main door. "You, move to your right and cover that side of the house. And you," he said to the man next to him, "move to the far left. Lindsay and I will watch the stairs and patio. Marcia, I want you upstairs, positioned outside her room. Kill anyone that approaches. And Marcia, if it looks like we'll be overrun, make sure that the last thing you do is put a bullet through her pretty head."

———

Dud jumped at the first gunshot and smiled. For the first time, the sound of automatic fire was welcome. Somehow, the guys had found him. Maybe advanced tracking software his new English friend had devised, or just dogged determination and the cast iron will to succeed.

The room he was in sat at the rear corner of the property. As he was led here, he'd made a mental note of every part of the building he could see; from the entrance, to the fire exit on the side of the building, to the windowless room at the rear where his captor had pushed him.

It would be difficult to break in. There was no access at the rear of the house or this side. The exits opened from the inside, and a thump on the rear wall confirmed his fears there. It was solid. The only access point was the front, and even that was protected by the harbor and layers of landscaping.

It was a brilliant design for a safe house.

More shots sounded, followed by a shout through the door, and then retreating footsteps. It seemed fortuitous, but there was a chance that, if the guys were staging a full-on assault, his guard had left his post to help. There was only one way to find out.

He rapped his knuckles against the door. "Hey, I need to use the bathroom."

Silence.

A little louder. "Hey. Dipshit. I need the bathroom."

When no one replied, he tried the handle. The smooth brass slid in his grip. "Yeah," he whispered. "No one is that lucky."

He looked around the room. On one side, two sofas faced an open fireplace, separated by a wooden coffee table. Small cabinets lined a side wall, with a decorative lamp sat on top of them. Elaborately framed pictures and a fire extinguisher broke up the back wall, and the other side wall held nothing but the door.

The fire extinguisher was a solid, red metal canister. He lifted it from its hook, hefted its weight, and moved to the door. Solid brass hinges held the wood in place. The only weak spot was the handle. If he could gain access to its internal mechanism, picking it would be easy.

More gunshots sounded and, over the sound of breaking glass, he raised the extinguisher and brought it crashing down.

35

"We've got nothing to lose now," said English. With Marbles on one side and Kenzie on the other, he turned down the call volume on his phone and called Numbers.

Seconds after Numbers picked up, Sarge joined the call. "That didn't go to plan."

"No shit, Sherlock," said English. "Now we're pinned down with no way forward, although I appreciate your help with the guy in the window."

"Can't say as I feel good about it," said Sarge, "but he was a nuisance. They've wised up, though. Not seen anyone since. How's it looking in there, Numbers?"

There was a brief pause while Numbers assessed the situation. "Looks like a guy positioned at either side of the house, and then a cluster in the middle. They're too closely grouped to work out. This is weird, though. They're all stationary but one. There's a single signal moving at a snail's pace from the rear right of the house. That has to be Evie or Dud."

"I'm going with Dud," said Marbles. "Evie will be under lock and key. To be honest, I'm surprised they haven't used her as bait yet. Hopefully, she's too valuable to them."

"So, a frontal assault is out," said English. "Too much firepower. How about we flank them and hit them from the sides, maybe flush them out so Sarge can pick them off?"

"Don't bother," said Sarge. "I scoped out the side of the building. No windows and one fire door. There's no access there, so it's either from the front or over the top. You still have that rope? You could climb the side walls and rappel in through an upstairs window."

"Forget that," said Kenzie. "I used the rope."

"The front it is then, but we need a distraction. I can fire off a few shots from up here," said Sarge, "but I'd prefer not to waste ammo on glass. Glass doesn't fire back."

"Sit tight, guys," said Numbers. "The signal moving at the rear of the house? It's feet away from whoever is watching the right side of the building, and it's getting closer. If it's Dud, you might just be in luck."

---

The door was like many others Dud had come across; a solid, two-inch-thick slab of oak, with a heavy duty, solid brass handle. It looked and felt sturdy. Once the extinguisher smashed away the handle, the exposed inner workings were basic and flimsy, a thumb turn lock that easily moved in the opposite direction.

Beauty masking a cheap manufacturing job.

Since the door fit snug to the thick carpet beneath it, it was more of a challenge to crack it open than it was to unlock it. After a few attempts, Dud slid his fingers beneath it and pried it open enough to wedge his fingertips down the edge. He peeped through the gap and saw nothing but beige wall. Rustling steps and whispers carried from the house beyond the hallway. His fingernails buckled as they dragged across the wood, but he clawed at the door until it crept open enough to poke his head through.

The guard was gone.

He opened the door and stepped off thick carpet on to polished tile. To his right, the corridor ended at a bulkhead with an expensive looking picture hanging dead center on it. A small mahogany table sat beneath it, holding a vase filled with plastic roses.

To his left, the corridor ended at a T. He remembered from the way in that a left turn would take him to a kitchen. Right traveled back to the center of the house. With the entrance in mind, he crept along the hall until he reached the end, flattened himself against the wall and dared to look around the corner. Shards of glass littered the floor. Other than glass and open windows, the corridor, for at least the first ten feet he could see, was empty.

He pulled back and swung his head to look toward the kitchen. Through the open door, twenty feet away, the guard crouched beside a window. A lace curtain rested on his shoulder and twitched in the breeze as he swung his head from side to side, peering one way and then the other.

Dud stayed low and edged out into the corridor. Shadows moved in the archway to his right, but no one was visible. He slid his feet across the tile and moved toward the kitchen.

He was fifteen feet away when the guard froze. Dud stopped. At this range, he'd have no choice but to shoot. The guard tensed and peered a little further around the window frame, then shook his head, eased back and resumed his watch.

Dud let out a slow breath and continued to shuffle

forward. At ten feet, the kitchen interior came into view. Cast iron pans hung from hooks over a butcher-block island, and a knife block sat on the counter like an armory. At five feet, Dud decided he didn't need them. The guard held a 9mm pistol and, if he was any kind of soldier, it would have a full clip.

At three feet, he could see the parting and gray flecks in the guy's hair. His left hand bore a shiny gold wedding ring. Dud swallowed down the guilt and lunged.

He wrapped a hand around the guy's mouth and pulled him close. The guard's legs shot out and scrambled against the tile, his booted heels squeaking against the floor. He twisted his wrist to aim the pistol, but Dud gripped the hand, slid a finger behind the trigger, and dragged the guard into the kitchen. As they neared the counter, Dud twisted his body and slammed the guy's head against the granite edge. A muffled groan bled through his fingers but the guard struggled to stand upright. Thuds echoed around the kitchen as again, and again, Dud hammered his head into the stone. A red smear appeared until the gun hand relaxed and the guard slumped against him. Dud lowered him to the floor and slid the pistol from his hand.

Nothing moved in the kitchen doorway. Dud sat for a moment, partly to see if anyone had heard the disturbance, but also to catch his breath and let his heart rate settle. Nothing affected aim and judgment like a pounding heart. As the beating in his chest subsided, he rose to his knees and checked the guy's neck for a pulse. A faint, steady beat throbbed beneath his fingers. Dud rolled the body under the kitchen table and picked up the pistol. Sure enough, the magazine was full. Fifteen nine-millimeter hollow points, and one in the chamber.

Through the window, the plane bobbed and rocked on

the current. They hadn't left, so Evie was still in the house somewhere.

It made sense to separate them on arrival. She would be at the other end of the house or up the stairs he'd seen through the double doors when they were seated. The smart move would be upstairs. As daring as Evie was, she wouldn't risk trying to escape through a second-floor window.

Dud edged around the corner and moved along the hall. A curved archway hid everything but the center of the foyer, so he stayed below the windows and slid along with his back to the inside wall.

He was five feet from the arch when his shoe landed on a piece of glass. The crack sounded like a gunshot. As he froze, a familiar set of dreadlocks leaned back to peer around the wall.

"He's here," screamed the guide.

As he turned and the barrel of his gun appeared, Dud slid over to the opposite wall and opened fire.

---

When the gunfire sounded, Marbles, English and Kenzie ducked like a well drilled unit. When nothing disturbed the railing in front of them, Marbles raised his head and risked a glance through the concrete bars.

Even in the rising sunlight, muzzle flashes flared through a window to the right of the door. Matching flashes lit up the right side of the entrance door.

There was a firefight. Inside the building.

He lifted the phone and shouted. "Numbers. Anything?"

"I'd bet the house that it's Dud. Someone moved from

the rear, through the side of the house, and now they're level with whoever's by the door. There's another stationary signal behind him. I'd put money on our man causing trouble in there. You wanted a distraction? I think you've got one."

Before Marbles replied, another gunshot cannoned off the front of the house. The window on the left shattered before more shots rang out by the doorway.

"That's another one down," said Sarge. "I guess he got curious, or panicked and raised his head."

"That leaves two by the door, two further back, and the one we hope is Dud," said Numbers. "And I hope to God that one of those others is Evie. Guys, if you're moving, now's the time."

As Marbles reloaded the Sig, English raised his AR and turned to Kenzie. "This could get messy," he said. "Why don't you wait here and come in when we give you a wave?"

She blew out through her lips and let out a laugh. "The hell with that, mon. I've come this far. I might as well see it through."

"Fair enough," said English. "Watch our backs, Sarge. Ready folks?"

Marbles nodded.

"Okay. Let's go."

Sarge laid down covering fire. As the top of the door frame disintegrated into splinters, they stood and charged toward the door.

36

Lindsay counted the rounds as they left his pistol, a trick he'd learned after a vicious firefight left him powerless when he'd naively blind-fired every bullet he had over the hood of a car in downtown Kingston.

His weapon of choice at the house was a Glock 17, taken from a Jamaican cop during a bungled drug raid. Its very name made checking his ammunition fools play. Seventeen rounds, fifteen of which he'd just fired in a panic brought on by the element of surprise.

Somehow, the girl's husband had got away from Hector. Now, they were hemmed in from the side and the front. The headless body on the patio telegraphed the long-distance sniper. Nothing else left that kind of mess.

Ramirez shouted and screamed as soon as the bullets flew. He was used to protection. In the heat of battle, he scurried like the cockroach he was, but Lindsay knew that, if they were to survive this morning, they had to stick together.

Another shot whistled down the hallway and chipped away more plaster from the arch that covered them. "What do we do?" he said. "I have two rounds left. What do you have? I don't know how many people we are dealing with."

Panic flashed in his boss's eyes. He didn't know either.

"It's us and Marcia," said Lindsay. "What do we do?"

Ramirez pulled himself together. "Okay. Safety in numbers. And we move to higher ground. Stay to the right of the door and get upstairs. We'll take positions behind the balcony and, when they enter, pick them off from up there."

Lindsay considered their options. It was the only one left. The hostile fire from one side meant the guard was down. They'd heard the window shatter, followed by the slump of Alvarez's body. With each side blocked, as well as the front, back and up was the only way to go. "Okay. You have bullets left?"

Ramirez pulled back the slide to show a shiny brass casing nestled in the chamber. "Yes. On the count of three, we cross the hall and run up the stairs, okay?"

Lindsay nodded.

"Okay. One. Two..."

On three, Ramirez tensed. Lindsay followed, held his breath and prayed that a round wouldn't tear through him. He turned and launched himself across the open space toward the stairs. A shot rang out and whined past his head as he vaulted up the staircase. At the top, he sprawled across the carpet and lay flat, then turned and looked through the metal railing.

The coward Ramirez huddled like a child in the corner of the far wall and the archway. Lindsay spun his pistol as a noise sounded beside him. Marcia walked toward him from the bedroom, pistol in hand, as the door opened behind her and the woman appeared.

He held his finger to his lips and pointed downstairs. "We're penned in. That bastard let me run here to take the fire and didn't have the balls to follow me. You know what we have to do."

Marcia glanced over the balcony. "Who's left?"

"Us," said Lindsay. "And him."

"How many of them are out there? Do you know who it is?" she asked.

Evie stepped up to them. "It's my husband. I told you. I said he'd come for me." She glared at Lindsay. "Whatever happens next, you deserve it."

Anger fired through every nerve in Lindsay's body. Ignoring the danger below, he stood and punched the woman. She fell and crab-walked backwards as blood trickled from her nose.

He lifted his pistol. Two rounds left - one for her and one for him.

---

Marcia flinched as Lindsay struck Evie. She felt the blow herself as the woman fell to the ground and scrambled away in panic.

Lindsay was no different from Ramirez. Women were objects to them, items to be bought, sold, traded and used. He raised his pistol to finish her off.

Somehow, Evie's eyes remained dry. Faced with life threatening danger, she still had the strength to look evil in the eyes and deny it the thing it wanted most; that feeling of power and control. Lindsay was shaking with rage, yet Evie met his gaze and didn't flinch.

Instinct kicked in. As his finger tightened against the trigger, Marcia fired. He staggered back in surprise as the round tore through his chest. Evie stood and moved toward him. Marcia stood by to let her have her moment as Lindsay dropped his gun and crashed against the balcony railing. His upper body leaned over them as his huge shoulders weighted him backwards. Searching for balance, his arms wind-milled before gravity pulled him over.

---

Evie lunged, reached out and grabbed a fistful of dreadlocks.

Her fingers wrapped around them as he fell further backward. Their eyes met and, for a moment, time froze. Evie held his gaze, expecting to see panic. Pools of evil looked back. The same look she'd seen when she'd been loaded into a truck like cattle. The same look that had watched poor Lecia fall under the train, Lecia who would have been sixteen next week. She stared so hard that she looked into his soul and saw nothing but darkness.

She relaxed her grip. As the braids threaded through her fingers, Lindsay screamed and tumbled over the balcony. A sickening thud echoed around the vaulted room as he hit the tiles. As it faded, gunfire tore through the doorway.

"This is it," shouted Marcia, "Quickly, back to your room. If this is your husband, it wouldn't do for you to get hurt in any crossfire."

Evie turned to her. "Please," she pleaded, "I can tell you're a good person. Whatever happens, it's not too late. I beg you. Come back with me. I'll tell them you protected me."

Footsteps pounded up the staircase as the front doors crashed open. Ramirez turned and fired as a man burst through the doors and shot back. He screamed and fell to the stairs as a bullet ripped into his thigh. While blood seeped between his fingers, another man and a woman entered the house. The first man raised his pistol to shoot again.

Marcia lifted her hands in the air and shouted, "Stop. Please, enough killing."

Ramirez continued to claw his way up the staircase until he reached the top. "What are you doing?" he hissed.

As she opened her mouth to answer, a voice she hadn't heard in years spoke from the foyer.

"Yanika? Is that you?"

The voice she remembered was assertive and in control but, right now, it sounded timid and confused. At the sound of her given name, Marcia flinched. Suddenly, everyone around her ceased to exist.

She stepped forward to the edge of the balcony and looked down at the group of people. A man with weird eyes looked back. And another man. Then, Evie's husband joined them from the hallway. But she couldn't take her eyes off the woman. She recognized that face.

"Kenzie? Is that really you?"

Tears streamed down her sister's face, and she took a while to speak. When she did, her voice wavered and cracked. "Yanika? What are you doing here?"

"Who the fuck is Yanika," screamed Ramirez. He rolled onto his side, leveled his pistol at Evie, and pulled the trigger over and over. The first pull fired off a shot that thudded into the wall. The rest were dry clicks. In frustration, he screamed again and pulled himself up the staircase and into the bathroom.

The group below ran up the stairs. Evie dived forward and into the arms of her husband while the others hugged. From behind them, Kenzie climbed the staircase one step at a time, her eyes glazed in tears. As her sister grew closer, Marcia's nerves jumped and crackled.

Four years of hiding pushed down on her like a cloak. Choosing to leave behind their squalid home for this life of riches had seemed like the only way out for her. Her mind cast back to that day in the street when, at last, she plucked up the courage to run while Kenzie was distracted. For the first time, she considered how her family must have felt. No doubt like the families of all the girls Ramirez had sold or used. Ramirez, the worm who now hid like a coward in the bathroom, afraid to face his peers. And Kenzie's eyes must have looked like they did now. Confused and scared and brimming with tears.

Her sister stood before her and took her face in her hands. "Is it really you? Is this Yanika? You're alive?"

Marcia nodded and wept as she threw her arms around her sister. This familiar body in her arms brought the memories of her family flooding back. It was time to stop running. Marcia was dead. It was time for Yanika to go home.

There was just one more thing to do.

---

Ramirez sat on the side of the tub and tied a towel around his leg. Blood soaked through the white cloth in seconds. He glanced at the hook on the back of the door, for the bathrobe he'd hung there for Evie. That selfish bitch wore it now, and the belt would have been perfect to stem the blood flow.

Once they had him, they would kill him. Then again, if that was the case, they would already have kicked in the door to finish the job.

As if on cue, the handle rattled. With the firepower they

had, the people outside could easily blast open the flimsy lock.

There was a gentle knock.

His heart raced. This was it. This life was over. If they didn't kill him, they'd at least hand him over to the authorities. Perhaps he could buy his freedom. Everyone loved money, and he had more than he'd ever spend.

The knock sounded again.

He slid off the tub, turned the lock to open the door, and sat again to take the weight off his leg.

"It's open."

The door inched open and Marcia walked in.

This time his heart leaped. She was still alive. If they'd allowed her to live, he still had a chance.

She closed the door behind her as he held out his hands. "Marcia. Thank God, you're okay. I was worried about you. What did they mean? About Yanika?"

She smiled and stepped toward him, then reached out, ignored his hands, and pushed against his chest.

Evie's bath water was still warm. It seeped through his suit as he sank below the surface. Confusion whipped through his mind as the shimmering image of Marcia loomed over the edge of the tub. Finally, his face broke the surface, and he was able to speak.

"Marcia. What are you doing? I thought..."

"Say hello to Yanika, you son of a bitch," she interrupted. "This is the second and last time my hands will be in this tub today. And you are the only person Yanika will ever kill. This is for all the girls you've destroyed."

Her hands pushed against his face and forced his head back under the water. Porcelain slammed against the back of his head as water filled his ears, and she leaned over to hold him there.

In his mind, Ramirez screamed. It came out as a stream of bubbles. Pressure squeezed against his temples and his lungs burned as he thrashed his arms. Lights danced before his eyes as they bulged before the edge of his vision faded. Strong muscles grew weak and, as the panic subsided, he took a deep breath and a wave of euphoria washed through him.

Then it went dark.

37

"And you're sure you're okay?"

As Dud pulled her tighter, Evie leaned her head back and let the morning breeze catch her hair. The lower curve of the sun had finally made it over the farthest line of the horizon and the glowing orange ball sent shimmering fire rippling toward them. She opened her mouth to breathe in the fresh air and swung her legs over the edge of the wall. The ocean was a few feet away, but she ignored it and sat on the wall with her arm wrapped around her husband.

"I swear, babe. The only person who laid a finger on me was a woman."

"Oh, really?" said Dud. "So, we're going to have that conversation at a time like this?"

Evie laughed. Tears formed in her eyes, even though Dud thought she'd be cried out by now. "Marcia, or whatever her name is, took care of me. She is a good-looking woman though."

Now he laughed and fished out his phone.

Marbles and English were still in the house moving

bodies, wiping down surfaces and checking that they left as small a footprint as possible. Dud's phone had turned up in the kitchen, casually tossed behind the coffee maker.

Evie watched as he scrolled through the screens until his photo gallery appeared. The last picture was of the two of them, smiling in an excited-looking selfie. The roll bars of the jeep were behind them as sunlight splashed across their smiling faces. He touched the image, and it filled the screen.

"Wow," she said. "That was moments before we were run off the road."

"Yep. Look at how the sunlight lights us up." He pointed across the harbor. "That's the same sun, over there. Come on, babe. It started like this. Let's take one more picture and bookend this whole damned thing."

They slid off the wall, stood in the damp sand and turned their backs to the sun. Dud stretched out his arm and focused the camera. As the shutter clicked and recorded the moment, a voice drifted across the beach.

"Okay, lovebirds. I've heard how flying lead and danger can be an aphrodisiac, but could you at least wait until an old guy can avert his eyes?"

Sarge trudged toward them, wet sand sucking and grabbing at his shoes. A rifle rocked against his back with every step. He walked right up to them and grabbed Dud in a tight hug.

"I'm so glad to see you, buddy. Tell me it's over."

Dud pushed him back and held his gaze. "It's over. The guys are sweeping the house although I'm sure there will be questions later. Do you remember Kenzie talking about her sister?"

Sarge nodded as he swept Evie up in his arms. "Yeah, wasn't she taken from town?"

"Long story, but no, she wasn't taken. She's here, in the house with Kenzie. They commandeered the kitchen, and trust me, that'll be a much more complicated conversation than this one."

"Well I'll be damned. You're aware none of my weaponry is registered, right? So, we don't have to worry about that. What about the bad guys?"

"All gone. The main guy will be ridiculously clean by now, thanks to Kenzie's sister. All we have to do now is get home. Should be a piece of cake since Evie and I are probably the only ones with a passport."

"You haven't called our man at home yet?"

As Dud opened his mouth to speak, Marbles and English walked down the steps, followed by Kenzie and Yanika.

"All done," said Marbles. "Well, at least as well as it can be. Bodies and blood are mostly gone." He jumped off the wall and hugged Dud, then turned and hugged Evie too. "This is English," he said as he gestured to the man behind him, "and this is Kenzie. And you know the other girl from what I can tell."

"So, what's the plan?" asked English.

"I've been waiting for Numbers," said Dud. "Hang on, I'll call him."

The phone rang once and Numbers answered. "Okay. For the love of God, could you give a guy a few minutes? I think I've got you sorted."

"That sounds promising," said English. "Is the wife okay?"

"I'm right here, honey," shouted Jenny. "It's great to hear your voice."

"You too, Jen. What's the deal with the intruders?"

"The idiots were stupid enough to bring their wallets

with them. We've taken pictures of their driver's licenses; names, dates of birth, addresses, everything. Turns out they're brothers. Once we're done, we'll let them go. But we've warned them that if we ever see them again, or they mutter a word about this place..."

"That'd be enough for me," said Evie. "And thank you. It seems you were the glue holding this whole thing together."

There was silence for a moment and then Evie continued. "So, can the glue find a way to get us home?"

"Depends where home is," said Numbers. "Sounds like it might be in multiple places now."

Dud looked at the group. Everyone belonged back in Kentucky, except Kenzie and her sister. Kenzie caught his gaze and looked at Yanika.

"You ready to go home?" she said.

"Yes, I am. It won't be easy, but..."

"Your sister will be there for you," said Kenzie. "Don't worry, we'll work it out."

"Then yes. We have a lot of catching up to do."

"It's a split journey, Numbers," said Dud. "What can you do?"

"Can you guys hang out for a few hours? There's a military flight leaving Venezuela in nine hours. Could you all be in Jamaica by then?"

The group looked at Marbles and he looked into the harbor, at the small seaplane. "It might take a few trips," he said, "as long as I can stay awake. But I could get us all there."

"There's a landing strip, east of Montego Bay. I know a guy there. Get there within nine hours and he'll put you on a plane. I'll text the location."

"Numbers," interrupted Dud, "is that military flight a daily thing?"

There was silence for a moment, and then, "Yes. Why?"

"Because I started something I need to finish. Postpone it for a day and we'll be there."

The group stared in confusion.

"It's okay, guys. Trust me."

With the call disconnected, Yanika turned to Evie. "There are no words to tell you how sorry I am."

"No apologies needed," said Evie. "A while ago I saw a documentary about Nazi soldiers during World War Two. The most repeated phrase they used was that they were just following orders." She swallowed heavily. "I saw Ramirez. I felt his power. You have nothing to apologize for, I'm just glad you're out of it. In all of this, you turned out to be a friend. Thank you."

As the girls separated, Dud turned to Kenzie. "So, you kids..."

"We'll be just fine, mon," said Kenzie. "Drop us in Jamaica and I'll sort out the rest." Her eyes misted over as she pointed to Evie. "You're a good man. Look after this woman. And the next time you come here..."

Dud laughed. "I think we're almost done with Jamaica, but if you ever want to visit the States, we'll always have a room for you."

"That would be nice. I appreciate that."

"Is anyone else hungry?" asked Marbles. "I'm starving. Is there food at the house?"

Yanika giggled. "I'm sure I can fix us some breakfast."

They climbed the stairs, back to the house.

"Tell you what though," said English under his breath. "I could murder a McDonald's."

The sun bounced off the Caribbean as the bus rocked and jolted over potholes. A fragrant cloud of smoking ganja billowed from the driver's seat and drifted backwards over the passengers.

Kenzie laughed as Jameson told another joke in fluent patwa. Dud didn't pick up a word of it, but hugged Evie and laughed anyway. "At last, we're finally going to see Bob's place."

"Has this been a lifelong ambition of yours?" asked English from behind him.

"Not so much, but I always like to finish things I've started. We were headed this way when the shit hit the fan. And the best way to overcome shit like that is to take the experience and make it good."

Sarge clapped his shoulders. "I like that attitude, buddy, and it's a pleasure to be sharing it with you."

"Big fan of Bob then, Sarge?" asked Marbles.

"Heck, no. Can't stand it. Give me Lynyrd Skynyrd any day, and there's this new band called Blackberry Smoke..."

"The Beatles," said English. "Best band ever. Always will be."

Dud smiled. "Philistines. Wait until we get there and you get wrapped up in the atmosphere of peace and love."

"The Beatles did that first, too," said English.

"Washed away on a sea of drugs, more like," said Marbles.

Dud visibly tensed as the bus neared the curve in the road where his earlier visit had ended. Evie gripped his knee as they rounded the turn and continued up the hill and along the road to Nine Mile.

"Well babe, at least we got further than last time," he said.

Evie placed her head on his shoulder as his phone rang. He dug it from his pocket and looked at the screen. "Guys, it's Numbers. Seems he didn't want to miss out."

He hit connect and put the phone on speaker. "Numbers, how are you this morning?"

"Honestly," said the old man, "it might be morning for you, but it doesn't feel like it here. I gave you guys the night to catch up on some sleep, but we have a situation."

English leaned out of his seat. "Numbers, everything okay? Is the wife there?"

"I'm here, honey," said Jenny, "but listen up. This concerns you."

English walked to the front of the bus and slumped into the seat next to Dud. "Really? Go on."

"Remember the two guys who broke in?" said Numbers. "Turns out they didn't break in with ill intent. Once we took their gags off, they begged to speak to us before we turfed them out."

The club had gathered at the front of the bus as Jameson continued the drive.

"They knocked at the door," said Numbers, "a couple of times. We just didn't hear them. They didn't come here to steal anything; they came to deliver a message to you. Remember me saying they were brothers? Their dad is a Scottish man named John MacIntyre."

English sat bolt upright and gripped the seat. "Bloody hell, that's a blast from the past."

"You know the name?" asked Dud.

"Too bloody right I do. Bomb disposal expert. Macca saved my life a few times. Once literally. We served together. He actually defused an IED while I was standing on it. And he's bailed me out of more trouble than I've managed to get myself into."

Evie glanced at him.

"What? I used to be a bit of a boy before I met the wife."

"Still here," said Jenny over the speaker.

"Shit. Sorry babe. Yeah, me and Macca go way back. Carry on, Numbers."

"Thanks. So anyway, he's in trouble, English. Big trouble. He told his kids about you, and they worked out where you lived and came to get your help. Said you owed him and you said he could ask for it any time."

"That's the truth," said English. "So, what's up?"

"It's too much to say over the phone. You need to come home, all of you. Do you reckon we've got used to working together as a team?"

"The Old Farts Club," said Sarge. "It's a force to be reckoned with."

"Well, it looks like we're not retiring yet. This will be a team effort, and it'll involve another trip. First off, come home and meet these boys. I'll arrange the flight while Jenny keeps an eye on them."

"Keeps an eye on them?" said Marbles.

"Yeah, we gave them a bit of a kicking, but nothing that some painkillers and bandages won't fix. I've seen worse. They'll be okay. Probably."

English shook his head and glanced across to Dud. "I wouldn't ask mate, but..."

Dud leaned forward and patted Jameson's shoulder. "Turn the bus around, dude. Take us back to the hotel."

English nodded a silent thank you as the bus turned in the road.

"One day, Bob," said Dud, "I'll see you one day, but

more important things take precedence. You'd be proud, man. Dropping everything for one love."

Jameson laughed and burst into the Bob Marley song. Dud sang along.

While the rest of the bus clapped the rhythm, Sarge nodded his approval and smiled. "Oh yeah. The Old Farts Club is a force to be reckoned with."

Mick Williams wrote his first short story (which linked a local celebrity to a spate of killings) in High School. His teacher noted 'he has quite an imagination'...she never mentioned whether it was good or bad. Since then he has written a twisted romantic comedy and three adventure/thrillers.

After a decade in Kentucky, USA, he has recently relocated back to his hometown of Stoke-on-Trent, England, and shares a house with his wife and two demanding and needy cats, Crash and Thud.

In between working and writing, he is an avid reader and enjoys watching football. Both kinds.